Milwaukee Jihad

*Saudi Terrorists, Deep State Saviors
and Designated Survivors*

Books by Matthew J. Flynn

Bernie Weber: Math Genius series
Book 1: Milwaukee Jihad

Coming Soon!
Book 2: China Code
Book 3: Hunting Bernie Weber

Milwaukee Jihad

*Saudi Terrorists, Deep State Saviors
and Designated Survivors*

Matthew J. Flynn

SPEAKING VOLUMES, LLC
NAPLES, FLORIDA
2022

Milwaukee Jihad

ISBN 978-1-64540-672-3

To my wife, Mary.

Chapter One

Iman Zulkifar Malouf sat at a desk in the Riyadh headquarters of the Saudi Intelligence Agency, known inside the kingdom as Al Mukhabarat Al A'Amah. As the head of Mabahith, the Secret Police, he wore a traditional white thobe with a ghutra on his head, fastened by an agal. Malouf was stocky, with black eyes that seldom blinked.

The man sitting opposite him also wore the thobe and a head covering, but he was much taller than Malouf and more powerfully built.

"Iman Taqi Maghribi," Malouf said, his lips forming a gash he intended as a smile. "You've done good work in Syria. And in Iraq. The Islamic State has expressed their thanks for what you've done."

"Does the King and his family know what we are doing for the Islamic State?" said Maghribi. "Are we in danger?"

"They suspect. But they are powerless. We are appointed by the Wahhabi leaders. The King has made a devil's pact with us. The royal family vacations in Italy and France, with unlimited women and pleasures. In turn, our religious leaders keep the country on the correct course."

"And the Europeans do not suspect? The Americans do not know?"

"They suspect. But they are naive beyond belief. They admit Turkey to NATO, while we work with Turkey to support the Islamic State. There is only one thing Europe has done correctly where we have failed."

"What is that?"

"They beheaded their kings a long time ago. We are still a generation away from that."

Maghribi looked slowly around the room.

"Don't worry," said Malouf. "No bugs here. What I've said is true."

"You brought me here for a reason. How can I be of help?"

"I need you to take a trip. A long trip. You will be embedded in a city inside the United States."

"Am I assigned to a mosque?"

"No. They are all under surveillance. Your objective is to attract no attention. You will be embedded in Milwaukee."

"What is that?"

"A city."

"Where?"

"In a state called Wisconsin. A pleasant little backwater. A land of small towns and villages. Milwaukee is their only big city. The people are naive. Unsuspecting."

"You are joking!"

"I am not."

"It will not be possible for me to blend in. The people in the middle of the United States are mostly of European descent. I will stand out. They will attack me."

"You are wrong, my friend. They are hungry for diversity. Bland cheese demands bacteria to make a rich Gorgonzola. Another Wisconsin city, called Madison, imported people from Chicago because Northern Europeans fear the monochrome and the relentless snow. Most of them would like to live in Madagascar. The parrots and the dark skins fascinate them."

"I am not convinced."

"Look, it is not your job to be convinced. The Germans themselves imported a million people to bring jihad to Europe when it had been eliminated. They are bored by perfection. They crave a touch of murder and rape. Some say their crafty chancellor wanted to eliminate troublesome cartoonists; to require armed guards at synagogues; to import wolves to kill the rabbits. But I do not agree. It was simply ennui in a dying civilization."

"All I can say is that I know the people in America do not like us. After 9/11 and the Boston Marathon and San Bernardino and the rest. I will defend myself if I am attacked."

"You will not be attacked. You will be a zoo exhibit. The stranger you look to them, the better. They will gush over you and tell you how much they like couscous and shish kebob. You will have your selection of young women. They crave the exotic."

"So, what will I do there?"

"You will wait until you are activated."

"Activated for what?"

"Come here."

Malouf walked over to a large calendar mounted on a wall. The date of February 1st of the next year was circled in red.

"On February 1st of next year, the President of the United States will give his State of the Union address to a joint session of the House of Representatives and the Senate inside the Capitol building. His entire cabinet will be there. In the event of his death, all of his successors provided by law will be present. Except one."

Maghribi raised an eyebrow.

"Except one?"

"Yes. This one individual is loosely described as the 'designated survivor.' A weak joke. The idea is that if some misfortune occurs to the building during the Address, and all inside perish, one cabinet member will survive to run the government."

"How does that affect me? And you?"

Malouf smiled.

"This coming February 1st, for the first time in history, if everything goes according to plan, the designated survivor will become President. It is my job to make sure that the man selected is weak and favorable to us. That he is too weak and stupid to resist a flood of jihad through immigration into the United States. Like Merkel in Germany."

"And my job?"

"Your job is to lead the force that will destroy the building and everyone inside it."

Maghribi didn't smile. He had the face of a cadaver, with two lumps of shiny coal inserted into his eye sockets.

"You are joking, of course."

"I am not."

"We cannot even get close to the Capitol in Washington. The security around that event will freeze any flight within a hundred miles. If we flew into it, they would shoot us down."

"My friend, we will not use aircraft alone."

"What then?"

Malouf stared at him.

"You are secure? You may be trusted?"

"Of course."

"Forgive me. You are highly regarded in our agency. You are well liked. But you know the penalty for betraying us. The penalty for you. And for your family."

Maghribi stood up.

"My family? You forget that my brother gave his life on 9/11. He piloted one of the planes into the Towers. I also took the Oath. I will not spoil my eternity. I will sacrifice my life in the fight against the enemies of the Ummah."

Malouf rose to embrace him.

"You are a good man. I expected nothing less."

They sat down.

"We will have spectators sitting in the gallery," Malouf said, "watching the speech. They will carry explosives. At the signal, a fireball will sweep through the chamber. There will also be an external missile attack that I will disclose later. The walls will collapse."

"Are you crazy? They will not let us in the building. They will not let us anywhere *near* the building. And they will not let anyone into the building who is wired with anything."

"You are wrong, my friend. Our people will go in as skutnicks."

"What is that?"

"The role was invented in 1982 by President Ronald Reagan. At the time, a plane crashed into the Potomac River from ice accumulation, and a man named Skutnick survived. Reagan honored him by inviting him to sit in the gallery at the State of the Union address.

Reagan's favorite TV show from long ago was *Queen for a Day*, where distressed housewives degraded themselves to try to win a refrigerator. They each cried and overstated their degradation to curry favor with the rabble in the audience who selected the winner by applauding the loudest after the most pitiful story. Ever since Reagan, presidents have invited guests who they wave at to distract the audience from the bad job they are doing."

"Are you serious?"

"Yes. Republican skutnicks have included a rural clerk who denied a gay marriage license and a hunter with a thick beard and a few teeth who hunts and wrestles alligators."

"And the Democrats?"

"Their skutnicks have included a woman with children who took courses funded by a wasteful program and found a job helping her friends get welfare benefits. They also had a refugee from Syria who has so far refrained from murdering his hosts."

"But even if we go in as skutnicks, we will be searched."

"You are wrong, my friend."

"What?"

Malouf stood to look out the window.

"The laxity in security started under President Obama. He pursued diversity without regard to consequence. His security chief was incompetent. A man and a woman got into one of his White House parties without an invitation or screening. Fortunately for him, they were merely celebrity sniffers who meant no harm. And then the courts went further to help us."

"How?"

"Their courts ruled that a woman in a burka and niqab did not have to show her face or her body for inspection at an airport. In some states, she did not even have to show her face for her driver's license photo."

"But she still must have had to walk through a metal detector at the airport."

"True. But we have perfected the chemistry of recombination. This is currently a secret. It must not be disclosed."

"Of course."

"Our skutnicks are women. They will carry under their clothing components of our explosives that are separately not remarkable. The American courts do not permit them to be patted down, even by matrons, for religious reasons."

"What about dogs?"

"They may not sniff under their garments. And if there are dogs, they will not react to neutral chemicals that are only dangerous in combination."

Maghribi said nothing.

"Once inside, the women will visit the restroom. Together. When they are alone, they will assemble the chemicals, as instructed. They will return to the gallery. At the time arranged, they will detonate their suicide robes. The chamber and all of the people inside it will be consumed by a fireball."

"The women know they will die?"

"Of course. They welcome it. They welcome becoming martyrs for jihad."

"But why will I be sent to this small city far from Washington months before the attack? What purpose is served by doing this?"

"We are under constant surveillance in the U.S. If everyone showed up in Washington right before the event, it would trigger suspicion. Instead, you will each be embedded in different small cities throughout America. In your case, you will be sent as a visiting professor in the Department of Victim Studies at Milwaukee Community College. There will be no mystery about it."

"I am not a professor. I do not even have an undergraduate degree."

"I know."

Malouf smiled as he looked down at a sheet in front of him.

"You were expelled from university here for sexual offenses with women."

"They lied. They were whipped."

"Of course. But you were still expelled. Fortunately, that will not appear on any record the Americans will see."

"What do you mean?"

"Their college will be informed that you have a doctorate in public policy from our university."

"But I know absolutely nothing about public policy. I could not identify an undergraduate textbook."

Malouf chuckled, enjoying himself.

"So what? Public policy is whatever you choose to pull out of your ass according to your mood. Say anything you want. But do not make it too threatening. The prestige of a foreign doctorate will dazzle them.

They will fawn over you. Their women in particular dream about being abducted into a seraglio by someone with a black beard who resembles Omar Sharif, to endure unimaginably delicious ravishing at his hands. But only for a few days. You absolutely must not frighten or even startle them. They must think you are a tame bear until it is too late."

Maghribi almost smiled.

"It will be a pleasure."

"I thought so. You will be embedded in their college for the fall semester. At the signal we give, you will drive to Washington, D.C., just before the State of the Union speech."

"Why should I drive?"

"There must be no record of you on any flight, any train, or any bus. You will always stay at cheap motels and pay with cash, and you will pay cash for meals in cheap restaurants. You are forbidden to have a credit card. When you leave for Washington, you will vanish from the surveillance grid."

"Very well. But what am I supposed to do for this fall semester you mentioned? What am I supposed to teach the students?"

"An outline and all materials will be given to you by our experts. Your specialty is Islamophobia. You will impress them with the wrongs that the Crusaders have inflicted on our people. They will love it. They nuzzle the hand that beats them the hardest. It is the masochism of the West."

"One final question. It is inconceivable that this will not leak out to the Americans. They have placed spies we have not yet discovered. And they have broken into our encrypted traffic."

Malouf shook his head.

"All of the planning, including the skutnicks and support, has been offline. Beyond all administrative departments and personnel. Everyone involved is known to me personally as incorruptible."

"But the electronic communications?"

Malouf grinned.

"Come with me. A Yazidi man has provided our solution. A wondrous solution."

"A Yazidi man?"

"Yes. A Yazidi man who has not much longer to live. We are going to meet him. Come with me."

Chapter Two

Malouf and Maghribi entered a conference room with no windows. Seated inside at a table made of teak were eight men and a teenage girl, wearing a hijab. They all rose out of respect, and one man in particular struggled to get to his feet.

"The Yazidi man has Parkinson's Disease," Malouf whispered to Maghribi. "He needs a caretaker. That is the only reason his daughter sits in our presence."

Malouf motioned them back to their chairs.

"Good afternoon," he said. "We will begin. The girl will be escorted to another room to wait for her father."

One of the men stood up and motioned to the girl. Her father started to protest. She touched his arm.

"It's all right, father. I'll wait for you until you're done here."

As she walked toward the door, everyone seated stared. She looked older than her sixteen years. She was beautiful, fully developed, with large, dark eyes and long slim legs.

"Goodbye, Father. I'll be waiting."

"Goodbye, Dalal."

She left with the escort. Malouf tapped the table.

"We will begin. First, some introductions."

He pointed to the girl's father.

"This is Professor Jangir Khalaf, a Yazidi gentleman, a mathematician who has lectured at several universities here and in Europe. Professor Khalaf, the other men at the table are mathematicians from our country. They have studied your work. Some may have questions about your conclusions."

Professor Khalaf nodded.

"Relations with our Yazidi friends have not always been amicable," Malouf said, "but Professor Khalaf has offered to share with us his discoveries on quantum encryption on an exclusive basis. I believe your hope is that this contribution to our security may lead to better relations between our peoples, is that correct?"

Khalaf nodded again.

"Precisely," he said. "Our people have been attacked for years. Centuries. ISIS tried to exterminate us. We want to show that we are loyal citizens of a troubled area of the world that must see peace. Saudi Arabia has the wealth and stature to protect us . . . if you see fit."

"Excellent. Excellent."

Malouf rubbed his hands.

"Gentlemen, we have a problem. Our current military and diplomatic communications might as well be transmitted publicly. To be brief, our encryption is a joke. It has been penetrated by the Americans. And the Russians. And the Israelis. And the Iranians. And the British, French, Germans, and anyone else who has an interest. Professor, please explain what you have discovered and how it can help us."

"Gladly. My discovery involves quantum cryptography. In brief, it permits the encryption and transmission of information that cannot be intercepted by your enemies. Truly secure transmission of information is impossible using only classical, non-quantum techniques. By contrast, it is impossible to copy data encoded in a *quantum* state. If an enemy tried it, the quantum state would change just by the attempt to copy its data. This would also alert you to the attempted intrusion by a third party."

"All of you have been given the full book on Professor Khalaf's discoveries and proofs," said Malouf. "Instead of repeating it, let us open this up for questions. Of clarification. Of explanation."

A man in full traditional dress raised his hand. Malouf nodded for him to speak.

"Professor, are you proposing that we adopt purely quantum-based cryptography, or just quantum key distribution where the encryption itself is classical?"

"You could do both. My own opinion is that the pure quantum-based cryptography that I have proposed is the most secure. No one has figured out how to invade it. It is based on principles of quantum entanglement between two particles. We do not yet understand how two particles, far apart, even at opposite ends of the universe, are nevertheless entangled in some unknown way so that they can instantly affect one another. If these particles contain information, and someone does *anything* to either one of them, to try to capture or read them, for example, that very contact itself will affect the particles and make them unreadable. But, of course, my method permits the authorized recipient to receive and understand the information."

Another man, also in full traditional dress, raised his hand. Malouf nodded.

"Professor, your work seems to put little value on position-based quantum cryptography. That is where the geographical position of one of the authorized parties is its only credential. Why do you reject it?"

"I do not reject position-based quantum cryptography completely. It ensures that the recipient can only read the message if they are at a precise, predetermined position. But I have proven in my work that position-verification is ineffective using classical methods against collusion or adversaries."

The questions continued for an hour. Malouf finally called a halt to them.

"Enough. Professor Khalaf, the rest of us will discuss this by ourselves for a short time. You will be escorted to a waiting area nearby. We will summon you when we are ready."

"Can I join my daughter?"

"You will shortly. Not right now."

"Where is she?"

"Nearby. Escort the professor out!"

A young man sitting near Khalaf stood and motioned for him to get up. When the professor finally stood up, the escort put his hand firmly on Khalaf's shoulder and guided him out the door.

Malouf looked around the room after they had left.

"I do not have to remind you that our people at one time were the preeminent mathematicians in the world."

No one said a thing.

"We invented algebra itself. In 825, the glorious mathematician, al-Khwarizmi, wrote *Kitab al-Jabr*. The West translated his discovery as 'algebra' and his name as 'algorithm.' "

The men around the table nodded in silence.

"We will restore our preeminence in mathematics *now*! We have been attacked and insulted for centuries. We will no longer kneel to kiss the claws of the wolf. We will regain our rightful preeminence among *all* nations!"

"We support you forever, Iman Malouf," said an older man with a sparse grey beard. "Only tell us what to do, and we will obey."

"First, you are the premier mathematicians in our country. Are you absolutely certain that you understand the Yazidi's theories and his proofs?"

"Yes," said the older man.

"Even assuming the Yazidi fell ill for some reason and passed away? So that you could no longer consult him?"

"Yes."

The rest of the men nodded.

"And do you have sufficient information to build a quantum encryption system that would be unreadable by Western intelligence agencies?"

"Yes."

"But our authorized recipients would be able to receive and read the messages?"

"Of course."

"Very good, gentlemen."

Malouf grinned, as much as a sociopath is capable of smiling. Several men winced.

"This discussion and information are of the utmost secrecy. As I ordered when you were recruited and in the oath you took. You know the penalty for breaking this promise. It will do you no good to escape to Europe if you disclose any of this. A deserter is like a kite. He flies away, but the string is held in Riyadh. It is where your families live. You know what will happen to them if you flee."

"You do not have to worry about any of us, Iman. We are the sons of al-Khwarizmi. We will once again stride the earth."

All the men nodded again.

"Good. How long will it take to produce the encryption system in the proper computer?"

"Sixty days, Iman."

"You may have forty-five days. Do not fail me."

"We will not."

"You may go."

The men got up to leave while Malouf and Maghribi remained.

Chapter Three

"The Yazidis are heretics," Malouf said.

He stared at the ceiling.

"We should have exterminated them a hundred years ago."

"Our friends in ISIS are doing it now," Maghribi said. "The Turks intimidated Trump into allowing it. But, of course, the King would not agree that ISIS is our friend."

"He fears the fate of the European monarchs," Malouf said. "He fears the Wahhabi masters."

"What should we do with the Yazidi? He will disclose his work to the West."

"He must regrettably pass away. Like the Jamal Khashoggi matter you handled in Istanbul. Of natural causes."

Maghribi chuckled, a nasty, grunting chuckle that jarred even Malouf.

"I have to give Khashoggi credit. Fat and old, but he fought like an animal. He injured two of my men. The sound of the chain saw on him was a sweet relief. I will do the same with the Yazidi and his daughter."

"No, my friend."

"What?"

Malouf stood up to stretch.

"My ancestors were in the Bostanci. They guarded the palace of the Ottomans. When an execution was ordered, they performed it. I have given this much thought. You see, I have a conscience. Professor Khalaf has given us a great gift. We must do him honor. As a sign of our respect, you will use the bow string on him."

"What? But that was reserved for Grand Viziers. Or members of the royal family who had to be removed!"

"That was many centuries ago," Malouf said. "We have advanced since then. Because of his great contribution to the modern Caliphate, we will honor him with the bow string."

"As you say. Shall I do it here?"

"Yes. In the room where he is being held. Now."

"And the girl."

"She is also a heretic, beyond protection. She is also immodest. When you are done with her father, go to the cell where she is being held. Do as you wish with her for your pleasure. And when you are done, also the bow string."

"I will enjoy it."

"Maghribi! May I tell you something, my friend?"

"Of course."

Malouf trembled as he spoke.

"Our words are like ripe figs shaken from the tree by a strong wind! Their skins burst to show the sweet fruit! The restoration of the Caliphate has begun! Before February 1st is over, we will have won the greatest victory in our history. And the first casualty is the Yazidi. Go!"

Chapter Four

Lathrop Willis, quite elderly but still sporting a head of thick white hair, was the retired head of the CIA. Wayne Hawkin, more than twenty years younger, was the current head of the Agency. A third man, Maynard Gieck, was the chief mathematician of the NSA. The three men gathered around a conference room table inside a Georgetown townhouse, miles from CIA headquarters in Langley, Virginia.

"Maynard," Hawkin said, "tell us in more detail what we discussed when you called me this morning."

"Right. We monitor all traffic from all governments and all rogue organizations in the Middle East. Most of them use poor encryptions that are easily penetrated. We've recently been intercepting messages from sources that were historically associated with ISIS in Syria. But unlike all other communications we track, these are encrypted in a new way that we haven't yet been able to break. We believe they may have perfected a system of quantum encryption that can't be deciphered using presently known techniques. The communications have been increasing in number, which suggests to us that they involve an urgent matter."

"Do you have any context?"

"Yes. Most of the traffic from these sources before their new encryption were typical. Attack targets, direction of supplies, movements of Russian and Turkish forces. But the last message we could read only had one reference. 'February 1.' And one attachment. A map."

"February 1st? What does that mean?"

"Don't know. That was the subject line. The body of the message was empty."

"Sent by accident?"

"Maybe. Just as they were switching over to the new system."

"Is there any significance to the date?" Willis said. "Any grievances happen on that day that they would want to avenge?"

"We've run all significant historical events that happened on that day. Under both the Gregorian and Julian calendars. Nothing. All obscure stuff that wouldn't inflame anyone today."

"What about this coming February 1st?"

"Well, the State of the Union speech will be on that day. The Super Bowl will be played a few days later. The Oscars are held later in February. If an ISIS affiliate is looking for a venue to stage an attack with maximum attention, those are the obvious choices."

"Right," said Hawkin. "We'll take care of that. And what about the map?"

"Milwaukee."

Willis and Hawkin laughed.

"A map of Milwaukee?" Hawkin said. "Are you joking?"

"Not at all."

"Is there some significance to February 1st in Milwaukee? Some event? I can't imagine there is."

"There is not."

"What are you doing to solve the new encryption?"

"We have our team on it. Full attention, including the involvement of two top academics who won the Abel. That's the equivalent of the Nobel for Mathematics. And you know one other thing that's strange?"

"What?"

"The traffic that we could read before they switched. Lately, it's had some phraseology and references that make us believe that the Saudis are involved."

"The Saudi Royal Family hates ISIS. They fear them."

"I know. I wasn't referring to the Royal Family or the government. But I'm convinced that there is Saudi involvement in these messages other than through the government."

"Very well. Thank you, Maynard. Keep us informed."

"I will."

Gieck left the room. Hawkin walked over to a side table where he opened a silver globe and removed a bottle of sherry. He poured two glasses and handed one to Willis.

"Polula elevate," he said, raising his glass. "Nunc est bibendum."

"Bibemus."

"To your health, Z."

"And to yours, Z."

The two men drank. Each had been a member of Scroll and Key at Yale, although many years apart. Each had been Zanoni, the name given to the leader of the secret society during his senior year.

"Willis, what do you make of this February 1st business? And the Milwaukee reference?"

"I'm not sure. I will say that I wasn't at all pleased to be reminded of Milwaukee again. The Bernie Weber boy and all that."

"Well, he's not a boy anymore. He must be out of college by now. He did help us, of course."

"He did," said Willis. "But I don't like going to the brink on these crises and depending on a savant to save us."

"It won't come to that; I can assure you. Maynard's a good man. He has a good team. He'll crack this."

"And if he can't? Like last time? Then what?"

Hawkin drained his glass.

"Then we get Audrey Knapp involved again. Like last time. To get to Bernie Weber. She can handle him."

"Hawkin, I want to tell you something that we've never discussed, but it needs to be said."

"Go ahead."

"No people in the history of the world has ever meekly turned over a country, much less a continent, to invaders who would eliminate them and their culture."

"That's true, Willis."

"You know, Hawkin, when you and I were at Yale, everyone looked like us. We all went to similar schools. That isn't true anymore."

"I know."

"The goal then was becoming a well-rounded man. Athlete, scholar, man of letters and action. You fenced and I boxed."

"That's true."

"It isn't true anymore either. Now they say they want a well-rounded class. It's an identity zoo. Every peculiar specimen in the world has to be represented."

"Our country's going in that direction, too," Hawkin said. "So, what do we do?"

"I'll tell you what we do. We look to history. Consider this. Jihadists have invaded Europe since the seventh century. They were turned back at the Battle of Tours by Charles Martel. And at the Battle of Lepanto by the European fleet. And at the Siege of Vienna by Polish cavalry and Austrian soldiers."

Willis sipped his sherry.

"Yet still they come," he continued. "This time as immigrants. In time, we will become like Lebanon, with sectarian power sharing and frequent bombings. But you know what? We can't permit that to happen."

"I agree with you. But what do you propose?"

"That we follow the Kelly doctrine."

"And what might that be?"

"It's named for Frank Kelly, a long-serving attorney general of Michigan and well liked. When he would bump into a newly elected attorney general from another state, he would say 'Always remember two things. First, the people of your state want their attorney general to be against gambling. Second, the people of your state want to gamble.' "

Hawkin chuckled.

"Crafty sort. But I don't see the point."

"The people of the United States don't want to exclude anyone. But they also don't want marathons bombed and night clubs shot up. We have to pay lip service to their vanity on the first point. To the conceit of the rabble, their presumption, their pretense of innocence. But we also have to eliminate all vestiges of jihad in the United States."

Hawkin raised his glass.

"History is unlikely as it happens and inevitable afterward. It's time to act!"

Willis raised his glass.

"Pocula elevate. Nunc est bibendum!"

Hawkin raised his higher.

"Bibemus!"

Chapter Five

A goat-bearded African American man in a sport jacket rapped gently on a conference table inside a conference room at Milwaukee Community College. The dozen men and women at the faculty meeting quieted down.

"I am Professor Gravegoods Beaker," he said. "I am the acting chair of the Department of Victim Studies and professor of indigenous public policy. I am the acting chair because our department head, Professor Praisesong Brideprice, is currently on leave as a visiting professor at the University of New Mexico."

In his early life in Detroit, Beaker was known as Malice Parsons. He had endured a rough childhood. He survived by learning to apply serious leather to certain citizens who tried to jump him as he fought his way home from school each day. After graduating against all odds from a small college with a degree in anthropology, he applied for jobs in various universities.

What's in a name? Plenty, he found out. Malice Parsons received no interviews or even responses. As Gravegoods Beaker, however, he received three offers. Milwaukee Community College offered the most money, so he moved to Wisconsin.

"First, as we start a new semester, let us go around the table and introduce ourselves."   Beaker nodded at a woman sitting to his left. She wore a shawl with a picture of a cat pinned to it.

"I am Bronwyn Ferkwell," she said, "professor of women's studies with a specialty in Renaissance victimology. I am a ginger, nonbinary, transfemme, partnered scholar who loves my Plushy."

She pointed to her pin.

"My pronouns are they, them, their."

Beaker pointed to a thin man with sparse hair who sat next to her.

"Yes," the man said. "I am Digby Brayboy, professor of sociology with a specialty in post enlightenment victimology. I am a nerdy Slav who identifies as gender fluid and pansexual. My pronouns are zie, zim, zir."

A young man with light brown hair and blue eyes squirmed in his chair next to Brayboy. Beaker nodded at him.

"Yeah. Okay. I'm Bernie Weber. They just hired me here to be a lecturer in math and physics. I'm getting my PhD in math at Madison. I'm not part of the Department of Victim Studies, but my chairman told me to come here to check it out."

Bronwyn Ferkwell gave him a big friendly smile.

"I think I've heard of you," she said. "Are you the PC-loving trans man gamer-geek from California who just got here?"

"No, ma'am. That wouldn't be me. I'm from here. Wisconsin. I attended this college as an undergrad."

"I suppose then you're binary white cis het."

"No, ma'am."

"Yes, you are," said Beaker. "You're good, Bro. Don't worry."

Ferkwell frowned.

"I do object, Chair. That is a normative statement. It's not good or bad."

"I stand corrected," said Beaker.

"And what are your pronouns, Bernie?" Ferkwell said.

"Uh, I guess I don't have any."

"Yes, you do," Beaker said. "The usual. Next."

And so it went until the last person at the table spoke.

"Welcome all of you," said Beaker. "And now before we start the agenda, I have an announcement to make."

The room became quiet.

"We are getting a new member of our Department of Victim Studies. A visiting professor from Saudi Arabia. His name is Professor Taqi Maghribi. He is an expert in Islamophobia."

Beaker looked down at a sheet of paper.

"Professor Maghribi has his doctorate in public policy from Iman Muhammad ibn Saud Islamic University. He will teach two courses. One is 'The Golden Age of the Caliphate in Spain' and the other is 'The Crimes of the Crusaders.' "

"When does he get here?" said Digby Brayboy.

"Next week. We're going to have a reception to welcome him. As you know, we don't get many visiting scholars. This is good for our reputation."

"Awesome," said Brayboy.

"Most excellent," Ferkwell said, nodding his approval. "This is an important addition to our study of modern victimology."

Gravegoods Beaker sighed as he looked at his colleagues without a hint of pleasure.

More crazy shit. But it's a living.

He continued through the rest of his agenda before dismissing the meeting.

Chapter Six

Waiting at the Milwaukee airport baggage claim was a tall man in full Saudi dress. Finally, he yanked his bag off the carousel and walked toward the exit. Someone was holding a sign that said "Al Maghribi". The Saudi man approached him and handed over his bag.

"Are you Al?" the man said.

Maghribi barely nodded.

"Where is the car?"

"Right outside."

"Take me to my motel. I am staying at a place called the Magnolia on Wisconsin Avenue. Near 27th Street."

Maghribi stared out into the darkness as they passed beyond the downtown Milwaukee skyline and headed west. Soon, the driver pulled up to a seamy motel with several cars parked outside two of the rooms.

"Payment has been arranged in advance?" Maghribi said.

"Yes."

Maghribi took his bag and entered the small lobby. The young woman sitting behind the desk was short and stocky with a blue streak through her blonde hair. She was looking at wedding dresses in a bridal magazine. Occasionally, she glanced down at the diamond on her ring finger.

"I am here for my room!"

She looked up at the tall man in the white gown and head covering.

"I have a room reserved," he said. "For two nights until I move into my apartment. It is under Maghribi."

The woman's lips trembled.

"Just a minute. Have to call my manager. About something."

She pulled out her cell as she stepped into the next room. It rang twice before someone answered.

"Officer Schmidt. Who is this? Jesus, Cindy! You know you can't call me when I'm working, when I'm on duty!"

Schmidt shrugged as he looked at the officer in the passenger seat of his squad car.

"I'm scared, Rudy!"

"What's up?"

"ISIS! We got ISIS here!"

"What?"

"I'm at work. It's one of them. I swear. He walked in and looked me over. I'm all alone here. He's got the uniform on, too. Get over here, Rudy! Quick."

"On the way!"

Officer Schmidt hit the siren. Cars pulled over to the curb as he sped toward the Magnolia and hit the radio.

"Squad 7022 here. 1033. Felony in progress at the Magnolia Motel. 27th and Wisconsin. Squad 7022 on the way. 1033. Request K-9."

The dispatcher came right back.

"Roger seven zero two two. Roger ten thirty-three. Squads in area seven zero proceed immediately."

Schmidt and his partner pulled up to the Magnolia just as two other squads arrived. All the officers got out and hurried to the door. One of them held a magnificent German shepherd on a leash.

Schmidt drew his weapon, pushed the door in and trained his gun on Maghribi.

"On the floor!" he screamed. "Down! Now!"

"I have done nothing wrong! The girl disappeared. Where is my room?"

Two officers ran over to the Saudi. One held a pair of handcuffs.

"You're under arrest. Put your hands behind your back."

"I will not."

An officer tased Maghribi, who went down immediately. The German shepherd jumped on him and tried to sniff under his robe.

"AAAGHGH! Help me! Keep the dog away!"

They rolled him over and handcuffed him.

Cindy reappeared as they hauled Maghribi to his feet and shoved him out the door. Her eyes were wet, but she had composed herself. She ran over to give her fiancé a hug.

"You're so brave, Rudy! Thank you, guys!"

"You okay, Babe?"

"I am now."

Rudy kissed Cindy and headed out the door.

Chapter Seven

Wayne Hawken's secretary poked her head around the partially opened door to his office.

"Audrey Knapp's here."

"Show her in."

An extremely attractive woman with thick auburn hair held back by a tortoise shell clip walked into Hawken's office. She was about forty, dressed in a dark skirt, white blouse, and low heels. Hawkin stood up to greet her. They shook hands. He motioned her to a seat near the window.

"It's good to see you again, Audrey."

"Same. But tell me you're not sending me to Milwaukee again to guard Bernie Weber."

She chuckled as she said it, an absurd idea, funny because it was impossible. Hawkin laughed with her.

"Good one. Going to Milwaukee to guard Bernie again! That's rich."

They both chuckled some more.

"So why did you ask me to come here?"

Hawkin stopped laughing.

"I want you to go to Milwaukee to guard Bernie Weber again."

"All right. Very funny. What do you want?"

"I want you to go to Milwaukee and contact Bernie Weber. Not exactly guard him. I hope it won't come to that. But we need him. Badly. And you're the only one in the Agency he trusts."

Hawkin handed her a copy of an email, with "February 1" in the subject line. A map of Milwaukee was clipped to it.

"We intercepted that email from an ISIS affiliate in Saudi Arabia."

"I thought ISIS was outlawed in Saudi?"

"It is. Members of the Royal Family fear for their lives. But the Wahhabi jihadists who control Saudi society are in bed with ISIS. They've developed an encryption technology that we can't break. Yet. This email was the last one to come through that we can read."

"What's the significance? Is something happening in Milwaukee on February 1st?"

"No. But something's happening in Washington that day. The State of the Union. We think they're planning to disrupt the speech. Or to do something to compete with it for attention."

"Why is Milwaukee involved?"

"Don't know."

"What do you want me to do?"

"I want you on the response team."

"Tell me more."

"Are you familiar with quantum encryption? You have a PhD in math."

"My dissertation was in number theory. I'm familiar with quantum theory. And a little bit with encryption strategies. But if you're looking for an expert, I'm not your girl."

"I'm not looking to you for that expertise, Audrey. But you did excellent work last time getting Bernie to help us break the Chinese. Someone in Saudi has figured out quantum encryption. I'm very concerned that an attack by jihadists is being planned, and as things stand now, we can't prevent it. Because we don't know what it is."

"Where are Maynard and the NSA mathematicians on this?"

"They're working hard. And maybe they'll solve it. But I have an uneasy feeling that they won't. That's where you come in. With Bernie."

"Quantum theory is a lot of physics, as well as math. Do you think Bernie can realistically solve this in a few months? It's July already. Even assuming he agrees to work on it, how can it be done so quickly?'

"Audrey. A lot of people out here think Bernie is a fluke. A savant who got lucky when he helped us last time. I don't agree with them. I think Bernie is a genius. A young man with an extraordinary gift. It can't hurt to get him involved. If Maynard's team does the job, no harm done. But they didn't last time, and Bernie did."

"All right. Give me my orders."

Hawkin stood up and looked out the window.

"You will work directly for me, and report only to me. Your communications will be verbal only. Personnel records will show you on leave. You will go to Milwaukee and recruit Bernie to penetrate this code. No other line officers in the Agency have anywhere near your mathematical knowledge. You'll be his handler. And one other thing."

"What?"

"You'll report to Langley for training in certain combat techniques. Just in case."

"I've already had combat training."

"Not this kind. You will get Bernie to start working on this. Maynard will brief you. And if anyone gets wind of this and tries to stop him in any way, you will protect him."

"Right. When do I start?"

"When you leave this office."

"Yes, sir."

Chapter Eight

Inside Milwaukee Community College, Bernie Weber looked at his Intro to Math and Physics class of two dozen students. He didn't appear old enough to be the teacher. He was dressed more like a teenager in khaki pants, a blue, long-sleeved shirt, and sneakers. With his bushy light brown hair, pale blue eyes, and exceptionally clear skin, he didn't even look old enough to shave. He could have been mistaken for a smart high school kid who'd been cleared to get college credits after he'd tested out of his senior courses.

The class was made up of aspiring physics and math majors, a few other students who were knocking out their science requirements, and a handful of grey-haired retirees. Wisconsin lets anyone over sixty audit courses in the State University System for free.

"Good afternoon, class," Bernie said.

A few "good afternoons" came in response.

"Welcome to Intro to Math and Physics. I'm Bernie Weber. I'm a lecturer. I'm actually getting my PhD in math from UW-Madison."

After years of attacks and cuts by vandal legislators, most campuses in the state system used non tenure track lecturers at peanut wages to teach many of their courses.

"This course assumes that you've had high school math through calculus, and physics. But I've been given pretty wide latitude in how we go about this. Math is really a language, a beautiful language, and physics is its literature. Think of it that way. We'll cover plenty of equations and all that, but I also want you to dream. By that, I mean you can ask me anytime about things that may seem crazy to you but capture your imagination. So, let's start now. Throw out a crazy question that you've been thinking about."

One of the elderly auditors raised her hand.

"Yes."

"I was wondering, because I've heard it both ways. Can anything go faster than the speed of light?"

"Yes and no," said Bernie.

"What?"

"Nothing in the universe can go faster than the speed of light. But the universe itself is expanding faster than the speed of light."

"What does that mean?" the woman said. "What's it expanding into?"

"Good question," said Bernie. "We'll get to that later in the course. Now let me throw something else out that I'm working on in my dissertation. Under quantum theory, two particles can be entangled, and can affect each other instantly, even if they're billions of light years away from each other. Does their effect on each other violate the rule that nothing in the universe can go faster than light? Or is it somehow innate, more biological, like genes? But if it is, how do they communicate?"

Silence. No one spoke for a solid minute. Finally, an undergraduate raised his hand.

"Yes."

"I'm like an econ major? I'm taking this for my science requirement? This is supposed to be like an intro course, right?"

"Absolutely," Bernie said. "Nothing like what we just talked about will be on the exam. But I like to consider some crazy ideas. Throw them out when you want."

He turned to the whiteboard and wrote an equation on the board.

"Okay. I want to review the first problem in the course outline. I know it's a lot of material, but we go through it more quickly in summer school. Consider this: a rock is dropped off a cliff a hundred meters high. How long does it take to reach the ground?"

Bernie went through the rest of the outline. When the hour ended, he gathered his notes and followed his students out into the hall. Gabriel Bay, the chairman of the Math Department, was standing outside, waiting to speak with him.

"Bernie. Got a minute?"

Bay seemed agitated.

"Just wanted to make sure you're attending the Victim Studies meeting."

"I was at the last one, Mr. Bay."

"Call me Gabe. They're meeting again in an hour. I need one of us there."

"This is just the reception to welcome a new guy. I didn't think . . ."

"They're dragging the university down, Bernie! It's an umbrella group of professional victims and identity freaks. They're killing us on money, increments, and resources. Always with their hands out, wincing, begging, and whining. We've got to keep an eye on them. You're it."

"Yes, sir."

"Report back to me after you meet."

"Okay. Will do."

People had already started to file into the dean's office when Bernie arrived. A tray of cheese, crackers, and peeled shrimp was set on a credenza. Several bottles of wine, with plastic glasses, and cans of beer and water cooled in a tub.

Through a closed glass door leading into the dean's private meeting area, Bernie could see a tall man in Arab dress sitting by himself, typing on a laptop.

Digby Brayboy interrupted him. He sipped from a glass of white wine.

"So, tell me what you're teaching, Bernie. And about your dissertation."

"I'm teaching Intro for now. My dissertation is on quantum encryption."

"That sounds distressingly technical."

"It's fun. Basically, here's the issue. Let me explain."

While Bernie spoke, the Arab kept typing, paying no attention to anything else.

Chapter Nine

"Ready for conference. Have limited time."

As Taqi Maghribi typed these words in Arabic, the word ENCRYPTED flashed in blue letters at the top of the screen and then froze.

"Are you in a secure place?" came the response.

"In private conference room of Dean. Door closed."

"They cannot read this remotely. But can anyone see the screen?"

"No."

"Nevertheless, we will postpone until this evening when you are alone. But I have a question. What happened out there? You were arrested checking into a motel? You were not up to any mischief with women?"

"No. They are a simple people, afraid of foreigners. You insisted I stay at cheap hotels in bad parts of town to keep a low profile."

"You must remain anonymous. But the story has been reported. We are deciding how to handle it. Perhaps to own the story, we will sue the police for Islamophobia."

"Is that wise? It will draw more attention to me."

"You have already drawn press attention. Now you may have to hide in plain sight. Bringing suit would be expected. No decision has been made. This conference is adjourned until seven p.m. your time tonight."

"Understood."

Maghribi closed his laptop. Gravegoods Beaker took him by the arm as soon as he came out into the dean's office.

"Welcome, Professor Taqi Maghribi!"

The small group of faculty applauded.

"We will introduce ourselves," said Beaker. "I am Professor Grave-goods Beaker, acting chair of the Department of Victim Studies. I have an interest in urban education policy. I spent many years in Detroit under an assumed name doing research on seemingly mundane issues; for instance, how a student gets safely to school and back to his apartment."

Digby Brayboy, Bernie, and Bronwyn Ferkwell went next. Ferkwell then nodded to the man next to her.

"Yes. I am Uri Diggleboots. I am a professor of anthropology with an interest in Sumerian victimology and evidence of victim presence in prehistory. Stone Age middens are my specialty. I am a motorcycle-riding, Stonewall-surviving, Texan foodie who identifies as gender fluid. My pronouns are tey, ter, tem, ters, and terself."

And so it went, until everyone had gotten in touch with his inner weasels and brandished them for approval.

"And yourself, Professor Maghribi," Beaker said. "Tell us about you and your specialty."

"Yes. Of course. I am Professor Taqi Maghribi. I am a scholar, from the faculty of Iman Muhammad ibn Saud Islamic University, where I received my doctorate in public policy. The courses I will teach here are the Golden Age of the Caliphate in Spain and Crimes of the Crusaders."

"What are your pronouns?" said Bronwyn Ferkwell.

Maghribi hesitated.

"They are Iman and Professor."

"It was horrible what happened to you when you tried to check into your motel, "Uri Diggleboots said. "We heard about it this morning. It must gall you every day to see white privilege exercised in this fashion."

Maghribi pretended to look sad. He lowered his head.

You triumphant, ascendant, insincere prick! You are secretly pleased that they tased me and a big dog stuck his wet nose under my robe. Are you not? Beheading with a penknife would be too good for you.

"It is difficult," he said softly.

"Tell me," said Diggleboots. "Purely as an academic question. I was reading a document that set out the ISIS rules of slavery. What does the term 'al-sabi' mean?"

"It means a non-Muslim woman who has been captured by Muslims. Please understand that we reject ISIS. Of course."

"Right. But the article seemed to say that once she is captured, she is the slave of her captors, and they can enjoy her sexually as they please."

"That is true. There is support for that . . . but, of course, we reject such an interpretation. The proper focus must be on the Crusaders. But tell me more about yourselves!"

The conversation was brisk, and the shrimp went quickly as they mingled. It wasn't long before just a few crackers and bits of cheese remained.

Digby Brayboy led Bernie over to meet Maghribi.

"I want you to meet Bernie Weber. One of the few scientists who comes to our meetings. Probably the only one. And probably because Gabe Bay makes him."

Brayboy chuckled.

"Even paranoids have enemies. Gabe, I mean. Not Bernie."

He chuckled some more.

"What is your subject?" Maghribi said.

"Math. Well, I'm teaching Intro to Math and Physics, but my PhD will be in math."

"Tell him the topic, Bernie," said Brayboy.

"It's on quantum encryption."

Maghribi frowned.

"Interesting. What is your progress? What is your conclusion?"

"I'm not done yet. I'm still a grad student in Madison."

"You are just starting out!" Maghribi said. "Still a boy! Very good. Very good."

Brayboy expertly snagged the last piece of cheese as the rest of the faculty clustered around Maghribi.

Chapter Ten

Bernie sat on a bench in Milwaukee's Lake Park, near the softball field, just past the Indian Burial Mound. It was a beautiful August evening, in the low eighties, with no clouds. He stretched and looked impatiently down the path.

A woman in shorts and a blouse, wearing sunglasses, sauntered down the path. Bernie stood up, and she hugged him.

"Hi, Ms. Knapp," he said, shifting awkwardly.

"It's Audrey, Bernie. You know that. Sit down."

He looked at her, then looked away, trying to smile.

"I haven't seen you in a long time, Bernie. Since the Riemann adventure."

"Right."

"Are things good with you? Your mom and dad? Your uncle?"

"Yeah. Kinda. Dad's still in the hospital. Joe and Franny are good. Moms good. So is Terry Norris."

"I'm glad to hear that."

"Why'd you call me?"

"Bernie, here's what's happened. I need you again. *We* need you again."

"I thought so. But you know I don't want to be with spies and such. I don't mean you! Not you! I like you! But the others."

"I know, Bernie. But here's the thing. Nobody we're after knows about you. They don't know I'm here. But something terrible is going to happen if we can't read some messages from some very bad people."

"What do you need me for?"

"Here's the problem. Some people who hate this country have started to encrypt their messages so we can't read them. But just before they did, they sent a message that clearly mentioned the date February 1st, and they attached a map of Milwaukee."

"What does that mean?"

"February 1st is the date of the President's State of the Union Address. Six months away. We don't know why they included the map."

"What do you want me to do?"

"The NSA says the messages are protected by some form of quantum encryption that we can't penetrate. Yet. Their mathematicians are working hard to pierce it. But frankly, I don't have a lot of confidence they'll succeed. Neither does my boss. We both have a lot of faith in you. We want you to work on it separately, just like before."

"Can't you just, like, guard the Capitol that day? Keep them away?"

"Of course. And we would anyway. But I think they're up to something that could be lethal for a lot of people. We need to know exactly what they're doing."

Bernie looked toward the Indian Mound. He didn't answer right away.

"And I suppose I should ask you the obvious, Bernie. Do you even know anything about quantum theory? And especially about quantum encryption? In any of your courses? It would be unfair to ask you to do this if you had to start from ground zero."

"Yeah. I do know some things. In my grad work in Madison."

"So, will you help us, Bernie? Please help us."

Bernie sighed.

"Okay. I'll help you."

"Thank you, Bernie! Thank you! You'll be getting a package delivered to your apartment with a secure computer and instructions on how to log on to a special site to read the messages I'm talking about. That site contains an outline of where they came from, and context info. It shows the approaches that the NSA is currently taking to break them."

"Am I supposed to have that stuff?"

"Of course not. It's eyes only for just a few people. But how do you help us break the messages if you can't see them?"

Bernie nodded.

"Right. Okay."

"And let me dig into something, Bernie. We have to assess how likely it is that you can help on this. We don't have a lot of time. Can you give me an idea of your grad work? What you're trying to accomplish?"

"Sure. But I'm not telling people about it now. I mean generally. I want to spring it on them when I finish my dissertation."

"Bernie, what you tell me is as secret as the package I'm sending you. Only my Agency head will know. You remember him from last time. Wayne Hawkin."

"Yeah. I remember him."

"And when the time is right, he'll give the results of your work to the NSA. Their head mathematician. That's it."

"That's okay, Audrey. So, here's what I'm doing. Have you ever heard of a guy named John Bell? John Stewart Bell?"

"I've heard the name. That's all."

"He was a famous physicist. Anyway, in 1964 he proved that a theory Einstein and two other guys proposed in 1935 was wrong. Einstein never liked quantum theory. The idea of two entangled particles billions of light years away from each other affecting each other instantaneously bothered him. He called it 'spooky action at a distance.' He said it would mean information between them traveled faster than the speed of light, which is impossible. He said that there must be hidden variables, so that the results of the experiments were preordained."

"What did Bell do to change that?" said Audrey.

"Bell proved that Einstein was wrong. At least that's the current view. Not on relativity, but on quantum theory. Bell showed that the hidden variables Einstein proposed were nonlocal. He proved that the results of certain kinds of measurements of one entangled particle depended instantaneously on certain measurements of the other entangled particle. Even if they're billions of light years apart! In other words, once subatomic particles become entangled, an action performed on one will have an instant effect on the other, no matter how far apart they are."

"You're getting a little deep here, Bernie," Audrey said. "Where are you taking this?"

"I read up on Bell. A lot. Did you know that he did some work at the University of Wisconsin? At Madison? He was from Belfast. And he worked in Switzerland, but he actually spent time here."

"No, I didn't know that."

"I was sitting in my carrel at the library one day, and I thought, what if he left some papers? Or notes? He died thirty years ago. So I went over to the library and asked if they kept papers from any of the professors. They said sometimes they did."

"What did you find?"

"There's this room in the basement with boxes on wooden racks. They had a section for math. They let me look. One box said JSB. So I opened it up and went through it."

"Did you find anything?"

"It was him! Bell! His stuff. And then it hit me."

"What hit you?"

"Bell initially agreed with Einstein. I'll boil it down. See, other physicists believed that quantum theory meant that particles don't have definite values for stuff like position and velocity. They believed that particles hang in a probability cloud until they're measured, and then they get definite only when they're measured."

"You're saying Einstein didn't like that, right?"

"Right. And neither did Bell. And neither do I. Some of these other physicists didn't believe the world exists independently of our observing it. They didn't even believe the moon existed unless someone was looking at it."

"But Bell proved that Einstein was wrong?"

"Right. But I think even Bell was surprised by his proof, and I don't think he was ever satisfied that it was the final answer."

"What do you think now, Bernie?"

"I don't think this is the final answer. Bell's proof became the basis of new fields. Quantum information theory, quantum computing, quantum encryption. I realized that if someone can prove that a particle actually has a real position and velocity that isn't dependent on being measured and isn't dependent on measurements to another particle light years away, then any encryption based only on Bell's proof is compromised."

"What did you find in the box, Bernie?"

"Lots of equations and notes."

Bernie was getting excited.

"Bell was working on a theory to explain his proof! He obviously still believed that any physical object must actually be located somewhere and that it must have a definite velocity even if it's never measured by anybody. He didn't finish this work when he was here at Madison. And then he suddenly died. But I think I can follow his train of thought from his notes!"

"That's amazing, Bernie. But six months isn't a lot of time. Can you do it?"

"I'll try. I think I can."

They got up to leave. Audrey hugged him again.

"I'm staying in town, Bernie. Just let me know if I can help you at all. The way to contact me is in the package you'll be receiving."

"Okay.

"We'll talk soon, Bernie."

"Bye, Audrey."

Chapter Eleven

Taqi Maghribi sat in front of a computer screen in his apartment on Brewers Hill. The date and time read September 1, 7:30 p.m. A blue legend flashed and froze.

ENCRYPTED.

Then came the first question in Arabic.

'Are you secure?'

He typed in 'Yes.'

'Is anyone with you?'

'No.'

'Can anyone see your screen?'

'No.'

'I have news. But first, you have been there two months. What progress have you made?'

'To blend into this community?'

'Yes.'

'Could not be going better.'

'Except for your arrest at the motel the day you arrived.'

'I was released. It was not my fault.'

'I was joking. Proceed.'

'The masochism of these people is beyond belief. I say what I want about the decay of their culture and country, and they beg for more. The women especially are fond of firm treatment.'

'Be very careful with that. We want no scandal.'

'I spent the early weeks meeting people and preparing my courses. The materials you provided are very helpful. The semester starts this week. How are the others doing?'

'Good. It's really funny. Our asset in Chicago was part of a demonstration against immigration bias. When he was questioned by the press about certain military operations our soldiers took in defense of the Ummah, he mentioned the Crusades and attacked the FBI, as instructed. He has become quite popular in his university.'

'Is that wise? Shouldn't we be invisible?'

'We have concluded that that is impossible in this climate. The best strategy is to hide in plain view. A modest profile shows we have nothing to hide. Their government wouldn't believe that our assets could have the boldness to be public before we strike.'

Maghribi frowned.

'I hope you are right.'

'This implicates you. We have decided you will bring a lawsuit against the City of Milwaukee for police brutality. You were simply checking into a hotel. You were wearing your traditional dress, which is your right under their first amendment. The police shot you. You were bitten by their dog."

'Well, I was shot with a taser, and the dog put his head under my robe.'

'Same thing. This must be presented for maximum sympathy.'

'Won't my colleagues here be angry with me?'

'On the contrary. Our strategy in all countries that we initially penetrate through immigration is to ally with the left. The right would kill us on sight. But the left hate themselves and their culture. They demand to be flogged by an unsparing hand. Their women hear of our culture where women obey men. Where women cannot show their bodies or appear alone in public. Where honor killings are the result of disobedience to the father. And they scream for our culture to come to them.'

'You are exaggerating.'

'Not by much. Homosexuals are executed over here. But left-wing homosexuals scream to loosen the immigration laws to let our people into their country. We prosper in the fertile fields of the far left, until the time is right to act.'

'How shall I proceed on the lawsuit?'

'Do nothing for now. We will select the right lawyers and instruct you.'

'As you say.'

'I am not done. There is a matter of great urgency I must discuss with you.'

'What?'

'We have received certain information from sources in the American Congress and in their security agency.'

'How is that possible? Are they reliable?'

'The Americans are naive. They scream for diversity even in their most sensitive organs of government. They hired a Chinese national in the CIA, and he betrayed them for thirty years. All their informants in China were executed. But still, they feel they must hire Chinese nationals.'

'But for us? Aren't they more careful?'

'No. Their congressmen are permitted to hire whoever they want as staff. One of them is an excellent source. He passes on useful rumors. And we have a low-level hire in their CIA who does the same. What I am about to tell you is only a rumor, revealed by a secretary in bed with our man. But it must be investigated.'

'What?'

'There is a professor at the college you are visiting, named Bernie Weber.'

Maghribi snickered.

'You ARE joking!'

'Why do you say that?'

'I met this 'professor'. He is a boy. They are using him to teach an introductory course. He is still a graduate student. He is not a professor. He knows nothing but basic concepts.'

'We can't assume that. The secretary says that an agent has been assigned by the head of the agency to get Weber to penetrate our communications. This agent is a woman.'

'I haven't seen or heard of a woman or anyone else out here for this purpose. Or even to see the Weber boy.'

'Nevertheless, you are instructed to monitor Weber and anyone contacting him. Engage him in conversation. Determine what he knows. If a bitch from the CIA appears, tell us immediately. We will determine whether you or someone else will stop her. Permanently. And him.'

'I understand. I will obey.'

'Good. Out.'

Chapter Twelve

Nine men and four women sat around a conference table in a small room inside the Rayburn House Office Building on Independence Avenue in Washington, D.C. The door was locked. No staff were present. No notice of the meeting appeared on the daily congressional schedule of events.

A man sitting in the middle tapped his fingers on the table.

"You all know me. I am Lamar Patterson of Texas. To my right is Mr. Wayne Hawkin, director of the Central Intelligence Agency. On behalf of the rest of us Representatives, we welcome our two colleagues from the Senate who are with us."

He nodded at a man and a woman sitting across from him.

"And we are especially honored to have the chief justice of the United States Supreme Court. Mr. Chief Justice."

He nodded toward a man at the end of the table.

"I am now going to turn this meeting over to Director Hawkin, who requested we convene it. You will all remember the reason this committee was formed in the first place. With the rise of more foreign-born members of Congress and more foreign-born staff from non-Western cultures, the CIA became reluctant to share with us the most sensitive information that could endanger our assets in the field. When several of our other members were suspected of collaborating with Russia, and receiving payments from the commie Russkies, including our president, Mr. Hawkin insisted that we form an ad hoc committee from both parties of members and Senators who the Agency is certain are not compromised. This committee is unknown to the press and the rest of Congress, and no written record will be made of our discussions. With that, Mr. Hawkin has the floor."

"Thank you, Lamar, Mr. Chairman. We have a matter of the utmost urgency. I will first state the problem we face, and its history. Then, I will propose a solution and ask for your approval of the action we propose.

"The problem. For fourteen hundred years, from the founding of Islam in the early seventh century until now, the West has battled jihadist forces seeking to destroy us. The jihadists quickly overran Spain and Portugal thirteen hundred years ago and held them for centuries. Eventually, they were thrown out of France in the Battle of Tours Poitiers. Their fleet was driven out of the Mediterranean at the Battle of Lepanto. They were driven out of Austria in the Siege of Vienna. They occupied the Balkans for nearly five hundred years until they were mostly driven out in the late nineteenth century.

"The Ottoman Empire, the seat of jihadist violence against the West, was called the sick man of Europe. After the First World War, we divided up their empire to neuter it and it remained that way—until now. Stopping the resurgence of jihadist violence against the West is my top priority, and it is why I asked for this meeting."

"Some of the Muslim countries are allied with us, at least on paper," said one of the Senators. She looked down at her notes. "Saudi Arabia, Turkey, Pakistan and others. Is it possible they have changed?"

"No," Hawkin said. "It is not. Their governments will ally with us if they are given enough money and weapons. But the cultural imperative to commit jihad against us is engrained in the people. I remind you of 9/11, the Boston Marathon, San Bernardino, Orlando, Fort Hood, Chattanooga, Chelsea, Ohio State, and the Manhattan Bike Path Murders. Saudi Arabia masterminded 9/11. Their ambassador to the U.S. had a slip of paper in his pocket with the phone number of one of the hijackers. Twenty-five pages of the 9/11 report are sealed because they show involvement by the Saudi government. Pakistan hid Osama Bin Laden from us. Turkey slaughters the Kurds and defies us at will."

"What is the present problem?" said a congressman.

"The West has lost its historical memory," said Hawkin. "Angela Merkel let a million people from jihadist cultures into Germany. She had to have known that they would go to Paris and London and elsewhere. They have shown their gratitude by unleashing murderous anti-Semitism and attacking churches, priests, newspapers, and the general populace in France, Germany, Britain, Spain, and Belgium. As their numbers increase, it gets harder to simply remove them."

No one responded.

"At one time, Egypt was a hundred per cent Christian," Hawkin said. "Iran, Malaysia, and Afghanistan were not Muslim countries. But when jihadist culture takes root, either through conquest or immigration, the cultural imperative of jihad demands the forced conversion or murder of the host population. That is what happened in Asia, and it is happening in Africa right now. Europe will be more than ten percent Muslim in a generation if their leaders don't show some backbone. In an advanced country like ours, you either give in to blackmail and murder and slowly change your culture, or you remove millions of people and become a police state. We have to stop it before it starts."

"Wayne, what are you asking us to do?" said Lamar Patterson.

"Here is the present problem in the United States. The jihadist presence is increasing. We have active terrorist investigations in all fifty states. When we catch a terrorist, we are required to try them in civilian courts. But civilian juries can be threatened or bribed. We had one case in New York where we prepared an indictment with more than two hundred counts. The defense lawyers argued that the bomber they were defending was being discriminated against and the jury bought it. We had physical evidence of the bombing, a confession, an accomplice's testimony, and a wired conversation before the bombing about the plan. But the rabble are easily manipulated and acquit their tribe."

"He got off?" Lamar said.

"No. The jury found him not guilty on all but one count. They thought they were throwing us a harmless bone, to make it look as if they were on the up and up. Fortunately, the count they convicted him on was conspiracy, so he got life in prison. But we can't keep doing this. The illegal Mexican immigrant in California who shot the girl in front of her father on the pier was acquitted by a jury, even though he was caught immediately and admitted he'd done it. We can't allow that to happen in a bombing case."

"Isn't there a bill pending in Congress?" said another congressman. "In effect it would declare that a state of war exists with jihad. All trials would take place in Guantanamo with military lawyers and judges, and all appeals would be expedited to the FISA court outside of public view?"

"Yes," said Hawkin. "And it has no chance of passage. I pointed out that in a war, you have abbreviated process. When we captured Nazi spies in North Carolina in 1943, we gave them a military trial and executed them. But that bill is still buried in committee."

"Tell us what you'd like to do, and what it is you're asking us to approve," said the Chief Justice.

"Let me get to the point. We have an immediate danger. We believe that there may be a jihadist attack planned on the Capitol during the State of the Union Address in February. We do not know the specifics. I am requesting authority from this committee to use any means necessary, even deadly force, to prevent that attack. And to use it in advance, outside of any judicial process."

The room was completely silent.

"And let me add something," Hawkin said. "I strongly feel that our democracy requires both the appearance and the reality of legislative and judicial control over the use of deadly force by the government. The reason that I asked Lamar to assemble this committee is that all members of Congress here were duly elected, are trustworthy, and are respected throughout our government. The chief justice was duly appointed and is widely respected. If I brought my request to the entire Congress, or to the public judicial process of the lower courts, it would have no chance of being approved. But we absolutely need it as jihadist attacks become bolder, and the West refuses to expel jihad from its borders."

"Why couldn't you bring this in secret before the FISA court?" said the Chief Justice.

"No chance," said Hawkin. "That court, as you know, does not have the jurisdiction for this. They would not go out on a limb, and the newspapers constantly attack the FISA process anyway. They attack the FISA court and the CIA for not playing by Marquis of Queensbury rules against assassins."

"I'm not sure I like a James Bond type roaming around bumping people off," said a congresswoman. "What kind of controls on him do you propose?"

"Do not assume it will be a *James* Bond," Hawkin said. "Could be a *Jane*. But the identity will not be disclosed. As to controls, this person would report directly to me. Offline, and not through the normal processes of our agency. I give strict orders on boundaries and objectives."

"Would you require your personal approval in advance before action is taken by this individual?"

"Wherever possible. But remember, in the present threat, we do not know most of the details. I can envision circumstances where our agent would have a chance to terminate a jihadist who might escape before they could make a phone call."

"Wayne," said Lamar. "Why don't you step outside the room? We want to discuss your request in private."

"Gladly. Thank you."

Hawkin left the room. He walked into an adjacent room and texted.

'Audrey, come home. Need to see you day after tomorrow at 9 a.m.'

He walked back into the hallway and waited. Half an hour later, Lamar Patterson poked his head out.

"Come back in, Wayne."

Hawkin followed him in and sat down.

"Wayne," said Patterson. "You have our approval. Your actions must be discreet. They must be essential to the defense of our country from enemy attack. And any reasonable person should be able to agree that what you and your men do is right."

"Thank you. Thank you very much for your confidence in me and the Agency."

No one spoke. Hawkin got up and left the room.

Chapter Thirteen

Wayne Hawkin's secretary opened his door and poked her head in.

"Audrey's here."

"Send her in."

Audrey Knapp took a seat near Hawkin's desk.

"What's up?"

"Plenty. First, how are you doing in Milwaukee? Is Bernie getting anywhere?"

"Yes, he is. The approach he's taking is really extraordinary. How is the NSA doing on it? Maynard?"

"I don't have much confidence. He briefs me. I don't know beans about the subject, but no one has been able to break quantum encrypted communications. It's too new. Frankly, we're going under the assumption that the traffic on the February 1st strike will be unreadable. We're assuming the worst and tightening security around the Capitol."

"I'll keep pressing Bernie hard. But why are we meeting now?"

"Two reasons."

Hawkin took a laptop on his desk and turned it toward her.

"Look at this."

Audrey leaned closer to the screen. She saw a picture of an Arab man with a heavy beard dressed in full, traditional Arab dress. He was not smiling. He was identified beneath the picture as Iman Taqi Maghribi.

"Why are you showing me this?"

"Have you ever seen him?"

"No."

"Well, he's in Milwaukee."

"How do you know?"

"Pure chance. I saw a newsfeed about an Arab man assaulted by police in Milwaukee. I ran the name through our data base. He's one of the men who murdered Jamal Khashoggi in Istanbul in 2018."

"Okay."

"And the search kicked out a press release from Milwaukee Community College. The man is a visiting professor at the college this semester."

"What's he teaching?"

"Courses on Islamophobia. In their Department of Victim Studies."

"Oh, brother!"

"Here's the best for last. You're in the file, Audrey."

"What?"

"Not by name. We intercepted a message from a Wahabi plant in the Saudi Department for Western Immigration to a contact in Virginia. Normal encryption. It mentions, as they put it, 'a CIA bitch in Milwaukee who may be a problem.' Congratulations!"

"What do you want me to do?"

"A lot. Protect yourself. Monitor him. We'll seed his car, his office, his apartment. And give me a plan for getting him out of the picture. But you know, how the hell did they hear about you? Recruiting Bernie? How did they possibly get to Milwaukee so quickly?"

"Maybe it originally had nothing to do with Bernie. I'll find out. But you didn't call me here just for this. We didn't need a face-to-face for that. What's up?"

Hawkin stood and looked out the window.

"Audrey, jihad is a mortal threat to our civilization. Angela Merkel betrayed Europe by inviting it back in after it had been driven out over many centuries. When a tumor gets too large, the surgery to remove it can also kill the patient. Europe will have to decide before too long whether to expel all vestiges of jihad or succumb to it. I have no intention of seeing the United States succumb to anyone."

"What can I do to help?"

"In the short run, we have to stop the imminent threat. But we can't effectively derail the attack on the Capitol with conventional arrest and prosecution techniques. I've asked a committee of members of Congress and the judiciary to authorize us to use deadly force, at our discretion, outside of judicial and legislative review."

"How can a committee give that authority? The Constitution is pretty clear about what's required."

Hawkin took his time to respond.

"Audrey, we are a nation of laws. But invaders have found a way to use our laws to destroy us. This demands a response. We have declared war on jihad. Not the Congress on the record, but its leadership through private communication with me, and the leader of the Judiciary. Our rules are now the rules of war."

"But why did you want me here today?"

"I agreed with Lamar Patterson that for now I would designate one agent to have this responsibility. You're it."

"Me?"

"Yes, you."

"Wayne. Look. I've never turned down an assignment. And I never will. But there are far more qualified people than me to fill this role."

"There's no one more qualified than you."

"What do you mean?"

Hawkin walked back from the window and sat down.

"Audrey, on its face, this procedure seems to violate all that our democracy stands for. In peacetime, it would deny due process and be unconstitutional for many other reasons. As an act of war, it is justified, but the declaration of war here is . . . irregular. It is of the highest importance to me, to the Agency, and to our government that decisions in this singular procedure be made by someone of the highest integrity who acts in absolute good faith, who represents the essence of our culture. Of the Judeo-Christian tradition. Of Western civilization."

"That's very flattering, but how am I different from anyone else?"

"I've reviewed every course you took from high school through graduate school. I've read all the comments and recommendations by your teachers and coaches that you submitted when you applied to the Agency. At Elmhurst, you took math, physics, and chemistry, but also Latin and Greek. At Boston College, you majored in mathematics, but you took a wide range of liberal arts courses. You read Hesiod and Pindar in Greek. You read Vergil in Latin. You are the embodiment of our culture. I trust you to refrain from killing needlessly and to act *only* when necessary. And by the way, I loved your high school essay about your spider box."

Audrey covered her eyes, pretending to be embarrassed.

"You keep a lidded container in the kitchen to catch insects. Then, you shake them out the back door so they can live. You will not casually kill anybody. You will not get buck fever and blast away because it feels good. That's what I want."

"Wayne! I forgot about the spider box. You're very thorough."

"That's all, Audrey. Go back to Milwaukee. And by the way, don't let all this go to your head. As good as you are, I do have one reservation about you."

"What?"

"It's related to the spider box. I have no fear that you will abuse your power. But I do worry that you will hesitate to use it in time when it's absolutely necessary. That could get you killed. Do not hesitate. That's an order."

"Understood."

She stood up and walked to the door.

"Thanks, Wayne."

Audrey took out her phone as she walked down the hall. A new text.

'Sister Geraldine is in hospice. She is failing. If you intend to visit her, come immediately.'

Audrey put the phone back in her purse and trotted down the hall-way.

Chapter Fourteen

Taqi Maghribi's class met on the first floor of Enderis Hall at Milwaukee Community College. "Crimes of the Crusaders" was printed on the whiteboard. Apart from two older students auditing the class, greyhaired relics of the anti-war protests of the sixties, the room was full of earnest, wide-eyed undergraduates, some sporting tattoos and electric, pastel-dyed hair.

Maghribi looked at them with contempt.

"So, we will take up where we left off yesterday," he said, "about the crimes committed by the Crusaders against the innocent people of what is today called the Middle East. We, I say we, because I am descended from these victims."

A student raised his hand.

"Yes?"

"I have a question from yesterday's discussion."

"Go ahead."

"Is it permissible in your opinion for an individual to blow himself up to target a group that owes allegiance to the Syrian regime, even if this causes casualties among civilians?"

"Very good question," said Maghribi. "Yusufal-Qaradawi of the Muslim Brotherhood has provided the answer."

He took out his phone and scrolled through it.

"I want the precise directive. Let's see. Yes. Iman Yusufal-Qaradawi states, 'Generally individuals should fight and die in combat, however, if the need arises, individuals should only blow themselves up if the Jamaa decides that it is necessary for those individuals to blow themselves up. These are matters that are not left to individuals, who should surrender themselves to the Jamaa, and it is the Jamaa that determines how to utilize individuals according to its needs.' "

"Thank you."

Maghribi gave the students a minute to finish their notes.

A senior auditor raised his hand.

"Yes?"

"What is the directive on whether all unbelieving women may be taken captive?"

"Yes. The directive, and all scholars are in consensus, is that all un-believing women, kufr asli, may be captured."

"Thank you."

"All right. We will now discuss the crimes of the so-called King Richard the Lionheart. Up until now, your teachers have used historical debris to cover up the actual truth of history."

Professor Uri Diggleboots entered the room toward the end of the class and sat in the back. Maghribi dismissed his students a few minutes early and turned to Diggleboots.

"Can I help you?"

"I hope so. Are you busy tonight?"

Maghribi hesitated.

"Possibly. What are you thinking of?"

"I'm sure you're interested in learning more about Milwaukee and our culture. It is very diverse. I wanted to invite you to be my guest at Fur Fest this evening."

"What is that?"

"A festival of Furdom. You'll love it."

"Well, all right."

I will become acquainted with their sick culture before we destroy it.

"Where shall I go?"

"I will pick you up at seven p.m. outside Curtin Hall."

"Very well. Thank you."

Maghribi returned to his apartment. He sat at his desk and turned on his PC. A blue 'ENCRYPTED' legend appeared, then a text.

'Respond immediately.'

'I am here.'

'You are alone? No one can see your screen?'

'Correct.'

'You have an assignment. This so-called boy, Weber, is a problem. More than you told us.'

'What do you mean?'

'We had our asset at the University of Wisconsin in Madison monitor him. Our asset is a graduate student in physics. Weber has been going to the basement of their library. Our asset chatted up a girl at the desk. Weber has been researching papers of the physicist Bell.'

'The significance of that?'

'The Yazidi on whom you bestowed the bowstring plowed the same ground. His, I mean our, cryptography is based on Bell's work. These papers Weber has reviewed were unknown to us. And to everyone. They may contain insights that could compromise us.'

'Shall I take them and burn them?'

'Too late. The girl told our asset that Weber has copied them.'

'This is speculative. He is a student researching a physicist. Not unusual.'

'Not unusual, except you recall the CIA has sent an agent to recruit him. Not unusual, except that our asset tells us this Weber is exceptionally respected by the mathematics faculty at the University. One professor told him that Weber is the finest mathematician he ever met.'

'What do you want me to do?'

'Weber must be eliminated. Do it in Madison to avoid any link to you or to Milwaukee. Our asset is trained in these matters. You will guide him. And the agent sent to recruit Weber must also be eliminated. It must also be done without any trace of your involvement. We have assets in Milwaukee. They will be identified to you.'

'I understand. The timing?'

'Up to you. But as quickly as possible. We will not let anything compromise our plan. Out.'

Maghribi stood in front of Curtin Hall a few minutes before seven. Uri Diggleboots pulled up in a fifteen-year-old Lexus.

Maghribi stared at him through the window. Diggleboots was dressed as a leopard. The fine spotted fur of his costume blended in with the leopard skin upholstery of the seats. Diggleboots had applied makeup to give himself whiskers.

"Hop in, Taqi! This is my fursona."

Maghribi slowly got into his seat.

"I must ask you a question."

"Fire away, Gridley!"

"You are not a pervert, are you?"

Diggleboots took offense.

"Fuck you and the horse you rode in on! Pot calling the kettle black. What kind of question is that? There's no such thing."

It became a long, two-mile ride to the Festival Grounds. Diggleboots chattered away about Furry culture.

"Furdom is not monolithic. Most of the Furries are lefties, but a handful are hard right. You'll see all kinds. You will be welcome here."

They parked near the Italian Community Center, a couple blocks from the festival gate. Dozens of men and women in animal costumes walked along with them. There were cats and dogs, lions, tigers, birds, deer, an ostrich, and a fox.

Diggleboots paid for their tickets.

"I'll introduce you to O'Furr. He owns a bar on Bluemound. Knows everybody. He's our unofficial chairman."

The Festival Grounds were filling with Furries. Diggleboots took Maghribi over to a man dressed as a Panda.

"Mr. O'Furr, I'd like you to meet a visiting scholar from Saudi Arabia, Professor Taqi Maghribi. Professor, Mr. O'Furr is a prominent local businessman."

Instead of extending a paw, O'Furr simply inclined his head.

"Welcome. Uri, I assume your friend is not yet out of the cage? Professor, perhaps you will develop a fursona after your experience tonight."

Maghribi frowned and stood rigid, without responding.

Suddenly, they heard loud voices in the distance.

"Hail, Catler!"

"Hail, Catler!"

"It's the Furred Reich!" said O'Furr. It is Catler! The Furrer."

"I thought we told the Alt-Furries not to come," Diggleboots said. "They're not invited."

"Right. But they show up, hide their armbands, and pay the admission."

A group of Furries dressed as wolves hurried around the corner. Four Furries dressed as sheep walked along on all fours. A large Furry, dressed as a cat, rode in a sedan chair balanced on the sheeps' backs, guided and supported by four wolves.

All the wolves wore black-and-red armbands with a paw print on the white center. As they moved along, some in the crowd shouted "Hail, Catler!" and gave the stiff-arm salute.

Each time, the cat in the sedan chair took his exceptionally long and bushy tail in his hand and thumped it against the chair in approval.

"Hail, Catler!"

Thump, thump, thump.

As the parade passed by O'Furr and Diggleboots. Maghribi's face revealed his rage.

"You have desecrated the great man himself! He almost accomplished . . . and you perverts ridicule him?"

The parade stopped. Catler stared down at him. The wolves looked at Catler for instruction.

"Who are you? Who are you who insults Catler?"

"He's a visiting scholar," Diggleboots said. "He doesn't mean to insult you."

"He is not of our elk!" said Catler.

"He is not of our elk!" shouted the wolves. "He is not of our elk!"

"Pounce on him, boys!" said Catler. "Give him a good tickling! Throw him out of here!"

A few wolves leaped on Maghribi. One threw his arm into his jaw, which knocked him down. The wolves jumped on him and pummeled him with their paws.

"Stop it!"

Diggleboots jumped in and was punched to the ground. O'Furr dialed 911 as fights broke out between the Alt-Furries and the rest. The sound of police sirens came closer. The wolves dragging Maghribi by the ankles and wrists toward the exit dropped him and disappeared into the festival grounds. Maghribi and Diggleboots were barely back on their feet when officers from three squad cars came running into the crowd with billy clubs.

Chapter Fifteen

Audrey Knapp drove up a long elm-tree-lined drive in Portsmouth, Rhode Island. A sign said Elmhurst Academy of the Sacred Heart, Founded 1872. She parked in front of the Manor House. "Can I help you, Ma'am?"

The young girl at the desk wore the same plaid skirt and dark blazer that Elmhurst girls wore in Audrey's class and for years into the past.

"I'm here to see Sister Geraldine. She's expecting me."

"She is sick. I think she's resting now."

"I know. She sent for me."

"Thank you. I'll check."

The girl had a brief conversation and turned back to Audrey.

"Yes, you can go up now. Sister is on the second floor in the room at the end of the hall."

Audrey walked up to her room and knocked.

"Come in."

The voice was faint.

Audrey opened the door and hurried over to a woman in her nineties. She was sitting in a recliner with a blanket over her lap.

"How are you, my darling Audrey?"

Audrey hugged her. She kneeled at her side, brushing away tears.

"It's so good to see you, Audrey. Sit here with me."

Sister Geraldine pointed to a chair by the bed. Audrey sat and continued to hold her hand.

"Tell me everything you've been doing, Audrey."

"Well, I'm working for a department of the government. Doing mathematics. I live in Washington, D.C., when I'm not traveling. And I'm happy."

Sister Geraldine squeezed her hand.

"I'm so glad. You were the best student I ever had, Audrey. And you were my favorite!"   She grinned.

"I'm not supposed to say that. But it's true!"

"Sister, tell me what's happening with you. Truly. What is the prognosis?"

Sister Geraldine settled back in the chair and put her hands under the blanket. She shivered slightly.

"I have congestive heart failure. And COPD. The truth is, I will be with the Lord sooner than you might think."

Audrey hugged her again.

"Audrey, have you met a good man? A man who cares for you?"

Audrey looked down.

"No, Sister. I thought I had once. But I was wrong."

"It will happen. You are a beautiful girl, Audrey. I mean, woman. You always were. In every respect. There must be men out there like that, too."

"Sister, do you remember your Thought for the Day? Every Friday, you would give us a sheet with a thought for the day. You don't know what an influence that was."

"Did you really pay attention to them? I always wondered if the girls thought about them at all."

"They were really important. 'Be considerate even of people you dislike.' 'Be courteous even in the presence of rudeness.' And we always loved the ones when we had a Friday night tea dance with the boys from Portsmouth Priory or LaSalle."

Sister Geraldine chuckled.

"Remember that your body is a temple of the Holy Spirit."

They both laughed and Audrey hugged her.

" 'And keep away from occasions of sin.' The only problem was, it sounded as if *we* were the occasions of sin!"

Sister Geraldine laughed harder.

They spoke for a long time about Audrey's classmates, about the other nuns on the faculty, and the progress of the school since Audrey had graduated. At last, Sister Geraldine changed the subject.

"Audrey, can I say something?"

"Of course."

"I know you. You seem sad for some reason. Is something bothering you?"

"Your health, Sister, I'm worried about you."

"Yes. I know. But it's not just that. What else is worrying you?"

Audrey hesitated.

"I can't describe it fully. But I may have to do things, that with all my being, I do not want to do."

"What are they?"

Audrey bowed her head. She didn't answer immediately.

"Sister, I may be ordered to take a human life."

"Oh, my!"

Sister Geraldine looked away.

"What kind of math are you doing for the government?"

Audrey tried to smile.

"Do you remember our course on the just war?" Sister Geraldine said. "From Grotius to Kellogg-Briand to Viet Nam?"

"Very well."

"Life is sacred. All life. But sometimes, in a rare instance, it is necessary to do something that is abhorrent to you. I'm thinking of my oldest brother, Gerald. Gerry. He was nineteen when he enlisted in the Marine Corps after Pearl Harbor. Gerry couldn't hurt a fly. An insect. But he enlisted after Pearl Harbor."

"I never heard you speak about him before, Sister."

"After basic training, he was troubled. He told me he spoke with our pastor at St. Nicholas of Tolentine in the Bronx. On Fordham Road. Father Philip. Philip Wilson. A good man."

The memory seemed difficult for Sister Geraldine. Audrey held her hand.

"Gerry told me he said, 'Father, I may land on a beach with a rifle and a bayonet. I may have to kill someone.' "

She paused.

"He told me Father Philip said it is wrong to kill in almost all cases. But when you defend your country, from people who would kill us, you may stop them. Even if you must take a life."

Sister Geraldine sat back and closed her eyes. She was getting tired.

"Father Philip was a good and holy man. And he was right, Audrey."

"I never heard you speak of Gerry before, Sister. Is he still alive?"

Sister Geraldine shook her head.

"He died in 1945. At Iwo Jima."

Audrey wiped tears from her cheeks. A nurse opened the door.

"Oh, I'm sorry," she said. "I'll stop back."

As she ducked out, Audrey stood up.

"I have to be going, Sister. But would you do something for me?"

"Anything."

"Would you bless me?"

"But I am not a priest, Audrey!"

"You should have been. Please, bless me."

"All right."

Audrey kneeled by her chair. Sister Geraldine put her hand on Audrey's head.

"May God watch over you, my daughter. May all you have learned from us protect you. It is not easy to be a woman. You have gone far beyond all the subjects we taught you here. In the name of the Father, the Son, and the Holy Spirit, I bless you, and ask Him and the Blessed Virgin Mary to hold you in their hands and protect you from harm."

Audrey was crying when she stood up.

"Thank you for all you did for me, Sister."

"We will meet again, Audrey. In the presence of the Lord."

"Sister, could I ask you one last favor? It seems strange."

"Of course."

"Could you write me one last Thought for the Day?"

"Of course. I want to think about it."

"Yes."

Audrey handed her a card.

"This is an address where I can receive mail."

"Goodbye, Audrey."

Audrey knelt and hugged her tightly.

"Goodbye, Sister."

Chapter Sixteen

The New York Times' editorial board sat around a table in a conference room in their midtown headquarters on Eighth Avenue in New York City. Laura Penner, the chairwoman of the board, gaveled it to order. She was a handsome woman in her sixties, with long, blonde hair and small earrings, dressed in a dark brown pantsuit and blue blouse, open at the collar.

"We have a full agenda today, so let's get started. You have the action items in the materials in front of you. They are three; admonition to our chief music critic, Gianfranco Vergili; potential discipline of our ombudsman, Wesley Scroggins; and guidance to our reporter Cenk Rut on a very important story on Islamophobia in Milwaukee."

She nodded to one of the editors near the door.

"Fatima, would you please ask Mr. Vergili to come in?"

The woman left the room, to return with the short and balding Gianfranco Vergili. *The Times'* chief music critic wore a tailored dark suit, white shirt with spread collar, and silk maroon tie. He kept stroking his waxed moustache as he sat in the only empty chair.

"Mr. Vergili . . . Gianfranco, the board has reviewed your proposed article on the ten greatest musical geniuses in history, in ranked order. We have a deep concern about your ranking and will ask that you respond to our comments. I will ask one of our associate editors, Sir Basil Hartmann, to voice our concerns. Sir Basil, please."

A tall, thin man in a linen sport jacket, denim work shirt, and Lululemon trousers took off his glasses.

Sir Basil had been born Stuart Hartmann. He grew up on University Avenue in the Bronx. He had married well, into the family that owned the paper and was known for his extensive philanthropy. An enormous gift to the Royal Opera in London had secured him a knighthood. He chose to be knighted as Basil, chiefly because there were no Basils in the Bronx, or at least not on University Avenue, Jerome Avenue, or the Grand Concourse, where Sir Basil was acquainted.

"Mr. Vergili, Gianfranco? I can call you Gianfranco, right? We're friends. We've been friends for a long time. Haven't we, Gianfranco?"

"Of course."

"Gianfranco, you were asked by the board to rank the ten greatest musical geniuses in history. We have grave concerns with your list."

Sir Basil adjusted his glasses.

"You listed Mozart as number one."

He looked accusingly at Vergili.

"You listed Beethoven as number two. And Bach as number three. And worse, the list is not diverse."

The board was silent. Laura Penner, Fatima, and the rest looked on without pity as Vergili got a taste of the lash.

"There are no English composers on the list. That sceptered isle deserves representation."

Sir Basil suffered from stage 4 pancreatic Anglophilia, excessive even for a *Times* editor.

"There are no women. Only one person of color."

Vergili took out an ironed handkerchief and applied it to his forehead.

"What are you suggesting?"

"We have taken the liberty of redrafting the list for you. Give us your comments."

Sir Basil handed him a sheet. Gianfranco trembled as he read.

"Absurd! Can't possibly do it! Not under my name!"

"What's the matter?"

"What's the matter? You have Mozart ranked number three! Bach number one! Beethoven number two!"

"So?"

"So? Saying that Bach, Beethoven, and Mozart are the three greatest composers in history in that order is like saying that Plato, Aristotle, and God are the three greatest philosophers in history, in that order! It is not possible. Not possible!"

"Gianfranco, Bach was nourished by the fresh springs and verdant pastures of the Reformation. Mozart was not nourished by them. And you seem to be unduly fond of only a certain kind of opera. You disregard the magnificence of Beethoven's *Fidelio*?"

"What? Magnificence? Listening to *Fidelio* is like listening to an obese man choking off the largest turd in the history of mankind."

"We will ignore that comment. What else bothers you?"

"You crossed out Puccini! My beloved Pooch! His arias are second only to Mozart."

"Redundant. We don't need Verdi and Puccini. One Italian is enough. And what about an English composer? Who is the greatest native-born English musical genius?"

"Paul McCartney."

Sir Basil frowned.

"I'm not in the mood for jokes."

"I'm not joking."

"Look, Gianfranco. You have a good position here. You shared with me that in your youth you tossed pizzas in a slice joint in Queens behind a bulletproof window while the kids gawked. Work with us."

"So, suddenly it's a slice joint? So, now you're Mr. Fancypants?"

Gianfranco Vergili got up and stood at attention.

"I will make a statement. I will put Mozart third. I will delete my beloved Pooch. But if you make me list the Beatles or the Stones or

Herman's Hermits; that I will not do. For that, I will go back to Queens and toss pizzas."

"Relax."

Sir Basil gestured with his hands down.

"Relax. McCartney was Irish anyway. Just work with us. More diversity. Find a woman."

"Really?"

"And I have a question."

Laura Penner looked down at the sheet.

"Where is Philip Glass?"

"Where is Philip Glass? You ask me that? In a group home for the tone deaf in Jersey! That's where he is! My God! You trifle with me."

"That's all, Gianfranco," said Sir Basil. "We're done. You get the picture. A little more modern. A little more diverse. Too many Europeans. You get the picture."

Gianfranco Vergili inclined his head slightly and stalked out.

"Bring in Wesley Scroggins," said Laura Penner.

Fatima left the room and returned with Scroggins. He sat in the empty chair, looking around at unsmiling faces.

"Let me start this," said Laura Penner. "Wesley, you are our ombudsman. But your last few pieces were unusable. I don't think you understand the mission of this paper. Let's look at them, shall we? First, your piece on Supreme Court Justice Brett Kavanagh. Why did you write it?"

"I'm not for or against him. I do *not* belong to a party. I don't vote, so that I can be truly objective. But the paper's article on the front page had a lengthy account of a party at Yale thirty-five years ago that said Kavanaugh was drunk and groped a girl's breasts. A witness said he personally observed it."

"And your objection is?"

"The alleged victim denied it happened. But that is not mentioned in the article."

"It was omitted because of space considerations," said an editor.

" 'The victim denies it' are four words. It's the most relevant fact in the scenario."

"Racism and sexism are increasingly prevalent in our culture," said an editor, wearing a bow tie and John Lennon glasses sitting next to Scroggins. "Many of us are rethinking the concept of objectivity and how it's used to maintain hierarchies of status and power. Perhaps public policy is more important than objectivity given our imperative to weaken status hierarchies."

"Let's move on," said Penner. "Your piece about the EgyptAir employees removing trash. Why did you write it?"

"Removing trash? The headline was 'How taking others' trash helped keep city safe.' Islamic terrorists planted two bombs in New York. One went off. The other did not. Two security guards from EgyptAir just happened to find it in a trash can—just happened to take the bag, which had evidence like fingerprints and DNA—but left the bomb. It was only inactivated by accident. They flew back to Egypt and refused to be questioned by the FBI. They won't produce the bag. You praised them for keeping the city safe. You compared it to people finding salad bowls and jackets in the trash."

No one spoke.

"Your criticism of cultural comparison of dress was disrespectful," Fatima finally said.

"Disrespectful? You juxtaposed two pictures of women, one a German woman in a bikini, the other a woman in a burka. The caption read 'Which one is freer?' I did criticize that."

"In fact, you said it reminded you of something that would appear in *The Onion*."

"Right. And you also caricatured the prime minister of Israel as a dog, and a priest with a wolf's face."

"And you said they belonged in a Berlin paper in the 1930s. Why did you say that?"

"Because I believe it to be true."

More silence.

"Wesley," Penner finally said, "we are most concerned with a piece you had on your computer that you have not submitted for publication. Can you explain it?"

"I know what you're talking about. So you know, it was not intended to be submitted to you for publication. They were random thoughts. I had the impression that my computer was private unless I chose to give you a piece in the course of my job."

"That is not the case. We own the computer and the system."

"Okay. What is it about the piece you'd like to know?"

"It's long, and frankly it's disturbing."

Penner looked down at a transcript.

"I'll just read one paragraph, which pretty much sums it up. 'The ultimate goal of *The New York Times* is to see a world without race, gender, religion, or ethnicity. Everyone will look slightly bronzed, like present-day Hawaiians. Everyone's gender and sexual orientation will be uncertain. Western Civilization and the Judeo-Christian tradition will be remembered only for having been responsible for thousands of years of oppression and violence. Every atrocity by a jihadist is minimized or ignored by the paper, and Western institutions are attacked with unrelenting fury.' "

She looked at Scroggins.

"Little strong, don't you think? Why did you write that?"

"Because it's what I believe."

Sir Basil tapped his fingers on the table.

"Wesley, you have to understand something. Let me put it in terms of rivers. Okay? It's true that suffering, violence, and racism occur everywhere. But the racism of the Nile and the Euphrates can be managed through tribute and flattery. The racism of the Rhine and the Danube cannot. It is incurable."

"Okay." said Penner. "That concludes the meeting. Wesley, we will get back to you."

He left.

"Where did he get his degree?" said Fatima.

Penner looked at his folder. She frowned.

"Ohio State."

"Why do we even have an ombudsman?" said Sir Basil. "They're a pain in the ass. Nosy as hell."

"Here's the plan," Penner said. "We are eliminating the ombudsman position. It is unnecessary. Transfer Scroggins to the Staten Island bureau. In six months, after his brain atrophies, pension him."

Everyone around the table nodded.

"Okay," said Penner. "Now our last agenda item. Bring in Cenk Rut."

Fatima left the room once again, and returned with a short, thin, dark-haired man.

"Welcome, Cenk!"

Unlike Vergili and Scroggins, Rut basked in miles and miles and piles of smiles around the table.

Cenk," Penner said, "we're sending you on special assignment. To Milwaukee, of all places. Let me give you the objective."

Shall I hold up on my piece on parochial schools?"

"For now. Here's what we want you to do."

Penner picked up a remote. A picture appeared on the side of a screen. Board members on that side turned their chairs to look.

"This is a picture of downtown Milwaukee. It has been called the Vienna of the Midwest. It even has a river, although it's hardly the Danube."

Rut examined the picture. Most of the buildings were small, a few stories high. There was a cluster of taller buildings that looked new, in the eastern part of the downtown. The Calatrava-designed art museum was shown, and beyond it a portion of Lake Michigan.

"It looks pretty," he said.

"Pretty masks a darker reality," said Penner. "We believe it masks a deep-seated Islamophobia that must be brought to light."

"Got it."

"A distinguished Islamic scholar agreed to serve as a visiting professor in Milwaukee Community College. The night he checked into his hotel, the Milwaukee police menaced him with guns, tased him, and set a German shepherd on him. The dog kind."

"Incredible!"

"Right. And a few days ago, the same scholar was researching a festival of nonbinary, species-fluid persons who were exploring what it means to experience intersectional identities and to empower themselves as marginalized individuals."

A thin man at the end of the table raised his hand.

"I can identify. I'm checking in with some anger. I know it's not very yogic, but I haven't had a drag-it-out cry since I was in high school."

"I know what you mean, Bruce."

Several other editors nodded.

"Sometimes, I'm afraid to be with myself," said Bruce. "I come with a lot of victimhood. The group makes me feel strong."

"Right, Bruce," Penner said. "But in Milwaukee, the Islamic scholar and the persons at the festival were attacked and beaten with batons by the Milwaukee police!"

Heads shook in disbelief.

"Cenk, here are the bones of the story. Milwaukee is emblematic of the Midwest. And the Midwest is emblematic of America itself. The friendly face of Milwaukee conceals a deep-seated Islamophobia."

She handed Rut a folder.

"Here's a memo with talking points, an outline, and suggested bites for the story. All contact information for relevant people we're aware of, including officials, police, and college. Of course, you'll interview locals for color. Interview the scholar. Sit in on one of his classes. Sniff them out. Their deep-seated prejudices. We're talking Pulitzer, Cenk!"

Cenk Rut got up quickly.

"I'll get 'em."

Chapter Seventeen

Taqi Maghribi sat in the anteroom of Gravegoods Beaker's office. An African-American man in a blue suit and white shirt with no tie sat across from him, holding a folder. He wore a nametag that read, "Mr. Pronoun Jackson." He was powerfully built, with a massive chest and arms, and several scars on his cheeks and forehead that demanded explanation. Despite the scars, he smiled at Maghribi, a pure and guileless smile.

The department secretary looked up from her phone.

"Chairman Beaker will see you now, Mr. Maghribi."

Gravegoods Beaker was sitting at his desk, chewing on a toothpick. He waved Maghribi to the chair near his desk.

"So, how's it going, Taqi? You enjoying it?"

"Good so far."

"Good. Good. You're wondering why I asked you to come by."

"Somewhat."

"Right. Right. Taqi, here is the situation. We got a lot of crazy shit in this place. Diggleboots. Ferkwell. Brayboy. Me, even. But you got to be smoove with your shit. You got to know your way around decent junk. The Man is crazy. He puts up with a lot of crazy. To a point, that is."

"What do you mean? What man?"

"The Man."

Beaker looked annoyed.

"We all got a good thing going here. But there's some things The Man won't put up with. He'll get pissed off. And once he gets pissed, this all goes away, see?"

"What does that mean to me?"

"Taqi, I got some complaints from your class. Blowing up the Jamaa and shit. Capturing female slaves and shit. You're kind of an intense individual. You need to put some glide in your stride. Chill."

"I was speaking hypothetically, in response to questions. First of all, you don't blow up the Jamaa. The Jamaa decides if you blow yourself up. But it's all theoretical. Today, I was talking about the crimes of Richard the Lionheart."

"Taqi, you can shove it up Richard the Lionheart's ass all you want. You can shove it up Friar Tuck's ass. But you ain't shovin' it up my ass! Dig?"

"Dig? How does it affect you?"

"How does it affect me? If The Man cancels this department, who you think could find work? I'll tell you. None of us. We got a good gig here. Pay's good. Offices are good. You can preach all the crazy shit you want, and The Man is entertained, see? You can attack him up to a point, and he loves it. Makes him feel superior. But only up to a point. You spin some crazy shit about blowing him up and making his wife your slave? Your dead ass gonna be hanging on the wall with the moose head in the Dew Drop Inn in Sheboygan. Dig?"

"I have my First Amendment rights! I have an absolute right to advocate whatever I want! This is the price we must pay for freedom."

Beaker's face got hard.

"You lay off the extreme shit, dig? We don't like that much diversity, dig? We got a living to make. We got a good think going here. Ain't no one fuckin it up for us, dig?"

Beaker's secretary poked her head in.

"Mr. Pronoun Jackson is here for the interview."

"Bring him in."

"That's all," Beaker said to Maghribi. "I want no more complaints."

Pronoun Jackson smiled at Maghribi as he walked by him to shake hands with Gravegoods Beaker.

Chapter Eighteen

Taqi Maghribi sat at his computer in his apartment. The blue ENCRYPTED legend appeared, and then instructions.

'Respond Immediately.'

'I am here.'

'Are you alone?'

'Yes. In my apartment.'

'What is your explanation?'

'For the police encounter?'

'All of it. You attended a party with perverts dressed as animals. The police came to arrest them. You were arrested and then released?'

'Correct. One of the faculty at the college invited me to a festival. My orders were to blend in, to accept social invitations as any visiting scholar would. I had no idea what to expect. When I realized what it was, I made plans to immediately leave. Fights broke out among the animals, and someone called the police.'

'We may add this to your claim against the city. It would look transparent. But Maghribi. One more arrest under strange circumstances, and we may have to pull you.'

'I understand. There will be no more controversies.'

'Good. Now let me tell you the purpose of this contact. It's about Weber. Our asset in Madison has monitored him. He has penetrated Weber's research area. He sent us several screen shots of Weber's computer that make it urgent to remove him.'

'That has great risk. What is the urgency?'

'We showed the screen shots to the mathematicians on our team who applied the work of the Yazidi to our purposes. They expressed alarm. They believe that Weber is on the path to prove that measurements to a so-called entangled particle cannot depend on simultaneous measurements to its 'entangled' partner light years away. This would overturn the physicist Bell's refutation of Einstein's conjecture. It would ultimately defeat our cryptology that is based on Bell's work.'

'Isn't this speculative? It's not clear that Weber can do it at all. And it's very unlikely that he can do it in the few months before February 1. His murder would be catastrophic if it is traced to us.'

'We have decided that the risk of that is far outweighed by the risk of his defeating our code, no matter how uncertain. Our defeat would have geopolitical consequences that would set back the Caliphate a hundred years. The risk of discovery is easily minimized. Do not permit it to be traced to you. Do not bungle it. You have more training and experience than any of our men.'

'Will do.'

'These are your orders. Do it in Madison. He has a meeting scheduled at 4 p.m. tomorrow in the Physics Department of the University in Madison. Use our asset there. Direct him. And do not fail.'

'I will not fail.'

Chapter Nineteen

Bernie Weber and Audrey Knapp sat at a kitchen table in Bernie's apartment on Humboldt Boulevard in the Riverwest neighborhood of Milwaukee.

"Fill me in, Bernie. Where are you on it?"

"I'm getting there. I've finished the work to disprove Bell's initial hypothesis. His papers in Madison really helped. The messages you showed me were encrypted, based on it. Now, I'm figuring out how to break an encryption with an erroneous foundation."

"Tell me more about what you did with Bell's work that changes the current thinking. Don't you have a heavy burden on that? Every physicist over the past fifty years has supported Bell's initial work, correct?"

"Not really. Bell's notes show that even *he* had doubts. And a bunch of others said they didn't believe there could be an instantaneous cause-and-effect relationship between two particles billions of light years apart without exceeding the speed of light. A guy who won the Nobel Prize called it flapdoodle."

"Flapdoodle?

Bernie nodded.

"Well, tell me more about what you did so far."

"Okay. The basis of Bell's theory initially was . . ."

"Vehicle 1 exiting garage onto Kenwood Boulevard west . . ."

The low GPS voice came from Audrey's phone. She turned off the sound and laid the phone on her lap.

"Go ahead, Bernie. Sorry."

"That's okay. I have a little time. I need to go to Madison this afternoon to meet with my adviser at four. So, I'll boil it down for you. Particles don't have a definite position and a definite velocity. At least according to quantum theory. They sort of float in a probability dimension. It's only when they're measured that one definite position or velocity is somehow selected from all possibilities."

"I get it. Go on."

"Here's the weird thing. The math shows that if two photons are entangled, for example, and are billions of light years apart, then if you successfully measure the spin around an axis of one of them, the other simultaneously and automatically pops out of the probability dimension and has to adopt the same spin."

"Even if any transmission between them would take billions of years to get there at the speed of light?"

"Right."

"Are you saying Bell's math was wrong?"

"Almost. I'm saying it was wrong because it's incomplete. No one can repeal the principle of cause and effect. And cause and effect can only occur within the speed of light. I'm convinced that in his gut he knew it, too. I cleaned up his math."

"Bernie, you're amazing. But how does that affect cryptography?"

"I'm not sure yet. Theoretically if a cryptography system is based on wrong or incomplete equations, it should be vulnerable. That's what I'm working on now."

Bernie looked at his phone.

"I've got to go."

"Where is your meeting in Madison?"

"The physics building. Chamberlin Hall on University Avenue."

Audrey had parked a block away. She turned on the ignition. Two GPS screens lit up on the dashboard. She turned the sound back on.

'Vehicle 1 merging onto I-94 West toward Madison.'

Her phone rang as she was pulling out onto the street.

"Yes?"

"Audrey? It's Judy. Can I talk?"

"What's up?"

"I'm screening your mail. But there's a letter you might want to hear."

"Who's it from?"

"Elmhurst Academy."

"Read it to me."

"Actually, it's a letter with a note inside. The letter is dated two days ago. It says "Dear Ms. Knapp: It is with the deepest regret that we inform you that our beloved Sister Geraldine Calabrese passed away in her sleep last night. Sister was a fixture in the life of the school for more than fifty years. Funeral arrangements are pending. She had asked me to mail the enclosed note to you the day before she died. I enclose it now. Sincerely, Anne Kelly, Manor House Secretary.' "

Audrey closed her eyes.

"What does the note say?"

"It's addressed to you and sealed."

"Open it, please."

"Okay. Let me see. It's handwritten and says, 'My dearest Audrey. I don't think we shall see one another again in this world, but I can't tell you enough how wonderful it was to see you again and to spend time with you. As you left, you asked me to write you one last Thought for the Day. I gave it much thought, and here is my final thought for you: Whatever you do, shoot first. Do not die at Iwo Jima. All my love, Sister Geraldine.' "

Audrey wiped hot tears from her cheeks as she drove downtown to access the highway to Madison.

"I'm sorry for your loss," Judy said.

"Thank you, Judy. Goodbye."

'Vehicle 2 merging onto I-94 toward Madison.'

The GPS flashed on one screen. The second screen showed Vehicle 1 a few miles ahead.

The light ahead turned yellow. Audrey jammed her foot down on the accelerator and ran the intersection as she headed onto the I-94 entrance ramp.

Chapter Twenty

Taqi Maghribi pulled into the Lake Street parking ramp in Madison and finally found a spot on an upper floor.

'Arrived.'

He texted and stayed in his car. Soon, a thin man in his twenties knocked on the passenger door. Maghribi popped the lock.

"You are on time. Good."

"I am always on time."

"Weber has a meeting at Chamberlin at four. Where is he likely to park?"

"A lot nearby for faculty and graduate students."

Audrey Knapp sat in a car several blocks away, listening.

"Do it in the parking lot if possible. Do they have cameras?"

"Assume they do."

"Disguise yourself. Have you brought what you need?"

"Yes. Let's go."

"It's early. We've got at least an hour."

"All right. I'll go to the student union to prepare."

"I'll walk with you. I have a few more things to discuss."

Audrey heard a door slamming shut. She got out of her car and plugged the meter.

Maghribi and his companion heard a crowd clapping as they neared the Memorial Union. They turned onto State Street. Hundreds of people were gathered on the Mall. A dais had been set up with a banner:

MADISON'S PROGRESSIVE GESAMKUNSTWERK

Two women and a man holding microphones faced the crowd. A small stage was set up behind them.

"Good afternoon, Progressives!" shouted the man into his microphone. "I am Woke Fetish, the editor of *ProgCheck*, the newspaper of progressives in Madison!"

Fetish had been born Seymour Balz in Froid, Montana, population 185. He realized early on that there was only one way out of Froid. By changing his name to Woke Fetish, a wondrous world opened. He found work. He was regarded as an intellectual in Madison. Rumored to be ABD from Harvard in public policy.

ProgCheck had once been published on paper until people stopped paying to read it. When it resurfaced as a blog, Fetish forwarded its link widely, to the surprise and annoyance of many.

"This afternoon we are presenting the Progressive Gesamkunstwerk," Fetish said. "The composer, Wagner, proposed this, a total work of art that combines all forms and stimulates the senses. We are liberating it from its foul origins. We are rescuing art from the controlling hands of the Eurocentric, misogynistic, patriarchal fucks who have hoarded institutional knowledge and kept it from the people!"

"Wagner was a Nazi!"

As someone shouted from the crowd, a group of frat boys swilling beer from thermos bottles laughed and jeered.

"Wagner's music is better than it sounds," one shouted back.

"Fuck Wagner!"

"The poor have no opera!"

"Opera is for the one percent!"

"Bed is the poor man's opera!"

"The poor demand art!"

"Who's Art?"

Fetish held up his hand.

"Please, please citizens."

He waited for the catcalls to subside.

"It now gives me great pleasure to introduce the two progressive Madison leaders who produced and directed this event. First, I call on Leader Kundt to speak."

A ferret-faced woman, gaunt, with hollow eyes and long, stringy hair, waved at the crowd. She was dressed in bib overalls and a baseball cap that said, BOY BYE.

"Good afternoon, Progressives! I am Krissie Kundt, and I want to introduce my colleague, Leader McCoy!"

Kundt started to clap while the other woman waved to the crowd. She had cold eyes that appeared to have seen much suffering and found it wanting. Her name was McCoy and she called herself Roy, but everyone knew her as Spikey. In Madison, she was known as Krissie's Sancho Panza, her Leporello. Or for those who browse in bait shops, her Sagebrush, her Tonto. McCoy was dressed in cargo pants and an XXL tee shirt that said, ART IS POWER.

Maghribi looked at his companion and shrugged.

"I want to watch a little more. This degraded culture."

"And now," said Krissie, "the Spikester, and I present our first act."

She pointed to a man standing next to the stage.

"Ganymede!"

The man nodded. He had a thick black beard and wore a pink knit Pussy Hat from The Women's March. He held up a cardboard sign:

THE DYING BAT

A heavy girl with one leg in a cast came hopping out from around the stage, dragging her cast behind her and waving her arms around.

Suddenly, a two-hundred-pound, bearded nymph in a tutu came running out, shrieking and waving his hands. He was pursued and pounced on by several small satyrs with large breasts who pretended to hump him while shouting threats in high, squeaky voices.

The girl with the cast looked up to the heavens, shouting to the gods to intervene. At last, she tumbled to the ground and laid on her back. The crowd went crazy. The frat boys howled and shouted at her. The rest clapped and cheered. She finally stood up and waved.

"Namaste, my bitches!" she shouted. "Unsheathe your claws!"

She bowed and exited.

"Ganymede," said Kundt. "The second act!"

Ganymede held up a second sign:

MO'S ART

Two men carried the frame of a piano with no keys out from behind the stage. A man in his sixties wearing a costume shop tux and an Einstein wig bowed to the crowd. He suddenly started jumping around, slapping the piano from different sides, attacking and withdrawing. He jumped and slapped his thighs and calves, like a Swiss dancer at the Wilhelm Tell festival. Then, he slapped the piano frame again, abruptly stopped and bowed to loud applause, along with some insults and obscenities.

"Ganymede, the third act!"

Ganymede held up a sign:

PAINTING BY AN ASSHOLE

A skinny man, naked except for a raspberry-colored jockstrap, had worked a thin paint brush into his butt, dripping blue paint. An elfin figure with a mohawk and waxed eyebrows spread a long sheet of butcher paper in front of him. The artist duckwalked down the paper, dripping a blue streak behind him.

The crowd went nuts. More mad applause, more insults and obscenities.

Leader Kundt grabbed the microphone.

"We need the People's Art! Are you with us, Citizens?"

"We are with you, Citizen!"

They had gone full-frontal progressive. Beyond Glass and Adams, who had keys on their pianos. Beyond Jackson Pollack, who used his hands to fling paint onto a canvas. Beyond the prize-winning recording of farts that had won a poetry contest in Madison a year earlier. Beyond the prize winning "Ultimate Dance" that had presented a coffin with a cadaver in it and five minutes of silence.

No one could out-progressive Madison!

The crowd quivered with the erotic stirrings of their absolute spoor-state masochism, degradation, and desire to lie under a tree and be urinated on by ISIS and wolves.

"Before we go to the next act," said the *ProgCheck* editor, "I think we all have to acknowledge the work of Leader Kundt and Leader McCoy. They have pried the skeleton fingers of Mozart and Michelangelo and Shakespeare from the people's throat. They have opened up new vistas for the progressive imagination!"

The crowd cheered.

"Let's leave," Maghribi said,

His companion nodded. They walked toward the Memorial Union.

"I'm leaving for Milwaukee. You know what to do."

"I do."

"Afterward, when it's safe, call me to report."

"I will."

Maghribi walked back toward the parking ramp. His companion went into the Union. The Rathskeller was crowded. He turned toward the stairway and walked down to the men's room on the lower level. A cleaning lady was mopping the floor outside. A yellow cone said CLOSED. He brushed by it and pushed open the door.

"Hey," she said. "It's closed."

He laughed as the door shut behind him. The cleaning lady shrugged. She put her mop into the bucket and wheeled it to the women's bathroom, pushed the door open and went inside.

The man put on a light brown wig. He adjusted a prosthetic chin and jaw. As he was applying makeup to give himself a scar on his right cheek, he heard the door open.

"Cleaning lady. Anybody here?"

He saw a woman with a scarf wound around her head come into view. He dropped his kit. As he reached for his gun, silent rounds tore through his back. He pitched over the sink, spilling blood into the basin before his body fell to the floor.

The woman turned and left the bathroom. The hall outside was still empty.

Chapter Twenty-One

Taqi Maghribi and Zulkifar Malouf sat at a corner table in a cafe in Times Square, speaking quietly in Arabic.

"What happened? How could you possibly have failed?"

"I instructed our man on his mission and technique. He was disguised properly. Naturally, I left the city to distance myself, and he was assassinated in a restroom at the university."

"I know all that. By whom?"

"I don't know precisely. Obviously one of their intelligence agencies. A forensic expert was quoted in the paper as saying that the gun was probably Russian, the kind used in Ukraine."

"It's unusual for them to be so bold. They can't read our messages."

"They suspect something. You told me they sent a woman to Milwaukee."

"Have you discovered her?"

"Not yet."

"You must find her. She and Weber must be removed."

"Is this starting to draw more attention than the risk is worth?"

"No. You are blameless in all that happened to you. You will not be seen as having any connection to the murder in Madison. There is a pattern of Islamophobia in Wisconsin that must be exposed. We will have their media and intellectuals on our side if we present a proper case."

"All right."

"We're meeting with the lawyers who will direct your lawsuit for the attacks on you. The law firm we've hired is one of the best in New York. In the U.S. They represented the bank that tutored Greece in how to commit accounting fraud to get more money from the E.U. They represented the bank that helped Malaysian leaders steal a billion dollars from their country. They never lose a case. They have agreed to represent us."

"What have we told them to do? Who do they think we are?"

"You are a professor from Saudi Arabia who is a visiting lecturer in Milwaukee. I represent the Saudi government. You were arrested, set on by dogs, shot, beaten with a billy club, and are afraid for your life. A Saudi graduate student in engineering at the Madison campus was murdered in a bathroom because of his race and religion. We want all of your rights under the law enforced, and all damages you are entitled to."

"I understand."

The two men left the cafe. They walked into the lobby of a building a block away and stood in line at the guard counter until they were waived forward.

"Who are you here to see?"

"Raptor, Hawk. Law firm."

"Name of lawyer?"

"Mr. Raptor."

"Your names?"

"Zulkifar Malouf and Taqi Maghribi."

"IDs?"

Malouf handed him their passports. The guard examined them and handed them back.

"Elevators on the left. 40th floor."

The two men got off on the 40th floor and stepped into a large lobby, with a window overlooking the city that extended the entire length of the room. Three neon sculptures mounted on walnut tables were placed between armchairs in the seating area. But the focus of the entire lobby was on a large replica of the statue of Hercules and Diomedes, two naked Greek wrestlers. Hercules holds Diomedes upside down and is about to throw him. Diomedes has his hand clenched around Hercules' penis. The title "IMPASSE" was carved into the pedestal.

"We're here to see Mr. Raptor," Malouf said.

"Your names?" said the receptionist.

"Malouf and Maghribi."

"Please take a seat."

Maghribi walked up to the statue of the wrestlers. Below "IMPASSE," more words were carved: "Commissioned by Cosimo 1 de Medici, 1519-1574. Re-commissioned by Napoleon Raptor, 1957-"

A few minutes later, four young lawyers hurried into the lobby. One extended his hand.

"I'm Weaver Dane. From Mr. Raptor's team."

He gestured to the others.

"My associates are also on the team. Please come with us."

They walked down a long hallway. Halfway down, they passed a dining room with a buffet table of shrimp, fruit, salads, and sushi. Two covered serving tubs were labeled "Veal Piccata" and "Pappardelle with Boar Ragu."

The tables to the side were covered with white tablecloths. People filed in and out, helping themselves.

"Are you hungry?" Dane said.

"No. We just had a coffee. How long have you had a dining room for the employees?"

"We've had it since we moved here."

"It must be expensive."

"It's more expensive to let them leave the building for lunch. They burn an hour and a half, two hours that way. We lose billable hours. If you feed them, they're back at their desks in half an hour."

They walked into a conference room at the end of the hall, an enormous room that looked more like a small theater. Two more associates were waiting for them.

"Please have a seat," Dane said. "Mr. Raptor is on his way."

They were barely seated when the door opened. A tall, bald man with a gray fringe of hair stepped in. He wore an Armani suit, a light blue shirt with a white collar, and no tie. His shoes were alligator.

"I am Napoleon Raptor. Gentlemen, welcome."

The associates had jumped to their feet. Weaver Dane hovered around Raptor while Maghribi and Malouf shook his hand.

"Everyone may be seated."

Raptor walked to the front of the room.

"Mr. Maghribi and Mr. Malouf, we welcome you. We have agreed to represent you and the Kingdom of Saudi Arabia. I want to say first that we are not the cheapest firm in the country."

Raptor chuckled. He dug a finger in his ear, scooped around, and examined his finger when it emerged.

"People do not understand how we win cases. We leave nothing to chance. Every statute, ordinance, rule, witness, document, judge, clerk, bailiff, opposing lawyer, expert, juror, exhibit, recording, affidavit, motion, brief, and judicial and administrative case is exhaustively researched by my team. No one escapes the talons of Raptor, Hawk!"

"How do you plan to proceed?" said Malouf.

Raptor nodded.

"We sue the world. We file a Notice of Claim against the City of Milwaukee for the police assault on you when you arrived. We sue the city if they reject the claim. We immediately sue the motel, the clerk who called the police, and the individual police officers. We sue the festival where you were beaten, the police who beat you, the festivalgoers who beat you, and the city once again."

"We also want to discuss our real objective," Maghribi said. "We want to impress on the public the danger of Islamophobia. We are planning a diplomatic initiative in the near future that will ultimately benefit our two countries in terms of immigration and exposure to our culture. This lawsuit must be presented discreetly to the press. The amount of damages is not as important as . . ."

"I understand all that."

Raptor dug into his ear once again and examined his finger.

"I fully understand your objectives. But we must discuss one vital thing, other than our fees. Something that could spin out of my control if we make a mistake. That is whom we will pick to be our local counsel in Milwaukee. The state requires that nonresident lawyers join with local counsel in all cases."

"But how important is that?" said Malouf.

"Very important. We require a firm that is overwhelmed with the prestige of working with us. They should not be competent in anything. They must be content to merely sign and file documents we send them, without comment. We want them to have status without ability."

"You're joking, of course."

"Gentlemen, let me tell you something. Napoleon Raptor does not lose. Not losing depends on total control. In my whole life, I have lost only one case. And that is because local counsel fucked it up. It will not happen again."

The associates all nodded.

"The local cretin was told only to file what I sent him. To say nothing to the press and to the court. But he fucked it up for us. He freelanced. And that will not happen again."

Raptor nodded to Weaver Dane. Dane picked up a remote. A large screen lit up with the words BURDEN, HEFTY in the center.

"We have found the dream pick to be our local counsel. The law firm of Burden, Hefty. A dysfunctional firm that has been compared to a malpractice factory managed by Bernie Madoff. Yet, the partners belong to the most prestigious clubs in town. They have status unencumbered by ability."

Maghribi and Malouf leaned back and chuckled, enjoying the warmup comedy before they hit the hard issues.

"Let's look at their management. Five partners. They address each other only by their nicknames. They loathe each other."

He nodded to Dane.

A diminutive individual sitting behind an enormous desk appeared on the screen.

"This is Frederick Burden Jr. He wrestled at ninety-eight pounds in high school, and once was pinned by an eighty-five-pound girl from a reform school. He loses every client referred to him. His nickname is Pocket Hercules."

The Saudis chuckled some more. Raptor nodded to Dane again. An enormous individual with small, cunning eyes appeared. Rolls of pink, hairless flesh rolled out of his collar and cuffs.

"This is Walter Hefty. He is widely mistrusted by all his partners because he cheated and slandered most of them. He clawed his way to the top through treachery and peasant cunning. His nickname is Bigfoot."

Another man appeared on the screen. He was an Asian man in his fifties who stared into the camera.

"This is Charlie. Milwaukee manufacturing companies were frequently cheated by Asian customers who didn't pay. When they sued, the customers disappeared into dozens of LLCs with no assets. Burden, Hefty hired Charlie as a sort of scarecrow. He sits in on meetings with Asian clients, saying nothing. His specialty is unknown. They hope his presence will deter fraud. Next."

Another picture appeared, of a stocky woman in her fifties with a bland expression and a watery, blond, shag hairdo.

"This is the Mullet. She was originally hired to defuse MeToo grenades. She eventually found a niche in their Stiffs and Gifts department protecting wealthy Alzheimer's patients from thieving nephews."

Dane pressed again. A picture of a man with a bad haircut, bristles of dark hair randomly sticking up across his head, showed on screen. He had a sad, defeated countenance, made worse by a dorky smile.

"And this is my favorite," Raptor said. "This is the Nurse. He is the head of their litigation department."

"The Nurse?"

Malouf frowned.

"Why such a name?"

"The Nurse committed malpractice in a small claims case. He spends all his time writing memos to his clients. Clients leave him for other law firms. In an exit interview, one client shouted, 'I needed a surgeon, and you gave me a nurse!' The name stuck."

"This is all amusing, but I really want . . ."

Raptor ignored Malouf.

"And the best of all? The Nurse has a rare kind of phobia. He is afraid of courtrooms!"

Raptor laughed, an unpleasant sound that was a combination of a gargle and a sneeze. The associate coyote pack howled along.

Raptor dabbed at his eyes.

"It is too perfect! Too wonderful! Sweet Jesus, how do I deserve such bounty? Our local can't fuck up! He's afraid of courtrooms!"

More howling, sneezing, and gargling. Malouf and Maghribi chuckled along with them.

"This is all very amusing, Napoleon. Can I call you Napoleon?"

"Call me Nate. I'll call you Zulky."

"Okay, Nate. Very funny, but let's get to the issue. Who do you recommend for our local counsel?"

"I just introduced them. Burden, Hefty."

Malouf was silent for a few seconds.

"But you just told us they are incompetent and strange!"

"Precisely. But they have large status in Milwaukee with business and the press. Look, Zulky, they are a wax museum to us. Mannequins. They will do nothing. Weaver Dane and two associates will move to Milwaukee. Expensive, yes, but guaranteed to win. They will work out of offices at Burden, Hefty. Everything we file, we send to them. It's all e-filing anyway. They will insert the Nurse's signature. The Nurse will never see the document. When they go to court, the Nurse will have laryngitis. Weaver will do all the arguing."

"Are you absolutely certain?"

"Absolutely certain. The only time we lost, local counsel fucked it up. That can never happen again. And if we use Burden, Hefty, that can never happen in Milwaukee."

"It's your decision. We put the case in your hands. But remember our real objective."

"I will. Now, come back to my office to discuss fees and terms of representation. How much time do you have?"

"Whatever you need. We have a lunch scheduled at one, but it can be moved."

"Plenty of time. Come with me."

Malouf and Maghribi followed Raptor out the door. The associates and Weaver Dane stayed behind.

Chapter Twenty-Two

Malouf and Maghribi walked into Trattoria Dell'Arte a few minutes after one. It was not crowded. A young, dark-haired man with a mous- tache waved to them from a table in the corner. They walked over and sat down.

"Marhaba."

"Marhaba."

"Your trip was good?"

"Very good."

"You know Tamerlane?" Malouf said.

He nodded to Maghribi.

"Of course. We worked together in Turkey. On Khashoggi."

The three men laughed.

"I forgot," Malouf said. "Now you will be working together again."

"I welcome it. But what is your plan?"

"Tamerlane will join you in Milwaukee. His skills are needed. We've decided that when the boy and the woman are eliminated, their bodies must disappear. No forensic work on the bodies that could arouse suspicion. The bodies will be flown in refrigerated diplomatic containers back to Saudi Arabia, unexamined. We will dispose of them there."

"You have the right man for that."

Maghribi pointed at Tamerlane.

"I know I do. Tamerlane, tell me your methods. You have done this before. Describe the process for me."

"When the bodies are delivered to me . . ."

"You will deliver them to yourself. Iman Maghribi will direct you. You will be the one to terminate them."

"Very good."

A waitress appeared to take their orders.

"What soup do you have?"

"Vegetable, lentil, tomato . . ."

Malouf put his menu down.

"Three bowls of lentil soup, bread, and tea. Bring us the check with the soup. Then leave us alone."

"Of course."

She took the menus and left.

"So, what do you do, and how long will it take?"

"It depends on their size."

"The boy is small. We have not yet identified the woman."

"If the woman is tall with a large chest and long legs, it will take longer. The joints of a sacrificial animal are easily split, but dismembering takes time."

"How much?"

"Perhaps several hours. I usually work on cadavers. I cut well. I only worked once on a warm body, as you know. But that will not be a problem."

Malouf and Maghribi were silent.

"Normally, while working on a cadaver, I put on my headphones and listen to music. I drink my coffee and smoke my cigarette."

"Do you have any questions of us?"

"Well, yes. When will you identify the woman?"

"Very soon. You will work with Iman Maghribi to identify and isolate her. Once she is eliminated, the boy will be easy."

"It is likely the woman meets with Weber," said Maghribi. "You are unknown. I will explain how to reach Weber and how you will track him until they are together."

"Who has the lentil?" said the waitress.

She smiled as she put the soup and bread and tea on a serving stand.

Malouf scowled.

"Very funny. Leave the check with the food. We need privacy."

"Of course."

She served the food and hurried away. The three men talked well into the afternoon.

Chapter Twenty-Three

Wayne Hawkin felt his phone vibrate as he stood at his desk.

"Hello?"

"It's Audrey. Can you talk?"

"Yes. Are you secure?"

"Yes."

"Good job, by the way. In Madison."

"Thank you. Returning your call."

"Right. They obviously suspect something about Bernie. And they mentioned a woman from the Agency. It's only a matter of time before they ID you. We have to secure you both."

"I agree."

"Move Bernie to a secure place. Stay with him. Whatever equipment he needs, tell Maynard."

"Will do."

"One other thing. I need you home here for a day of training. ASAP."

"I already had advanced training. Is there something more?"

"Yes. We need to train you at the Farm."

"I don't have experience in that."

"You'll get some now. Any questions?"

"None."

Chapter Twenty-Four

Representative Lamar Patterson sat at a table onstage inside a small amphitheater in Washington, D.C. A man in his forties, with short hair and pale blue eyes, sat next to him. He wore an old-fashioned blue blazer with gold buttons, grey flannel pants, and no tie.

A PowerPoint screen was mounted on an easel next to them. They faced an audience of about forty people, mostly men.

"Good afternoon, colleagues and friends."

Patterson touched the remote. The words "Skutnick Selection" appeared on the screen.

"We are here to discuss Skutnick Selection for the State of the Union Address, which is now only months away, and to receive advice from our consultant, Dr. Ramhardt Fluke. Dr. Fluke, these friends of mine are Republican members of Congress from the House and the Senate, who were selected by our caucuses to decide on skutnick strategy. And friends, it now gives me great pleasure to introduce our internationally known expert, Dr. Ramhardt Fluke."

The audience applauded. Fluke stood at attention, hands at his side.

"Dr. Fluke has two doctorates, one in paleontology and one in women's studies. He is a native of Linz, Austria, and has taught at universities in Vienna, Munich, and Passau. He advises our caucus on sensitivity training and gender relations. We have invited him to present his advice on skutnick selection. I give you Dr. Fluke."

More applause. A thin man with nervous eyes and curly hair raised his hand in the audience.

"I have an objection?"

"What is it, Senator?"

It was the Libertarian from Kentucky. Always fucking things up. Always. He stood up and waved some documents.

"I have in my hand an article from the Passau newspaper, saying Dr. Fluke has fake degrees. The headline: 'Summa cum fraude, not summa cum laude.' Here is a copy of an indictment of Dr. Fluke for falsely representing to the university that he had degrees. I renew my objection to his hiring, as I stated to Lamar in private."

The Senator sat down.

Dr. Fluke simply smiled.

"It is false. The work of Plagin Hood, a disgruntled opponent. He accused me of *Titelmissbrauch*. Abuse of titles. The chancellor herself claims to have a doctorate in chemistry. I express no opinion. Plagin Hood also attacked her."

"But you were indicted."

"Yes, but it was dismissed. We subpoenaed Plagin Hood and he did not show up. A Turk. They dismissed the charges."

"Why do you say he is a Turk, when you don't know who he is?"

"Only a Turk would accuse the flower of the German and Austrian intelligentsia of *Titelmissbrauch*."

"All right, thank you, Senator."

Patterson raised his hand.

"We have had this discussion privately. We are satisfied that Dr. Fluke brings great value to our selection. Let's move on. Dr. Fluke?"

"Thank you. The first thing to remember is that people watch to be entertained, *nein*? The rabble demand to see unthinkable things. A transvestite weightlifter with an enormous head and makeup. A man who has been mauled by a bear. But above all, they crave women who give the illusion of access. Who give the illusion they can be had. I am told that your caucus is given ten skutnick slots? And four will be used on

Saudi Arabian women because of certain . . . relationships that your party leaders have with the Crown Prince?"

Lamar Patterson jumped to his feet.

"You're misinformed, Doctor. Not because of relationships. Only because of recognition of support from a longtime ally."

"Of course. Of course. But the point is, we have really six to work with. The other four will reveal only their eyes. The remaining six must appeal to the secret dreams of the audience."

A picture of the actress Anita Ekberg in a teddy, kneeling before a fire, appeared on the screen.

"The Goddess Rackasaurus herself. We mourn her passing. But we must have the modern version. Give her an issue. Any issue that the rabble are talking about. Trade and jobs. But the audience must dream."

A woman in the audience raised her hand.

"I get it that sex sells. But we also want to be serious here. What about Yolanda Priore? She is a professor of economics at Columbia. Shortlisted for the Nobel in Economics last year."

"Do you have her picture?"

"Yes. Here on my phone."

"Send it to me."

Fluke pulled out his phone to examine the picture. He forwarded it to the PowerPoint. A pleasant looking woman, plump, about sixty with short, gray hair, appeared on the screen.

Fluke opened his mouth in exaggerated amazement.

"This is her picture?"

"Well, yes."

"A boner shrinker. *Nein.* You will lose. You must have women, yes? But you must also have their husbands."

Another woman raised her hand. A Stepford Wife with perfect hair, perfect makeup, blazing eyes, and teeth bared, fangs full of message.

"What about Jan Hawley? The famous network anchor. She taps into current issues. Spoke about being sexually harassed forty years ago."

"I remember the interview."

Fluke punched into his phone. He read for a few seconds and forwarded something to the PowerPoint. The anchor Jan Hawley was being interviewed.

"So, tell us what happened, Jan."

"It was forty years ago. A man invited me to lunch. And right there at the table, he asked me if I'd like to go to bed with him! But he knew that I was married! And he was married! I felt so violated!"

The interviewer nodded.

"Incredible."

Fluke stopped the video.

"Can I be blunt? There are only two men on the planet who can sit across the table from a woman at lunch and say, 'remove your clothing and report to my bed.' They are the President of the United States and the King of England."

He paused, as some of the men nodded.

"Women are controlled by their vanity. So are men. The woman wants to bear the son of the highest-prestige man in the room. But her vanity must be appeased."

A man raised his hand.

"But the most powerful man in film was just sent to prison for this. Why? He could give any actress any role."

"His picture. I have seen it. You can't be uglier than a pit bull's ass. The grotesque must be avoided. Except for the President and the King, a trace of foreplay must be present. Her vanity must be respected."

Fluke saw a few frowns among the nods. He raised his voice as he stood tall and stiff.

"You should know that I myself am a feminist. More of a quiet feminist. We *reject* the advice of Herr Friedrich Nietzsche that woman is recreation for the warrior!"

He looked around for approval. None was forthcoming.

"We *reject* the advice of Herr Nietzsche when he said, 'Are you going to woman? Do not forget to bring the whip!' "

More silence.

"The State of the Union Speech is a reunion of clowns and jesters performing for the entertainment of the rabble. The Chief Clown—and I do not offend anyone, correct? I do this for your benefit. He gives a clown monologue. The rabble enjoy it hugely. But the jesters who applaud him must also entertain. Your party must stand for action. Vote Republican for action. The Democrats will haul out ten victims, sorrowful sufferers. People will look away. But you will present pageant racks with long legs like giraffes in full flight from a lion. Mojoceratops. Rackasaurus. Wonderful dream channels. We produce *Herdengluck*, the happiness of the herd."

"Very interesting," Patterson said. "Very interesting. Are there any questions? Yes, Senator."

"Dr. Fluke, you are a European. Our party is concerned about the immigration issue. Europe has similar problems. What is your advice in light of your experience in Europe?"

"Let me be blunt. We fought to keep the Ottomans out of Europe for more than a millennium. The chancellor, a woman from Prussia who grew up under the communist Stasi, suddenly opened Europe to jihad. A man from Bavaria would not have done that. Yes?"

He saw several nods.

"She is crafty. It is not all historic guilt. By a simple act, she attacked London and Paris once again. Populations who had lived in peace are repeatedly under attack. Europe has lost its will. Through Frau Merkel,

Germany has once again launched an attack on Europe. You must understand an unpleasant fact. For Prussia, the primary enemy is not Mecca. It is Rome. Do not make her mistake."

Lamar Patterson stood up and clapped. The audience did the same.

"Thank you, Dr. Ramhardt Fluke! We will now go into closed session to discuss this."

Chapter Twenty-Five

On a Friday night in Milwaukee, Audrey Knapp and Bernie sat at a corner table in County Clare on Astor Street. A server handed them two menus as she filled their water glasses.

"Fish Fry is choice of cod, perch, or shrimp. Choice of coleslaw or German potato salad. Choice of fries, steak fries, or tater tots. Comes with rye bread. Drink orders?"

"We're ready to order," Audrey said. "Bernie, what sounds good to you?"

"Thanks. Just the fish fry with the cod, German potato salad, and regular fries. Extra tartar sauce. And a Miller Lite, please."

"That sounds good. I'll have the same, except no beer."

The server took their menus and left for the kitchen.

Families and children occupied most of the other tables. A young, dark-haired man with a moustache sat alone in the corner across the room. He held up his phone to scroll through his messages while he ate.

"You said you had to talk with me, Audrey. Is everything okay?"

"Overall."

She spoke quietly.

"I'll get to the point. People are following you. They'll try to kill you. You have to move apartments and go underground."

"How can I? I don't have anywhere to go. And how do they know about me?"

"Your name surfaced in some message traffic. We don't know yet how they know you. But it's certain that they're trying to kill you."

"Where can I go? I don't have a lot of money."

"We're taking care of it. You now have an apartment in the Cudahy on Wells. Do you know the building?"

"I know where it is."

"It's not in your name. The keys are in the envelope in front of me. When we leave, take them and go directly there. Do not leave the apartment. Groceries will be delivered."

"What about my stuff? My computer? In my apartment?"

"Tell me what you need, and it'll be brought to you."

"Can I go to Madison sometimes to work?"

"You shouldn't. Can you do it with the equipment you have in your apartment now?"

"Kind of. But there's some support I have in Madison that makes it easier."

"We'll transfer all your equipment in your apartment to the Cudahy. Let me know what support you have in Madison, and we'll duplicate it."

"That'd be too expensive. Tens of thousands of dollars."

"Let me worry about the cost. Just tell me everything you need, and we'll set it up."

"Okay. Thanks. Where are you going to be?"

"I'll be in the Cudahy, too. You'll be okay, Bernie. Tell me, what progress are you making? You said you had some good news?"

"Definitely. How much do you want to hear?"

"Everything. From the beginning."

"Okay. So, the problem all along is this. There was a guy named Werner Heisenberg in Germany in the 1920s. He came up with some equations that said that if you measure a particle's position, like a photon's position, you can't also know its velocity. And if you know its velocity, you can't also know its position. What he basically said is, a particle floats in a probability haze until it's measured. We talked about that before."

"I've heard of him. Do you disagree with him?"

"Particles are physical objects. They're real. All physical objects must have a position at any given point in time, and a velocity. Reality doesn't float in a haze. You may not know a particle's position or velocity, but that doesn't mean it doesn't have them."

"Can you prove that?"

"Yes. I have."

"Amazing. What else did Heisenberg say?"

The server returned with a tray holding two fish fries and a beer. She served them and left the check.

"Thanks," Bernie said.

They started to eat.

"Anyway, Heisenberg said that two particles that are entangled operate as one physical object, even if they're a billion light years apart. So, if you measure one of the particles, the other also pops out of the probability haze and yields the same measurement, even if they're far apart."

"We talked about that, too. And you still don't agree with that?"

"No. Neither did Einstein. He said it was spooky. That the result must have been predetermined locally before they were separated. You can't have an instant cause and effect that goes faster than the speed of light."

"Bernie, how does that fit into the code we can't read?"

"I told you about Bell and his papers in Madison and that what he did is come up with an experiment to prove that Heisenberg was right, and Einstein was wrong. I realized that if Heisenberg was wrong, then Bell was wrong. And if Bell was wrong, the encryption based on his equations has a flaw that we can get into."

"Do you have a plan now to exploit the flaw?"

"Yeah."

They continued eating. The dark-haired man in the corner left before they were done.

Chapter Twenty-Six

As the five law firm managers of Burden, Hefty sat inside a conference room, Pocket Hercules tapped a glass against the table.

"I will start with something I want to share with you, and then Foot has an announcement. I am sad to report that the Serpent, our partner, died last night."

He didn't look sad. In fact, his eyes sparkled as he spoke.

"Diet and exercise," said the Mullet. "I always said, diet and exercise."

"That wouldn't have helped him this time."

"How did he die?"

"He died in a full nelson."

"The Serpent was a wrestler?"

"In a manner of speaking. Nelson Rockefeller. He died in flagrante."

A silence followed.

"Our official position is that the cause of death is not entirely clear," said Pocket Hercules. "It will be revealed in due course. Mullet, you should send notice out in the firm Blurb. He died peacefully, surrounded by family. Arrangements pending. Charlie, if the associates committee has any questions, check with me before you answer. Okay?"

"Right, Herk. Who will get his office?"

"Any of you want it?"

"Not really."

"No."

"No."

"Who will get his clients?" the Nurse said.

"Foot and I will discuss that and make a recommendation. And now, Foot has an announcement."

Bigfoot's fleshy, hairless hands trembled as he set them down on the table.

"Good news! Unbelievable news! We got a new client!"

"Who?"

"Who is it?"

"You won't believe it! Saudi Arabia!"

"What? Why would they want us?"

"Long story. Short version: Nurse, you will be the liaison. We will be local counsel for Raptor, Hawk out of New York!"

"What am I supposed to do?" said the Nurse.

"Nothing! That's the beauty of it. Nothing! But we charge full rates. And I mean *full* rates!"

"Their Crown Prince just bought a yacht for five hundred million dollars," said Charlie.

"He bought a painting of an obscure artist for a hundred million," the Mullet said.

"He murdered a man in Istanbul," said the Nurse.

"Outstanding!"

Bigfoot rubbed his hands.

"Outstanding! Raptor, Hawk! Saudi Arabia! Big time! Big time!"

They discussed a few agenda items before Pocket Hercules ended the meeting.

"We're done for now. Same time next week."

Bigfoot stayed after the others had left and pulled a sheet of paper from his jacket.

"Herk, you've got to see this. I dictated an obit for the Serpent!"

Pocket Hercules started to read it out loud.

"Rick McDaniel, aka the Serpent, died in flagrante last night, at two a.m. in a Walmart parking lot. He was a devious prick, even by Burden, Hefty standards . . ."

"What is this?"

Bigfoot shook with laughter.

"Hee, hee hee! Just a spoof. Won't go beyond you and me. But we're rid of the prick! Herk, we're rid of the greedy prick!"

Pocket Hercules chuckled.

"Better erase this damned thing. But get me a copy. I want to read the rest of it."

"Will do."

"By the way. You're getting a new secretary?"

"Right. Mabel's been getting a little mutinous. A little short. I need enthusiasm."

"She's been here a long time."

"She has. But she'll find something."

"When are you doing it?"

"This afternoon. The team shows up at her carrel and escorts her out."

"Okay. See you later."

Bigfoot left. He went to a conference room and picked up the phone. "Yes?"

"Roger? Walt Hefty. Time to execute. You know the protocol. Take the team to her carrel and escort her out. She can take her purse and her coat. That's it. I'm hanging in the conference room until the deed is done."

"I'm on it."

Bigfoot sat back. He looked out over the lake, feeling well satisfied with his life.

Two floors above, Mabel Burke sat at her desk. She scowled at the document on the screen that her boss had dictated:

"Rick McDaniel, aka the Serpent, died in flagrante last night . . ."

She heard a noise and looked up to see Roger peering over the carrel. Two other messengers stood behind him.

"Mabel, I have some bad news. You've been terminated. Mr. Hefty asked me to escort you out. You can take your purse and your coat. But that's it."

"Oh, really? Really? Okay. Just have to sign out of this."

Before he could say anything, she hit Forward and typed in MEDIA-ALL.

"What are you doing? What are you doing?"

Roger lumbered around the carrel to grab her arm. With her other hand, she hit SEND.

"What are you doing!"

"You startled me. When I looked up, I thought it was a gorilla."

"Nice. Nice. Keep going."

"Ouch. That hurts. Are you supposed to be grabbing my arm?"

"Keep going."

Bigfoot lingered in the conference room until he was sure the coast was clear. When he returned to his office, Mabel was gone.

He hummed a few show tunes while he looked at his mail. At four o'clock, he grabbed his coat and left early.

He was still humming as he pulled out of the garage. When he got out on the street, his phone rang.

"Yes?"

"Walt Hefty? Roland Cheek, *Milwaukee Journal Sentinel*. Have a few minutes?"

"Of course."

Bigfoot was feeling jolly, expansive, and full of good will.

"I'm doing a feature on the obituary of your partner, Rick McDaniel. To begin with, he was called the Serpent and he died in flagrante? At two a.m. in a Walmart parking lot?"

119

"No! NOOOOO!"

Bigfoot screamed into the phone.

"It's a joke! He died of a stroke!"

"Hefty! Brilliant! 'It was a joke, he died of a stroke.' I smell headline, Hefty!"

"It was a mistake! A vengeful secretary. We fired her for stealing. She must have typed that up to hurt me!"

"Sure she did. Just a few more things. When you say 'he was a devious prick, even by Burden, Hefty standards,' what *are* your standards?"

"Cheek. So help me. If you publish that, I'll sue you for libel!"

"For publishing something you sent me? Good luck. Just a few more things. You say that you will bring a mirror to the wake to hold under his nose. Make sure it's not a scam. What kind of scam?"

"Cheek! I told you. The bitch stabbed me on the way out. It's a fake!"

"The bitch in question is your secretary?"

"Don't publish that! It's off the record, goddamn you!

"No worries. We don't publish bad words. Only some of the consonants. One more question. You say his proudest accomplishment was convincing a jury that an employee who was decapitated in an industrial accident felt no pain and suffering because his head was yanked off so quickly. Is that also your firm's proudest accomplishment, or just his?"

"Goddamn you, Cheek! Goddamn your eyes!"

Chapter Twenty-Seven

Inside the Willard Hotel in Washington, D.C., Taqi Maghribi sat at a conference table with Tamerlane and three other men. Zulkifar Malouf stood in a corner and dialed his phone.

"Raptor, Hawk. How may I help you?"

"I want Napoleon Raptor."

"Just a moment."

The operator transferred him.

"Mr. Raptor's office."

"I want Napoleon, Nate. I want him now."

"Who may I say is speaking?"

"Mr. Malouf."

Raptor came on almost immediately.

"Zulky! Good to hear from you. What's up?"

"Burden, Hefty! Did you read that article? It even showed up in the Post?"

"Which one? You mean Bigfoot calling his secretary a bitch and his partner croaking in a parking lot in the middle of the night? What's not to like?"

Raptor's sneeze and gargle laugh carried to the table. Malouf covered the receiver until the laughing stopped.

"They're incompetent. They hurt us. How can you continue to use them?"

"Zulky! Trust me, Zulky. It's exactly what we expected. All we want is their firm name. Weaver Dane is on his way out there. They won't have the stones to freelance on us. This is all a formality."

"We hired you. We have to rely on you. But I am uneasy about using them."

"And why would that be?"

More sneezing and gargling.

"Trust me, Zulky. Trust old Nate. This is a slam dunk."

"All right. Just so you saw the article."

Malouf sat down next to Maghribi. The other men were quiet.

"The woman and the boy. What progress has been made?"

"We identified the woman."

Tamerlane pushed copies of a photo toward each man.

"She was having dinner at a restaurant with Bernie Weber. I followed him there. When he left, I followed him to an apartment building. The Cudahy. It is different from Weber's address in the faculty records that Taqi gave me."

"He's hiding. Is she hiding with him?"

"Probably."

Tamerlane pointed to the other men.

"We will take turns watching the building. He has to leave sooner or later. And, of course he will see her again."

"Excellent! And you know your orders?"

Tamerlane and the others nodded.

"When they are alone, dispose of them in the way we discussed. There must be no evidence of what happened. There can be no witnesses. Their bodies must not remain in the U.S. They will simply disappear."

"We will do as you say."

"And, do it soon. Very soon."

"We will."

"Good. That is all. You may go."

Maghribi stayed seated as they left.

"You should know the status of Operation Cordoba," Malouf said.

"That's what you call it?"

"Yes. Cordoba was the headquarters of the Caliphate after it conquered Spain. The name will once again be known."

"Good."

"Cordoba will attack the Capitol by land and air."

"How will we penetrate their airspace? It will be closed to all flights."

"We will have men at every small airport in Delaware, Maryland, Pennsylvania, West Virginia, and Virginia that are within a hundred miles of the Capitol. Each piloting a private jet. At the appointed time, they will take off."

"The air traffic controllers will alert their military. They will be shot down."

"Some will be shot down. But not all. There are limits to how many military aircraft patrol a small urban area. You cannot shoot down a swarm of bees. At first, they will be astounded, hesitating to shoot a swarm of aircraft over the city. They will try to warn the planes away. When they do react, it will be too late."

"How many do you think will get through?"

"It may only be a few. But their cargo will blow the building apart."

"The pilots will die. It is a kamikaze mission. Do you trust them to do it?"

"Many of them are brothers or fathers of the mujahideen, the benefactors of the Ummah, who died on 9/11. They know their fate. They welcome it."

"What is the plan inside the building?"

"The skutnicks. Four women. A week before Cordoba launches, they will make their way to Washington. So will you."

"Where are they?"

"In different locations. One is in Chicago, one in Memphis, one in Atlanta, and one in Miami."

"What is their cover?"

"Two are students. One is in a company training program. And the other one works for the state government."

"Can they be trusted?"

"Yes. Each had family members who died in American bombings."

"What do you want me to do?"

"You will meet with the skutnicks two days before the State of the Union. I will join you. We will issue them their chemicals and explain how to use them. How to conceal them. What to say if they are questioned. And you will accompany them to the Capitol on February 1st."

"But not go in?"

"No. You are not to go in. You are too valuable to lose. And your name isn't on any list. If you even tried to go in, you would be arrested."

"What do you want me to do in the meantime?"

"Keep quiet in Milwaukee. Our lawsuit for your mistreatment is honorable and transparent. The lawyers will handle everything. Do nothing. Do not call any other attention to yourself."

"It will be as you say."

Chapter Twenty-Eight

Wayne Hawkin and Audrey Knapp drove up a long driveway in an isolated area near Williamsburg, Virginia.

"I've never been here before."

"NSA mathematicians don't need to come here. Now, your duties have changed. Welcome to the Farm, Audrey."

They passed by a long airstrip.

"Who uses that?"

"We do. It avoids troublesome formalities with commercial airports and air traffic controllers."

They pulled into a parking lot outside of a large wooden building. A man sitting on a chair outside the door stood up and approached them.

Hawkin pulled out his ID.

"Wayne Hawkin. And this is Audrey Knapp."

Audrey handed him her ID. He returned them both.

"Welcome to the Farm. You're here to see Joanne Martinez."

"Right."

"She's inside on the right."

The man sat down as Hawkin and Audrey went inside.

The door to the first room on the right was open. A woman in her early sixties sat at a desk, leaning back, her hands clasped behind her head. She was attractive, with perfect makeup. She wore a blouse buttoned to the throat and a blue skirt to just above the knee.

The room was decorated like a disorganized secondhand store. Shelves and end tables were overflowing with lamps, books, unopened liquor bottles, pots with no plants, wigs, false teeth, masks, prosthetic noses, lipstick, shoes, bricks, cameras, cigarette lighters, magazines, bars of soap, hotel size shampoo bottles, radios, mirrors, cereal boxes, plates, silverware, and other garage sale trophies.

The walls were covered with photographs, some of them framed. There were dozens of pictures of dogs in the passenger seats of cars, of identical twins, old women, young women, girls, boys, old men, and young men—all of different races.

The woman came out from behind her desk.

"So good to see you again, Wayne! And this must be Audrey? Welcome! I'm Joanne Martinez."

"It's very nice to meet you."

She motioned to two chairs and sat back behind her desk.

"Has Wayne told you what we're going to do today?"

"Somewhat. I'm eager to learn more."

"Wayne, do you want to start this?"

"Right. Joanne, Audrey will be on assignment in a venue where foreign assets may look for her. And also, where she needs to look for them without being identified. We want several disguises that she can put on without a handler helping her. Why don't you give her a tour of this room and explain what you do?"

"Glad to."

Martinez walked over to one of the shelves. Audrey and Hawkin followed her.

"Every item on these shelves and tables has a microphone in it, a camera installed, or it is used to conceal something."

She picked up a small camera and a copy of *People* magazine.

"This is a microdot camera. It reduces a photo to the size of a dot to conceal in the text of a magazine for example."

She opened the magazine and handed it to Audrey.

"You see the text on that page? Under the picture of five actresses? Read me the line just under the picture."

"One of these women will take the Oscar."

"See the period after Oscar?"

"Sure."

"That's a picture of a document."

"Very nice!"

"Are you going to be staying in a Moscow hotel room?"

"I hope not."

"Well, if you ever do, assume that everything has a camera and a microphone in it. The lamp. The radio. The pictures on the wall. The towel bar. The toilet. The smoke detector. Book bindings, lids of liquor bottles, plant pots. Donald Trump found that out the hard way."

Martinez walked over to some photographs. She pointed at one.

"What do you see in that picture?"

"A dog that looks like an Irish setter, sticking his head out of the window."

"And how about that one?"

"Another Irish setter in a car, head out the window."

"You're half right. One is a dog. The other is our agent. Which is which?"

Audrey looked closely at the photos.

"That's amazing! I can't tell."

"And how about that picture there?"

"It's an African American man, sitting on a bench."

"It's actually an Asian woman sitting on a bench. How about that one?"

"Two men who are identical twins."

"It's actually two men who look very different before they're made up."

"Excellent work!"

"You see, the successor to the KGB has thousands of officers in Moscow who follow all of our personnel everywhere 24/7. Everyone from the embassy, all U.S. government visitors, prominent businessmen. The same for the NATO countries. But they don't follow Irish setters. And if a man goes into a restaurant, they follow the first man who comes out who looks identical to him. The man himself slips out later."

"Joanne, we need a couple of disguises that Audrey can put on herself without anyone's help."

"Right. Man? Woman? Race?"

"Whatever Audrey thinks. You advise. I'll work down the hall until you're done."

"Will do. Audrey, please come with me."

Chapter Twenty-Nine

Taqi Maghribi sat in his apartment, skimming through Milwaukee's alternative newspaper. His face grew rigid as he looked at the pictures for gentlemen's clubs and adult chat. He began to read the classified ads below the pictures.

"Attractive young lady in need of discipline seeks generous older gentlemen for evening of instruction and adventure."

A telephone number followed.

Maghribi shook with anger. He went to the refrigerator and took out a package wrapped in butcher paper, which he removed, and placed a raw beef roast on the counter. As he dialed the number, he reached under the countertop and took out a whip. He raised the whip to lash down on the roast.

"Hello?"

It was a man's voice.

"I read the ad in the paper."

"Yes. It's two hundred dollars for an hour. Cash. Pay in advance."

Maghribi lashed the roast beef harder. Blood oozed onto the counter.

"All right. Where do I go?"

"On the corner of 35th Street and Wisconsin Avenue. In half an hour . . ."

"You do it in the street?"

"Plenty of alleys nearby. What is your name?"

"It is . . . Suleiman."

"Okay, Sully. My girl will meet you in half an hour."

Maghribi hung up and lashed the roast beef even harder.

In an art deco building on the bad side of town, Reginald Oliver hung up the phone. He was an African American man, powerfully built, with a moustache and hair clipped short. He wore a tee shirt that said, "Emperor Booty the First."

A very pretty African American woman sat next to him.

"Booty, what we got?"

"Half an hour. 35th and Wisconsin."

"What he sound like?"

"Foreign."

"They bad."

"We handle them. Let's go."

They drove an SUV with the plates removed to the corner of 35th and Wisconsin. A Walgreens drug store was open across the street, but few people were inside. The woman opened the passenger door.

"You staying, right, Booty?"

"You know I am. Pulling down the block here."

He parked half a block away, but in sight of the corner.

The woman stood leaning against a building just inside an alley.

A car pulled up ten minutes later. Maghribi got out and walked up to her.

"You the woman? Adventure and discipline?"

"That's me, honey!"

"Whore! Immodest whore!"

Maghribi slapped her.

"What you doin'?"

"Whore!"

He slapped her again.

"BOOTY! BOOTY!"

Booty came running down the block into the alley. He held a gun a foot from Maghribi's head."

"Lie down, bitch! Or I fan you down!"

"Who are you? She is a whore!"

"My shooter go off, bitch. Lie down! Ten, nine, eight, seven . . ."

Maghribi got down on the ground in the alley.

"Take off your clothes!"

"What? I won't."

"Ten, nine, eight, seven, six . . ."

Maghribi unbuttoned his shirt.

"Take them *all* off, bitch!"

Maghribi unhooked his belt but lay still.

"Pull them down, bitch."

Maghribi slowly surrendered his trousers. He lay there in his skivvies and shoes. Booty pocketed his wallet.

"Take off your shoes."

Maghribi complied.

"Roll over on your belly."

As Maghribi rolled over, Booty motioned to the woman.

"Get the handcuffs."

The woman ran to the car and returned with handcuffs.

"Put them on him."

As she snapped the cuffs on, Booty knelt down and put the gun to Maghribi's head.

"Now, stand up."

Maghribi struggled to stand with his wrists restrained behind his back. Booty grabbed him by the hair and got him to his feet.

"Now, walk toward that car."

Booty threw him across the back seat, face down.

"If your head pop up, I blow it off. Keep an eye on him."

"What you going to do with him, Booty?"

"Sell him!"

"No one buy him. He ain't a girl."

"I got a better idea!"

Booty chuckled.

"King Sugar steal my girls. Emperor higher than king. We dump him on Sugar's lawn and call the police."

A siren sounded in the distance. Booty turned left at 27th Street. They could hear more sirens.

"We got to get out of here, Booty. Woman must have called the police on her car. Got to get rid of it."

Booty didn't respond. He turned east. The sirens were getting louder. Booty turned onto Water Street. The Performing Arts Center was a block ahead.

"Dump him, Booty! Dump the car!"

Booty swerved up just beyond the drop-off area of the Arts Center. No one was in sight. He jumped out of the car, dragged Maghribi out, and threw him on the grass. He jumped back in, but the sirens were a block away. They pulled the car up in front of St. Kate's hotel and jumped out. The woman took Booty's arm as they walked down Water Street.

A crowd started to pour out of the Arts Center. Pocket Hercules walked with his wife in the middle, humming "O Mio Babbino Caro."

Damn, that was good. Pocket Hercules hummed a little louder. He heard voices yelling outside.

"Christo! Christo! Bravo!"

First a few, then many. He pushed through the crowd and saw an obese man in his underwear lying on the grass with his hands handcuffed behind his back.

What? Performance art? Some Riverwest wannabe honors Christo's memory by dumping a naked actor on the grass to make a statement? Progressives' revenge against the one percent?

Improbably, a few people started to shout "Banksy, Banksy!" Then even more improbably, "Shepard Fairey! Shepard Fairey!"

What? More progressive shit art? These prestige-starved assholes give a shoutout to anything they think is new? To show they're too cool for the old stuff? They bravo a handcuffed, naked, fat man? They see anything new and they're like starving cats on a saucer of cream? Of course, I like the masters. Anybody with a brain likes the masters. The new stuff is shit. But I get it. I understand it, even though it's shit. Have to show I understand it.

"Christo, Christo!"

Pocket Hercules yelled along with the others.

"Bravo, Christo!"

Chapter Thirty

Audrey Knapp's phone vibrated as she walked along Mason Street.

"Hello?"

"It's Wayne. Go home now. Log on. Joanne sent you some pix."

"Okay."

"From the apartment of the man in question. Four other men are now involved. It's urgent."

"Got it."

She was about to pass Polpetta's Italian Restaurant. A poster in the window said. "Taste my Grandma's Balls." Underneath was a picture of a smiling woman with her gray hair swept back in a bun, holding a tray of steaming meatballs.

A car with tinted windows pulled up. A man got out and walked toward her. Audrey ran to the door of the restaurant. She felt his hand in her back before she could open it.

"Get in the car, bitch. If you scream or run, I'll shoot. There will be no sound."

The door to Polpetta's opened and two men walked out.

"Ed, send me that letter and . . ."

Audrey pushed between them into the restaurant. The man from the car followed right behind, his hand still firmly in her back, the gun concealed.

"Table," Audrey said.

"No table," said the man. "Have to leave."

"Table!" said Audrey. "Just a quick lunch."

"Of course."

The hostess picked up two menus.

"Follow me."

The man held her arm firmly as they walked through the restaurant. The lunch crowd was almost all gone. The only occupied tables were near the front.

"That one. In the corner."

He pointed to a high-backed booth in the rear of the restaurant, behind a partition.

A waitress came to pour them each a glass of water.

"I'll be back to take your orders."

"Give us ten minutes," the man said. "We need time to discuss."

"Of course."

She left. They were alone. He wrapped a napkin around his hand.

"I have a gun. It makes no sound. Zero. If your hands go below the table, I shoot. I will say you are resting and leave."

Audrey's hands stayed on the table.

"What do you want with me?"

"I know who you are. You are a sneaky little whore. We are not having lunch. Get up now, slowly. Walk toward the door. Get in the car outside. Do it now."

Audrey leaned far into the table, looking at his eyes. She slowly unbuttoned the top button on her blouse. Then the next to show her bra. Then the next. The top of a magnificent breast came into view. His eyes gleamed. She leaned further over the table and pushed her bra down. Her breasts were fully exposed. He grinned at them as her other hand slipped down.

The first silent shot tore into his groin. The second into his belly. He pitched forward, his head slamming onto the table. Audrey threw a napkin over his head and jumped up. She buttoned her blouse, wrapped her scarf around her face and hurried to the door. The waitress was just emerging from the kitchen. Audrey stopped her.

"Get us two cups of decaf coffee. I will be back."

"Immediately."

"No, not immediately. The pot must be freshly brewed. And the cups must be cleaned again before they are served to us."

"Of course."

The waitress hurried away.

Audrey walked out the front door. The car with tinted windows was idling in front of the restaurant. She walked around to the driver's side and opened the back door.

The driver leered into the rearview mirror.

"Get in, bitch."

Two shots ripped through the seat and blew his back open. He collapsed against the steering wheel without a sound.

Audrey got out of the car. She hurried across the street into an alley and disappeared.

Chapter Thirty-One

Audrey sat on a sofa in her apartment, watching the local news.

"Welcome to the evening news with WISN-TV Channel 12. I'm Kathy Mykleby. We're going right now to Colleen Henry with breaking news, a horrible crime scene at Polpetta's Restaurant downtown. Colleen?"

Colleen Henry stood in front of the restaurant with a microphone. Yellow police tape ran from the front door out and around a car. Police officers moved in and out of Polpetta's.

"That's right, Kathy. A double murder at Polpetta's Restaurant on the corner of Mason and Milwaukee Streets here in downtown. Apparently, a man and a woman entered the restaurant for lunch. While they were seated, the man was shot twice. The woman left immediately. Shortly afterward, a man was shot in a car parked just outside. One of the waitresses, Carol Maltese, is here with me now. Carol, what did you observe just before the murders?"

"Jesus, Mary, and Joseph! Nothing! I swear to God! This lady walks in, scarf around her face. A man with her, possible Hispanic. They looked questionable, you know. My spidey senses started tingling. They took a table. I went to get them coffee. I came back, and he was lying on the floor, all bloody!"

"Carol, were they arguing? Could you hear them yelling?"

"Nope. Just having lunch."

"Thank you, Carol. Kathy, the police spokeswoman will make a statement shortly. An ambulance took the men away. The police are still looking at the car and the booth in the restaurant. Back to you, Kathy."

"Thanks, Colleen. News Team 12 coverage continues with exclusive interviews. Next, we go live with an expert at Milwaukee Community

College, Digby Brayboy, professor of sociology and an expert on hate crimes. Thank you for speaking with us, Professor. We have some questions about the murders at Polpetta's. What was your initial reaction to the news?"

"That was a pearl clutcher!"

Brayboy wore a dark corduroy sport jacket, blue shirt, and no tie. He sat in an armchair in his apartment.

"Professor, News Team 12 has discovered from a source in the police department that both of the murdered men were Saudi Arabian nationals. What is your opinion on whether this was a hate crime?"

"Very likely. It's statistically improbable that one Saudi man is shot in the restaurant and his driver is shot for an unrelated motive. And in broad daylight, in the heart of the business district! I eat there myself. I'm quite fond of their mushroom ravioli."

"Sounds yummy. But, Professor, what drives people to commit hate crimes?"

"Hatred of the other. Resentment of seeing foreigners advance economically while the perpetrator struggles. Low education. All undoubtedly present here."

"Thank you, Professor," said Mykleby. "We now go live to our exclusive interview with Pearly Stubbs, the Milwaukee Medical Examiner. Ms. Stubbs, thank you for speaking with us."

"Welcome."

Pearly was a middle-aged woman with a gray crewcut. She wore a dark green, gabardine jacket from the Army-Navy store over corduroy trousers. The head of a bull elk with enormous antlers, shot by Pearly in Montana, was mounted on the wall behind her.

Pearly had almost lost her job the previous year. Inspectors found thirty-five jars of testicles in formaldehyde in her office safe, trophies from years of autopsies, and, as it happened, the largest specimens she had encountered. Her defense was scientific research and the First Amendment. Eventually, Pearly was reinstated with back pay.

"Ms. Stubbs, what was the cause of death of the two men who were killed at Polpetta's? Have you officially determined it?"

"At this time, I have not completely examined the bodies."

Pearly's eyes glistened.

"We must examine the wounds carefully."

"The Saudi Arabian government has objected to the autopsies being performed by a woman. Our State Department has asked the city to consider shipping the bodies home without an autopsy to placate their government. What is your response?"

Pearly let out a grunting sort of laugh, with no evidence of humor.

"The law is the law. They will receive the bodies when I release them."

"You will proceed in spite of the wishes of a foreign government?"

"If wishes were fishes, they'd have some to fry. If wishes were horses, their beggars would ride."

"Thank you, Ms. Stubbs! We're told that the police spokeswoman is about to make a statement. Let's go there now."

An African American woman stood in front of Polpetta's, surrounded by four television cameras and a half dozen reporters.

"MPD will have no definitive statement until our investigation is complete. I can tell you that two males were shot this afternoon at Polpetta's, one in a booth and the other in a car, just outside the establishment. Both are dead. Their identities will be disclosed after their next of kin are notified. I will take questions."

"Do you have a motive?" said Colleen Henry.

"We have a working hypothesis, but no conclusion at this time. A person of interest is an unknown woman."

"What kind of weapon was used?" said another reporter.

"We're investigating that. Witnesses reported hearing no unusual sounds in the restaurant or on the street. The perpetrator must have used a silencer that is different from anything we've seen before."

"I am Cenk Rut from *The New York Times*," said a man. "An Islamic scholar here in Milwaukee was recently beaten by police while checking into a motel. He was beaten again at the Festival Grounds. He was then kidnapped, stripped, and thrown handcuffed on the sidewalk near the Performing Arts Center. Another scholar was murdered in a bathroom in Madison. Do you suspect a pattern of hate crimes?"

The spokeswoman rolled her eyes.

"We don't see a connection. No. That will be all until we have further information."

She stepped away from the TV cameras.

Kathy Mykleby appeared back on the screen.

"News Team 12 will continue to follow this story. And after a break, why one woman whose Bucks tickets were stolen didn't let that stop her from going to the game!"

Audrey turned off the TV. Her phone rang.

"It's Wayne. Can you talk?"

"Yes."

"Did you see Joanne's pix?"

"Yes."

Audrey clicked on her screen. A picture of Taqi Maghribi appeared. He was seated at a table in his apartment with four other men. She scrolled through several more pictures of the men from different angles.

"Joanne did an amazing job. How did she get these?"

"You spent time with her. All she needs is a vase or a book or a picture frame or a lamp. Her team seeds the room."

"What were they saying?"

"They know about you. You and Bernie are their targets."

"What are their plans?"

"Greatly changed now. You terminated two of them this afternoon. Bravo Zulu!"

"Thanks. But I can't let them get that close again. What else did they say?"

"Maghribi is the leader. It's clear that the rest are only in Milwaukee to get Bernie. And you. Whoever's above Maghribi takes Bernie's work as a serious threat to their encryption. But Maghribi hasn't said what they're planning to do. And we still can't read their message traffic."

"Got it. Any special requests of me?"

"Three things. Take care of yourself first. I worry about you. Two, take out the remaining two men. We'll track their movements and let you know. And three, take out Maghribi."

"Roger. Will do."

Chapter Thirty-Two

Taqi Maghribi looked at the words appearing on his screen.

'Are you secure?'

'Yes.'

'Now a good time?'

'Yes.'

'What is going on out there? You lost two more men? You were stripped, handcuffed, and dumped on the sidewalk? What are you doing?'

'I was taking a walk. I was attacked by a man with a gun. He stole my wallet and handcuffed me at gunpoint. This is a violent and lawless town. There is no respect for authority.'

'Plan to leave for Washington ahead of schedule. We can't have any more incidents. I will instruct you when. And the men in the restaurant? How did it happen?'

'They were careless. The bitch from the CIA got them. We know what she looks like. And we know where she and Weber live. It will be simple to neutralize them.'

'I'm glad it's so simple. It should also be simple to avoid being beaten, shot, and handcuffed. And it should be simple to take out a woman and a boy when you know what they look like and where they live. Just do it.'

'Do not be displeased with me.'

'I'm not the one you should worry about. It's the men I report to. You seem quick to excuse yourself. To brush this off. They are impatient. You still have relatives here. What should I tell them?'

'Tell them my words may seem light as a bird's feather, but my heart is as heavy as a mountain. We have lost two lions battling the enemies of the Ummah. I will avenge them. And I will give my life for our cause.'

'That's better. Let me know when the woman and the boy are dead.'

'I will.'

Chapter Thirty-Three

A succession of men in dark suits, white shirts, and black ties filed past a small, unlocked fence and entered a tomblike, unmarked, windowless building in New Haven, Connecticut.

None of them spoke a word as they each pulled open a large, engraved brass door and stepped into a small anteroom with another closed door.

"*Pocula elevate*," they said.

"*Nunc est bibendum*," said a man in a white coat, opening the door from inside to greet each of the visitors.

The hallway was dimly lit and led into a series of rooms.

"Welcome," he said. "Sherry is served in the Poculum."

"Thank you, Wamba."

Wayne Hawkin and Lathrop Willis filed in with the rest.

"Glad you twisted my arm, Hawkin. I haven't been to a Z session in years."

The Poculum in the Hall of Scroll and Key was crowded. Alumni who rarely saw each other sipped their drinks and caught up on the passage of lives.

"And by the way," Willis said, "The meeting afterward. In the Templum. Who are you inviting?"

"Only Agency veterans. You know them. You hired many of them. I want their input on some difficult questions."

"Very good."

Wamba summoned them to dinner. They walked into a large dining room. A round oak table that sat fifteen stood in front of a huge fireplace. Wamba occasionally added a log as the wood continued to crackle.

Banners and shields lined the stone walls. These were the arms of each of the fifteen pontiffs from the current class, banners from Scroll and Key classes of the past, and a large picture of a troubadour, kneeling in front of a woman with long hair in medieval dress.

Scroll and Key was founded at Yale University in 1842 as a nativist caricature of a papal court. The fifteen members tapped their successors each spring. Each had a name taken from mythology or history. The leader of the collegium, the Pontifex Maximus, was called Zanoni. He wore a black robe. His two principal assistants were Anselmo and Arbaces. They wore white robes. The rest of the pontiffs wore red robes.

The current members of Keys from the senior class sat at the round table. Three long tables were set up beyond the round table for the Keys alumni. Willis and Hawkin took seats near the back.

A young man stood up as the room quieted.

"Good evening, and welcome back to the Hall. I am Matt Ryan, the current Zanoni. We will now serve dinner, followed by the Z session. But first, I want to introduce our magnificent cook, who most of you know from your time in the Hall. I present with thanks, Mrs. Ella Scantlebury."

A middle-aged African American woman in an apron smiled and waved to the group. The applause was loud and sustained.

"Thank you. Thank you. So good to see you all back here! Thank you."

Ella Scantlebury had cooked at Scroll and Key for decades. She was also the elected treasurer of the City of New Haven.

Waiters began to serve a dinner of tenderloin, baked potato and string beans. Several of them were moonlighting members of the New Haven police department. In the late 1960s, during the Vietnam war, when some Keys men joined the New Haven police department to secure a draft deferment, they were sometimes served dinner at the Hall by their supervising lieutenants.

Bottles of port and Madeira were placed on the tables when the meal was over, and the staff retired. The young Zanoni stood up to strike a fork against his glass.

"Let the Z session start. We will begin by singing 'The Troubadour.' "

The whole room stood up to sing. Those who had been in the Whiffenpoofs carried the tune. The rest sang with great enthusiasm.

"Gaily the Troubadour touched his guitar, as he was hastening home from the war. Singing from Palestine . . ."

When the song was over, Matt Ryan waited for them to sit down.

"Thank you. I will start my address, which is called 'China: the real threat and how to contain it.' "

The roomful of investment bankers, professors, lawyers, diplomats, doctors, editors, CEOs, and philanthropists sat back and listened to a twenty-one-year-old graduating senior advise them on foreign policy. They applauded when he finished, nodding to one another.

"Shows promise."

"Smart boy."

"We'll hear about him some day."

"And now," the young Z went on, "Mr. Wayne Hawkin, Z '69, would like to see some of you in the Templum. You received his invitation. The rest of us will adjourn to the Poculum for more socializing. Thank you all for coming."

Hawkin and Willis walked up the stairs to the Templum. They were the first to enter. Hawkin sat on the throne of Zanoni. The arms of the throne ended in two carved lion heads. Over the throne hung the shield of Zanoni, saying "Hear and Obey," above an eagle with lightning bolts shooting from its talons.

Two smaller thrones, for Anselmo and Arbaces, flanked Zanoni. Twelve high-backed thrones were arranged, six on a side, connected by a platform. Over every throne stood a shield with the arms of another member.

A marble fireplace, unlit, lay along the far wall. Paintings from mythology covered the ceiling and upper walls. The lower walls were carved wood. The floor was marble.

Twenty more alumni filed into the Templum. Some sat in the remaining thrones. Wamba and his staff carried in chairs for the rest. As they left, Wamba pulled the door closed behind him.

"Gentlemen," said Hawkin. "Good of you to come. Arbaces '65, I see that you've brought your father. So good to see him. I believe he is the oldest living graduate of Yale?"

"Quite right."

A man in his seventies stood up and put his hand on his father's shoulder.

"Chilo '39, my dad just wouldn't miss it. And he's still quite acute."

The group collectively snapped their fingers. The old man stood up, supported by his son.

"Keep an eye on the Bolsheviks, gentlemen! Never let up. When I was with Wild Bill Donovan in the OSS, we were on to their game!"

Fingers snapping. Fingers snapping.

"Chilo, you have inspired us all," Hawkin said. "And I think of you every October 14th when I pick up *The New York Times* and read your magnificent annual ad: 'In Memory of Harold, the last Saxon King of England, slain this day in 1066 at the Battle of Hastings.' "

The old man nodded firmly.

"One must remember certain things."

"Right. Now, gentlemen, let's get to why I asked you to join me. You have all worked for the Agency. For those of you who have retired, I assume that you have still maintained your security clearances?"

"Yes."

"Absolutely."

"Of course."

"And for those of you who are still with the Agency, this briefing is confidential. It remains in the Templum."

"Right."

"I understand."

Others nodded.

"Good. Now, first let me give you background. Four disastrous presidencies, at least from a foreign policy viewpoint, have put us in grave danger. First, George H.W. Bush contrived a war with Iraq that set the stage for future disaster. He faced a tough reelection campaign in 1992 and had run up a three-hundred-billion-dollar deficit, astronomical for the time. He had his ambassador to Kuwait falsely signal to Saddam Hussein that the U.S. would not intervene if he invaded Kuwait. When Hussein was tricked into invading, Bush invaded Iraq. The ruse didn't save Bush in 1992, but it sowed the seeds of future destruction."

A man raised his hand.

"Yes. Guelph '69."

"He was a Bones man. What do you expect?"

"Very good. Right. Which leads me to his son, another Bones man. George W. Bush. He won the 2000 Presidential election under questionable circumstances in the Florida voting. Rumors of his cocaine use were fanned when he was asked if he'd ever used the drug, and he responded, 'not since my father became Vice President.' Of course, that was when W was thirty-four years old. Jay Leno showed a skit where W got out of a limousine in a cloud of white powder. His reelection in 2004 looked questionable. So, he invaded Iraq."

Another man raised his hand.

"Yes. Periander '68."

"Are you suggesting that he invaded in bad faith?"

"Yes. W knew that Saddam Hussein had no weapons of mass destruction. But when a President starts a war, any war, his ratings rocket upward. W won reelection in 2004, but at a terrible cost. Iraq is a contrived country, carved out by the Allies after World War I. It's predominantly a Shiite country but was ruled by Saddam Hussein, a Sunni. He kept the lid on things. His foreign minister was a Christian. When W killed Hussein, the Shiites rose up and drove the Sunnis out of power. Many of the exiled Sunnis formed ISIS, the terror scourge of the Middle East."

Another hand raised.

"Yes. Thales '72."

"You said there were four disastrous presidencies that brought us to our present dilemma?"

"Yes. The next was Barack Obama. He drew a red line on the use of chemical weapons in Syria. He told Bashar al-Assad that if he used chemical weapons against the opposition, the United States would retaliate. Assad called his bluff, and Obama did nothing. One of our German friends said that it was the beginning of the decline of American influence worldwide. It emboldened Russia, Iran, and Turkey to move in, and to effectively marginalize us in the Middle East. Obama also opened the United States to more immigration from jihadist cultures and did nothing to stop the spread of jihad through Africa."

Another hand.

"Yes. Glaucus '59."

"Should we have bombed Syria?"

"No. Assad is an Alawite. He has no choice but to ally himself with Shiites, and to show tolerance toward Christians. His opposition are Sunni Muslims. Most are more benign than their ISIS brethren, but it's not in our interest to bomb Assad and clear the way for a Sunni takeover. Obama should have not drawn a public red line that he couldn't defend. He should have pressured Assad privately through economic and diplomatic means."

"Thank you."

"Obama also rejected the idea of the exceptional nature of America, and the need for our ascendancy in the world to ensure international order. He endorsed the Mosque at ground zero, and said it was the 'right thing to do.' He bowed to the Emperor of Japan. He spoke at West Point, and instead of motivating our cadets, he cautioned them about the limits of American power. He secretly maneuvered a resolution against Israel in the U.N. and refused to veto it, further isolating Israel. Even the Egyptians were astonished. He minimized the murder of thirteen soldiers by Major Nidal Hassan in 2009 in Fort Hood by saying it was 'workplace violence.' "

"I understand. Thanks."

"Which leads me to the fourth disaster, Donald Trump. He has betrayed us to the Ruskies. He was funded by Russia for at least a decade. They also blackmailed him with the coprophile video in the Moscow hotel room that was mentioned in the Steele report. One of our men in Belarus got a source to let him see it, but not copy it. Of course, our Farm fit his glasses with a camera. Only Willis and I have access to it, but it's sufficient to say that Trump would do anything that Putin wanted to avoid disclosure."

Another hand was raised.

"Yes. Volero '64."

"But how did that affect our policy in the Middle East?"

"Trump is seen by the whole world as weak, beholden to Putin. We have been lowered in their esteem. Turkey was emboldened to defy us and to attack our Kurdish allies. Trump turned the white feather and betrayed the Kurds, who had taken heavy losses in beating ISIS as our surrogates. Putin pushed deeper into Ukraine, and Trump supported him. Trump tried to disband NATO and the EU. He acts like Putin's catamite."

A long silence and then another hand raised.

"Yes. Prasatagus '80."

"So much for the good news. What do you want of us?"

"Advice from all of you, my fellow Ponts. Here is the dilemma. Nature in phallic envy erodes mountains over time. Decayed civilizations attack tall buildings in the West for the same reason. They substitute murderous rage for accomplishment. When Angela Merkel let a million people from jihadist cultures into Europe without consulting other European countries, she sowed the seeds of Europe's destruction. Churches torched. Priests murdered. Airports blown up. Murderous anti-Semitic attacks. We need to stop that in the United States. No more 9/11s, Boston Marathons, San Bernardinos, Orlandos, Fort Hoods, Chattanoogas, Ohio States, Chelseas, and the Manhattan Bike Path killings. Neither political party will act. The Democratic Party is pickled in identity politics and victimhood. It will let in any culture, no matter how intent it is on destroying us. The Republican Party betrays us to Russia, Saudi Arabia, and anyone who pays it. It's run by its donors. If they had been at the Last Supper, they would have betrayed Jesus Christ so fast it would have scandalized Judas Iscariot. The Agency is all that stands between America and the jihadists and communists who would destroy us. And the Agency is Keys. We are it. No one else will defend our culture."

A longer silence followed, before the old man raised his hand.

"Yes. Chilo '39."

"I'm ever so fond of some of the wogs. Truly I am."

"I know, Chilo. You're quite generous with the doorman at Christmas."

"And how."

Another hand raised.

"Yes. Belus '69."

"You've given us the background. Well done. But to build on what Gus '80 asked, what are you thinking of doing? How can we help?"

"I want to hear your thoughts on how far we can go yet keep the support of the American public. We have to respect their vanity, their conceit of inclusion, their pretense of innocence when they still expect us to keep them safe. Obviously, we could take strong measures. Most of the senior military officers despise the President for his servility toward Russia and its interests. We could induce them to capture him, fly him to Guantanamo, and try him before a tribunal. But the people would be alarmed."

"You think?"

Eumenes '68 didn't wait to be recognized.

"We're not fuzzy-wuzzies. Military coups should be last resorts."

"Agreed. But in the meantime, we have a Russian asset in the White House who is destroying NATO, attacking the EU, and serving our enemies' interests."

"Beat him in an election."

"That would be nice. But between Russian hacking and chicanery at the polls, he might win again. The Bard said it best. 'And thus, I clothe my naked villainy/with odd old ends stol'n out of Holy Writ/and seem a saint when most I play the devil.' "

More hands were raised.

"Yes. Mago '79."

"What are your plans to stem the intrusion of jihadist culture in the U.S.?"

"Ideally, we'd stop its coming here, suspend the writ of habeas corpus, and mass deport all vestiges of jihadist culture in the country. But that's a messy business. Jihad is a glioblastoma. There is no chemo we can inject that will kill only the cancer. Some brain tissue will die also. In our culture it can't be done without temporarily turning into a police state. And police states are never temporary. How aggressive do you think we can be without losing popular support?"

A man raised his hand.

"Yes. Pironis '69."

"We have to be careful during all this in honoring the First Amendment. I strongly believe that it's the greatest human political accomplishment in history. If an evil day ever came when we lost the rest of the constitution but kept the First Amendment, the rest of the constitution would grow back in a generation. The absence of established religion, freedom of speech, freedom of the press, and freedom of assembly would grow it back again. But if an evil day ever came when we lost the First Amendment but kept the rest of the constitution, the rest of the constitution would wither and die within a generation. So, let me ask you this: how is what you're suggesting consistent with that?"

"Pironis. The question is this. Under the First Amendment, are we required to import and tolerate a doctrine of sectarian murder that is designed to kill the First Amendment and replace it with religious law? Simply because it labels itself a religion? On the contrary, we are required under the First Amendment to expel it from our shores to protect the free exercise of First Amendment rights by all others."

"Do you have legal authority for that?"

"Yes. The courts have held that heckling a speaker to interrupt his speech is not itself protected speech. Assassination is the ultimate form of heckling. The First Amendment requires us to exclude those who would perform the ultimate heckling of the exercise of our rights."

As Hawkin spoke, he saw a message on his phone from Joanne Martinez.

"Excuse me, gentlemen. I have to step out for a call. Please continue. Lathrop Willis, Z '50 will moderate in my absence."

Hawkin left the Templum to stand in an alcove outside the library.

"Hello? Joanne? It's Wayne."

"Thanks. I'll make this quick. Our tap shows that the people of interest are sending more assets to the venue in question. Our personnel should be notified."

"How many?"

"Don't know yet."

"What's their cover?"

"Some students. Some tourists. We don't have clarity yet on identities and photos for all of them."

"Okay. Thanks."

Hawkin called Audrey.

"Audrey, Wayne. Just spoke to Joanne Martinez. More assets are on the way to Milwaukee."

"Do you have them identified?"

"No. I'll get you that info ASAP."

"Wayne, one more thing. If I need to, request permission to use Puff the Magic Dragon."

"Granted. Use Puff."

"Got it."

Hawkin hung up. As he walked back toward the Templum, Wamba approached him.

"Sir, you have a message. From Arbaces '70."

"What is it?"

"He asked if you could meet him here at the Hall tomorrow morning. Eight a.m. Alone."

"Did he say what he wanted?"

"He did not."

"Thank you, Wamba. Please tell him I will see him then."

Chapter Thirty-Four

At exactly eight a.m., Wayne Hawkin opened the engraved outer door of the Hall. The inner door in the vestibule was metal with a brass knocker, which he used several times.

"*Pocula elevate*," said a voice inside.

"*Nunc est bibendum*," said Hawkin.

The door opened. A swarthy man of medium build grinned at him.

"Wayne!"

"Asad!"

Hawkin hugged him.

"I haven't seen you in years. You're a doctor? I need to hear what you've been up to."

"And you. Let's go inside. I switched on the coffee in the kitchen."

The Hall was empty. They went downstairs into the kitchen, which Mrs. Scantlebury had left in perfect order.

Hawkin took the pot of coffee, poured two cups, and handed one to Asad.

"To your health, Arbaces!"

"And to yours, Z!"

"Tell me everything. Your family's in good health? Your wife? Your children?"

"All good. And your family?"

"Same."

"I see your name in the news, Wayne. Occasionally."

"In my line of work, as little as possible."

"I understand."

"And you have quite a reputation as a cardiologist."

"That's kind of you to say."

"I don't say it lightly. A friend of mine was skiing in Aspen. He knows you and I are friends. He heard a conversation between two strangers ahead of him in line. They were talking about heart issues. One mentioned your name as his cardiologist. And the other one said, 'Oh, he's nationally known.' Two strangers!"

Hawkin toasted Asad's cup with his.

"Congratulations!"

"That's very kind. I've had a good life."

"How many years did you spend at the Mayo Clinic?"

"Ten years. I trained under the best. They were very kind to me."

"I remember when we spoke long ago, you told me wonderful stories of your boyhood in Pakistan."

"It was very happy. I grew up in Peshawar. Near the Lawless Region. My father was also a doctor."

"That's right near the border with Afghanistan. You know, there's one thing I've always wondered. With all the fighting, how do people in that area make a living?"

Asad laughed.

"You tell me."

"Touché. But seriously, how could a shopkeeper or a farmer stay in business?"

"You want to know?"

"Yes."

"Kidnapping."

Asad chuckled and sipped his coffee.

"What?"

"I'm serious. When they need money, they come into town and kidnap someone. Their relatives get a ransom note, and they pay."

"How do they treat their victims?"

"Very well. They feed them. They return them when they're paid. Sometimes, they kidnap them twice. I couldn't play in the yard without a bodyguard when I was young."

They both laughed.

"You know, you have conceptions about things, but people are the same everywhere. They quarrel, they flirt. The girls in Peshawar were covered from head to toe. But what they could do with their ankles! Ooh la la! You would know if she liked you."

Hawkin laughed.

"Do you ever go back?"

"No. It's too dangerous. After my parents passed away, I have no reason to go back. But how about you? What have you been up to? Although I know . . . somewhat."

"It's public. You read the paper. After Yale, I went into the Navy. Then, into the Agency. Charlie Barnes recruited me. Arbaces '33."

"I wondered."

"Wamba said you wanted to see me this morning. I'm glad you did. What can I do for you?"

"I need to talk to you, Z. It's urgent. Not in a physical sense. But for my piece of mind. For my happiness."

"That's mysterious and intriguing. Go ahead."

"Not here. Let's sit in the Templum."

"The Templum? All right."

The men walked up to the first floor, then upstairs again to the Templum. Hawkin sat on the throne of Zanoni. Asad sat to his left, on the throne of Arbaces.

"What is it, Asad? What's bothering you? How can I help?"

"This is difficult. I must start at the beginning of the story. I was the first Muslim tapped for Scroll and Key."

"That is true."

"You tapped me. You were criticized for it."

"Not for long. You made a lot of friends quickly."

"We were on the fencing team together. You fought saber, I fought foil."

"I remember our matches. Against Rutgers. Harvard. And all the rest."

"Z, I can see the clouds gathering. My culture is disliked. You must know that in your daily work. I wanted to tell you why I love my culture. And to see if you thought we can find peace."

"I'm sure we can. I don't dislike your culture. I'm concerned about violence. If everyone were like the two of us, there would be no issue. But from what I can see, if a reasonable and tolerant man in your culture reaches out to another culture, the mob murders him."

Asad didn't respond.

"There was the Christian woman in Pakistan, working in the fields with others. She was asked to get water. She quarreled with another woman, who falsely accused her of insulting the Prophet. The mob turned on her. When the governor publicly urged people to be tolerant of Christians, he was shot by his bodyguard, who was then shot by others. Thousands of people turned out for the funeral—for the bodyguard."

"That was terrible. Everyone I know condemns the rabble who did it. And I make no excuse. But I have wonderful memories of my childhood. The meal cooked by my grandmother when we broke fast during Ramadan. I close my eyes and taste her samosas, her pakora, and her chaat. I loved my grandmother. I sometimes think that religion is your love of your grandmother and her cooking!"

"I agree. I remember my grandmother's turkey dinner with mashed potatoes and creamed onions on Easter Sunday. It was a happy time."

They sat for a minute without speaking.

"You know what concerns me most, Asad? It's when a population from a jihadist culture grows large and they attack their own natural leaders. Their best people. People like you. Can fundamentalist violence be cleansed from a culture?"

"You managed it."

"How so?"

"The English people rose up in the 1600s and beheaded Charles the First. because he was too cozy with the disfavored religion. A few years later, they chased Charles the Second out of the country for the same reason. But in the long term, they settled down."

Hawkin smiled.

"I forgot you were also on the debate team. You were very good."

Asad stood up.

"I want to show you something, Z. Come with me."

Hawkin followed Asad out to the library. Its walls held the names of every pontiff in every collegium, back to 1842. Asad stood before the lists of the 1860s.

"Look, Z. William Edward Sims, Glaucus 1861. From Sligo, Mississippi. I looked him up in the vault. He was a private in the 21st Mississippi. Wounded and captured at Cedar Creek in 1864."

Asad looked at an earlier collegium.

"And see here. Frederick Callender Ogden, Glaucus 1860, from Newport, Rhode Island. He was a second lieutenant in the First U.S. Cavalry. Killed in action at Trevilians Station, Virginia, in 1864."

Hawkin said nothing.

"Did Glaucus '60 and Glaucus '61 meet earlier, at Gettysburg? Did they charge at each other? One tapped the other for Keys. If Glaucus '60 had slipped, would Glaucus '61 have run him through?"

"No."

"Not possible."

"Right."

"You would not raise your saber at me?"

"Never."

"And my foil would never point at you."

"Never."

"You're a powerful man, Z. I don't know anything about your daily life. Your normal decisions. But you're a good and decent man. And I wanted you to hear from me."

"I have to go," said Hawkin. "I feel great sadness, but also great hope. Until we meet again, Arbaces. My brother."

Hawkin reached out and hugged Asad. They walked together out to the street.

Chapter Thirty-Five

Bernie Weber's phone rang as he worked at his desk.

"Hi, Lovey! It's just Mom."

"Mom! Hi."

"I haven't seen you, Honey. Are you all right?"

"Yeah. Kind of. Actually, really good. Only thing is, I'm working on a project, and they want me to stay in this place until I'm done."

"What place? Where are you?"

"I'm not supposed to say."

"You can tell me."

"Well, it's in the Cudahy."

"Can you come over tonight? For dinner? I miss seeing you."

"I'm not supposed to go out, Mom. They made me promise."

"Who's they?"

"I don't know exactly."

"Be careful. There's more out than in. Are they paying you?"

"Yeah."

"You have to eat. Come home for dinner."

"Okay. I'll stop by my office to get some stuff. Then I'll come home."

"Okay, Lovey."

Bernie dialed Audrey's number. It went to message.

"Audrey, this is Bernie. Just wanted you to know that I'm going by my mom's tonight for dinner. Going to stop by my office first. I'll be fine."

Bernie took the elevator down to the garage. A woman and two children were getting into their car. Bernie pulled out of his space and followed them to the exit. He turned right toward Prospect Avenue. A car half a block away pulled out onto the street as the light at the corner turned red. It sped through as cars honked and followed Bernie north.

When Bernie reached the university, he turned into the entrance to the underground parking lot beneath the Student Union. He paid no attention to any of the traffic behind him, and parked close to an exit. Three girls with knapsacks were right behind him as he headed up the stairs to an outdoor exit. Two thin young men with dark moustaches ran down the parking lane toward the exit.

Bernie walked into Curtin Hall. The lobby was almost empty. As he stepped into the elevator, he heard someone yelling.

"Hey! Hey! Stop! Need to talk to you."

He saw two men running across the lobby to the elevator. Bernie pressed the close button. He got off at the seventh floor. The hallway was empty. Overhead, he saw the other elevator ascending.

The Department of Victim Studies offices were right across from the elevators. The door was open. Bernie ran in as the two men sprinted out of the elevator.

Gravegoods Beaker and Pronoun Jackson were talking in a department office. Beaker was sitting at his secretary's desk, and Jackson was standing near him. Beaker's office was open. Bernie ran past them right into it and slammed the door.

The two men ran in and stopped when they saw Beaker and Jackson.

"What you want?" Beaker said. "What the hell is this?"

"None of your fucking business. Get out of the way."

One of the men tried to shove Pronoun Jackson aside.

This was a bad idea. Pronoun Jackson had spent four years in a Michigan prison in the days when he was known as Quintaveous Jackson, due to a regrettable misunderstanding about the ownership of a car he had been driving. Inside prison, he learned a skill. Jackson was the Michigan Prison Boxing Champion for several years running. Even professional boxers who at first agreed to fight him for charity soon discovered unavoidable conflicts in their schedules.

Jackson punched the man. He tumbled across the floor but popped up with a bloody mouth and a gun in his hand. The other man trained his gun on Beaker.

"Lie down on the floor. Both of you. This doesn't involve you. We are undercover policemen. The boy stole money. He is under arrest. Do not interfere."

Beaker chuckled.

"You ain't police. You ain't shit. I just pressed the button under the desk. Security be here in two minutes. Put down the shooter and put up your hands."

One of the men ran toward the door to Beaker's office. Pronoun Jackson stood in front of it.

"Get out of the way! Out of the way!"

Jackson didn't move.

"One minute," Beaker said.

"Get out the way!"

"Thirty seconds."

The man with the bloody mouth turned to run out into the hallway. The other man followed. Beaker ran over to lock the door.

"Didn't know about the security button," Jackson said.

"Security button? Shit, we don't even have security. They on strike. Regents cut their pay."

Beaker knocked on his office door.

"Bernie?"

"What? Are they gone?"

"Yeah. Open the door."

"Okay."

"What's going on, Bernie? Who are those guys?"

"Don't know. I think it's something I'm working on."

From experience and Detroit custom, Gravegoods Beaker and Pronoun Jackson never expressed curiosity about why law enforcement or other troublesome gentlemen showed interest in anyone else.

"Cool. That's cool. Professor Jackson and I are going to walk you to your car. Let me drop some science on the situation. Stay away from here. Work remotely. Until this gets resolved to everybody's satisfaction."

"Got it. Absolutely. Thank you, guys."

Chapter Thirty-Six

A banner reading "Senate Debate" hung across the stage of the auditorium inside the Community College student union. Two lecterns were positioned on opposite sides of the stage, with a table and three microphones in the middle, facing the audience. Another mike stood off to the side. The crowd was largely seated, except for a few stragglers who took the few remaining seats.

Taqi Maghribi sat toward the back, on the aisle, with two other men. He leaned in to whisper instructions.

"Weber is getting an award before the debate. Follow him when he leaves. And don't fail this time. My patience is thin."

"Understood."

"I am leaving. What you do does not involve me."

"Understood."

A few rows behind them sat an elderly Asian man, reading a brochure. He looked up briefly as Maghribi left but resumed his reading.

"Ladies and Gentlemen."

A man in a suit stood at the side microphone and adjusted its height.

"I am Dr. Richard Perlman, president of Community College. This is a great night for us. We are honored to host the debate between the nominees for Wisconsin's U.S. Senate seat in the next election, which is being televised for broadcast around the state."

He gestured toward the bank of cameras.

"But first, we will present awards to three of our most impressive recent alumni who have gone on to pursue doctorates at other institutions."

The crowd clapped as Bernie Weber and two other students walked onto the stage and stood behind Perlman.

"Our first recipient is Johanna Voelcker, who graduated from Community College with a degree in Women's Studies and is now pursuing a doctorate at Northwestern University. Her chosen thesis topic is 'The Western Classics: how they traumatize, otherize, tokenize and pathologize, and strategies for combating educational oppression.' Johanna Voelcker!"

Voelcker stepped forward to receive her certificate to applause from the audience.

"Our second recipient is Mia Maloney, who graduated with a degree in sociology and is pursuing a doctorate at the University of Minnesota. Her chosen thesis topic is 'Applying bell hooks' intersectional feminism with a focus on overlapping identities through material culture theory.' Mia Maloney!"

Maloney shook Perlman's hand and received a certificate. More applause.

"Our final award goes to Bernie Weber. Bernie graduated from Community College with a degree in mathematics. He is pursuing a doctorate in mathematics at the University of Wisconsin-Madison. His thesis topic is 'Quantum Cryptography: breaking McEliece and lattice-based schemes to defeat post-quantum adversaries.' Bernie Weber!"

Bernie shook Perlman's hand and accepted his certificate. The crowd clapped again as he left the stage with the other two recipients. They sat together in the second row.

"The little bastard is staying for the whole thing," said one of Maghribi's men.

"Relax. We have no hurry."

"And now," Perlman said, "I turn the remainder of our program over to Kathy Mykleby, anchor of WISN-TV Channel 12 who will moderate the debate. Ms. Mykleby?"

Kathy Mykleby sat in the middle chair of the table, facing the lecterns. She stood and nodded to applause.

"I'm joined by two of my media colleagues," she said. "First, Colleen Henry, investigative reporter for WISN, and on my other side, Steve Olszyk, former political reporter and now news director of WISN. They will join me in asking questions."

Henry and Olszyk nodded as the crowd clapped.

"And now," Mykleby said, "we'll introduce the candidates."

She nodded to a student on the side, who disappeared through a door and re-emerged with two women. They walked over to stand before the lecterns.

"First," Mykleby said, "I'm pleased to introduce State Senator Mindy Krumbs, the Republican candidate for U.S. Senate. Senator Krumbs?"

She had a Botoxed face and perfect, seemingly plastic hair. She wore a dress, high heels, and a loosely tied scarf. As she waved over-enthusiastically to the audience, the applause was tepid.

"Next, I'm pleased to introduce Dane County Executive Pandora Berrycloth, the Democratic candidate for U.S. Senate. County Executive Berrycloth?"

Berrycloth stood to sustained applause. She wore trousers, a blazer over a blue shirt, and running shoes. Her small, searching eyes scanned the audience.

"We will now proceed to the opening statements, followed by questions from the panel. Each of you will have one minute for opening statements, one minute for closing statements, and one minute to answer each question. And as an innovation, you are each permitted to ask the other candidate one question at any time you choose during the debate. Only one, but the timing is up to you. By the coin toss, we start with Senator Krumbs. Senator, your opening statement?"

"Thank you."

Krumbs grinned at the audience, her anthracite eyes shining with submetallic luster as she fixed on the front row.

"Who am I? Why am I running? Good questions! Let me tell you about myself. I'm a mom. I'm a wife. I believe in local control. The state should not interfere with really anything. I believe in low taxes. Let's get off the backs of everybody. And I believe in the Second Amendment. My husband and I enjoy all kinds of hunting. We go turkey hunting and dove hunting. People complain about AK-47s? We hunt deer with an AK-47! If you vote for me, I will keep government off the backs of the people! Thank you."

She looked down modestly at the lectern.

"Thank you. And now, County Executive Berrycloth."

"Yes. Thank you. I am Pandora Berrycloth. Let me tell you about myself. I was raised by a single mom in poverty. My father was an alcoholic who ran out on us when I was two. I have been sexually assaulted. My mom was sexually assaulted by our landlord. I dropped out of high school and took to the streets. I finally went back, got my G.E.D., worked nights to get through college, and went to work for the county. I worked my way up until I became county executive. One way or another, we are all victims. I am here to ask for your vote."

Wild applause erupted from some of the students. The faculty were more measured.

Maghribi's two men looked at each other.

"Beyond belief."

"Women. Here they are allowed to run for parliament."

"Thank you," said Mykelby. "And now, my first question to Senator Krumbs. When you hunt deer with an AK-47, is there anything left but the hooves? Just kidding. And when you hunt doves, do you get much meat? Just kidding. My question is, when you said the state 'should not interfere with really anything,' what do you think the state should regulate, if anything?"

"I didn't say that."

"Well, you did. It's on TV."

"That's the liberal media talking. Fake news. What I said was, the state in general should refrain from interfering."

"Well, that's not what you said. But okay, what should the state regulate, from your point of view."

"A few things."

"Name two."

"I can't right now. But there are some."

"All right, the next question is from Steve Olszyk for county executive Berrycloth. Steve?"

"Yes. Thank you. County Executive Berrycloth, when you say we are all victims, the word victim implies a victimizer. In your view, who is the victimizer of all of us?"

"I have to be careful here. Let's just say this. Speaker Pelosi held a celebration when the number of white men in the Democratic Congressional Caucus fell below fifty percent. All eight members of the Madison School Board are now women. The Wisconsin Supreme Court now has six woman and one man. These are steps in the right direction."

"Thank you. The next question is from Colleen Henry for Senator Krumbs."

"Senator, you say you believe in local control. But you and the Republican legislature voted to strip county boards of any authority over pollution in their counties, minimum wages for county projects, and school funding. Why did you do that?"

"It's like anything else. I stand for limited government. That means limiting *local* government. We must use the power of state government to limit all government power."

"I will ask the next question of County Executive Berrycloth," Mykleby said. "County Executive Berrycloth, you defeated your predecessor in office by accusing him of 'hoarding institutional knowledge' and 'supporting segregationist candidates.' But the candidates he supported were Democratic incumbents who had been civil rights activists throughout their careers. You supported their primary opponents. My questions are, what institutional knowledge was your predecessor hoarding, and how were incumbent Democratic officeholders segregationists?"

"The institutional knowledge? There was a lot of it. Budgets. Know-how."

"Budgets are public. But what about the segregationist charge?"

"They were against Medicare for all."

"Anything else?"

"Not really."

"Isn't she marvelous?" Johanna Voelcker whispered to Bernie.

Bernie winced but said nothing.

The questions continued. Suddenly, Krumbs turned sharply toward Berrycloth.

"I will ask my question now. Ms. Berrycloth, you and your partner, the one with the tattoos, were arrested five years ago for marijuana. When the officer arrested your partner, she shoved him. My question is, how can we trust you?"

"You're lying, as usual. She's my sister. She doesn't have tattoos. Marijuana should be legal. The charges were dropped. And she didn't shove him. He was hurting her arm. There were no charges."

"Your sister? What, you adopted her?"

"All right, enough," said Mykleby. "The next question is . . ."

"I exercise my right to ask her a question," said Berrycloth.

"All right."

"Ms. Krumbs. You have a history of having powerful men advance your career. A man once gave you a brand new car. When you were a state representative, you attended a reception thrown by the governor at the executive residence. As people drove away, your head appeared briefly at the window on the second floor of the residence, where the governor's bedroom is located. My question is, what advice or services did you perform for the car and the governor's endorsement?"

Krumbs' eyes narrowed into metal slit holes.

"You lie, as you always have. I paid for the car. I wasn't invited to that reception."

"With what services did you pay for it? And you were listed as a host of the reception."

"All right, ladies, enough. Mr. Olszyk will now ask the next question of County Executive Berrycloth. Steve?"

The candidates droned on through the rest of the evening. They were finally asked to present their closing statements. When they were done, Perlman walked over to the microphone.

"Let's have a big round of applause for our two excellent Senate candidates!"

He cupped his ear to the audience.

"And now, let's have a big round of applause for our friends in the media who moderated this debate!"

He cupped his ear again.

"Thank you all for coming tonight for this great event!"

Johanna Voelcker touched Bernie's arm.

"Mia and I are going to Colectivo for coffee. Want to come?"

"Sure."

The three of them walked up the aisle with the crowd.

Maghribi's men got up slowly and filed out a few people behind them. The elderly Asian man also stepped out into the line in the aisle.

Colectivo wasn't crowded. The three students took a table in the corner. They didn't pay any attention to the two men with thin dark moustaches who sat a few tables away.

"So, Bernie, what are you going to do when you get your doctorate? Teach?"

"I don't know. Maybe teach. Maybe industry. How about you guys?"

"Teach," Johanna said. "And publish."

Mia nodded.

"Definitely teach."

"Awesome."

"What about the two women," one of Maghribi's men said.

"If he takes them home, we do all three."

"As you say."

"Time to get the weapons."

"Right."

One of the men got up and left the coffee shop. It was a cloudy night, with no stars visible and the moonlight was faint. He zipped up his jacket.

Their car was parked at the corner of the lot behind the coffee shop. There were no other people in sight. A tall hedge separated the lot from a dark, adjacent building. The man walked around the car along the hedge, opened the door, and leaned in.

Three silent shots blew his upper body into the vehicle. The elderly Asian man ran over to lift the man's legs and stuff the rest of his body into the front seat. He closed the door and walked away.

"Your theses were interesting," Bernie said. "So, Mia, what's the bell hooks thing you're doing?"

"So, there's a woman named bell hooks, who's like a major feminist. She's like big in intersectional feminism, you know? She doesn't use capital letters in her name. So, like 'bell' has a small 'b' and 'hooks' has a small 'h'."

"Got it. Okay. So, Johanna, what's the deal with the Western classics and the pathology thing. What classics are you concentrating on?"

The man at the table near them looked at his watch and took another sip of his drink.

"Well, really all of them. Like the chemistry department? It's oppressive. The pictures and that. They're, like, all men. White men. Mostly dead ones. And the same with philosophy and literature and that. I'm studying strategies to overcome it. But how about you? What's the McEliece thing?"

"It's really interesting!"

Bernie started to warm up.

"McEliece is a guy who invented a cryptosystem that's an asymmetric encryption algorithm. It uses randomization. The neat thing is that it's immune to attack from someone using Shor's algorithm. But I've come up with an algorithm to break it anyway."

"Awesome," Johanna said.

Mia nodded as she sipped her drink.

The man at the table near them got up and hurried out the door to the car. The clouds had gotten thicker, and the moon was barely visible. As he approached the car, he saw through the window the crumpled body on the passenger side. He ran around to open the passenger door. Before he reached it, a volley of silent shots blew him into the hedge. As he slid to the ground, the Asian man walked quickly away.

174

Chapter Thirty-Seven

The police spokeswoman called for attention at the presser inside the Police Administration Building. She frowned at the leapers and screamers, the reporters and TV cameras.

"I will make a statement. At approximately 9:30 p.m. yesterday evening, two males were shot and killed in the parking lot of the Colectivo coffee shop in Shorewood. They were foreign students legally in the country on student visas. Neither had criminal records. One attended the University of Southern Illinois. The other attended the University of Western Michigan. We have confirmation that they had just attended the Senate debate between Krumbs and Berrycloth at the Community College Student Union. Several people reported seeing an elderly Asian man walking on the sidewalk near the parking lot at the time, but we have no suspects. Several guns were found in their vehicle. They had not been fired. Investigation is ongoing. Any questions?"

Cenk Rut shot up a quivering hand.

"Cenk Rut, *New York Times*. We have information that the murder victims were from Saudi Arabia. If true, this makes five murders of Saudi nationals recently and the beating and handcuffing of a sixth. What steps are you taking to put an end to Islamophobia in Milwaukee?"

"Not sure what you mean. We haven't concluded there is any link between any of this. Investigation is ongoing."

Another hand shot up.

"Mike Crute, Talk 101.7 FM. What type of weapon was used in the murders?"

"We're looking into that. Basically, it fired small projectiles that blow through a target. But no one heard the shots, so it must have had a silencer that's more advanced than anything we know."

"What type of weapons were found in the car?"

"We're looking into that. We have been informed by the FBI that they are the type of weapons that Turkish paramilitaries are using in Syria."

"So, who put them in the car?"

"Don't have a conclusion at this point. Next question."

Roland Cheek raised his hand.

"Roland Cheek, *Milwaukee Journal Sentinel*. You say an elderly Asian man was lurking in the parking lot. He's an obvious suspect. Have you investigated Milwaukee's Asian community?"

"I didn't say he was lurking in the parking lot. I said some people saw someone of that description walking on the sidewalk by the parking lot. We haven't ruled anyone out. Investigation continues."

Another hand went up.

"Woke Fetish here, from *ProgCheck*, Madison. Many people are concerned with this senseless gun violence. Wouldn't you agree that background checks and a waiting period would have prevented this senseless tragedy?"

"I don't know. Investigation continues."

"And do you have a statement from Pearly Stubbs, the medical examiner? Why isn't she here?"

"She couldn't make it. I'm authorized to release this statement from Pearly Stubbs. Quote: 'There are many wounds that must be carefully inspected.' Unquote."

"Thank you."

"That's all, folks. When we have more information, we will release it."

The reporters scattered with their laptops to the work areas off the conference room. Woke Fetish sat down and started to type.

KILLINGS IN MILWAUKEE RAISE QUESTIONS.

Once again, senseless gun violence tragically took the lives of two students. The foreign nationals, lawfully here on student visas, stopped into one of Milwaukee's most progressive coffee shops and ordered nonalcoholic beverages after witnessing a debate between two candidates for U.S. Senate. They were murdered in the parking lot as they were getting into their car. While weapons from a foreign source were found in their car, experts would undoubtedly point out the improbability of students from Illinois and Michigan having access to weapons used by foreign resistance fighters. There is no direct evidence that the weapons were planted by the Milwaukee police, but a spokesman for the police said several times that the investigation continues.

Cenk Rut sat in an enclosed space nearby. He typed on his laptop for fifteen minutes and hit SEND. A few minutes later, a return email with a Zoom link popped up. He clicked on the link. The editorial board of *The New York Times* appeared on his screen.

"Can you hear me, Cenk? This is Fatima. We're at a board meeting."

"Yes. I can hear you. And see all of you."

"And we can see and hear you, Cenk," said Laura Penner. "I want to let you know that Fatima has been promoted to deputy editor. She will take the lead on your project. Fatima?"

"Yes. Cenk, outstanding story. We've made a few edits. I'll read them now. When you say, 'two more scholars were murdered in Milwaukee,' I've added the word gentle. It's now 'two more gentle scholars.' "

"Isn't that trite?" said Sir Basil Hartman. "We use that phrase a lot. Just asking."

"Not yet. Still room to use it. And Cenk, when you mention the guns found in the scholars' car, I'm tempted to delete that. Not relevant to their murder."

"Okay."

"But I'm also tempted to leave it in and say, 'sources tell us they were likely to have obtained the guns to defend themselves from Islamophobic attacks.' What do you think?"

"Either way is fine with me," Rut said.

"Who are the sources?" said Sir Basil.

"People I've spoken to," Fatima said. "I'm not at liberty to disclose them. But anytime scholars like this are armed, it is almost certainly in self-defense."

"There's one small problem," said Rut. "The police department said they are the kind of guns used by Turkish paramilitaries in Syria. It could be awkward explaining how they got them for self-defense."

"Good point."

Fatima nodded around the table.

"We'll just delete the guns in the car."

"Great."

"I love the rest of it," she said. " 'The victims were students who had attended a debate of Senate candidates to learn more about our democracy. They had just stopped in for a coffee at Colectivo, a working-class shop in Milwaukee that sells sustainable Fair-Trade coffee. This follows two more scholars murdered in a Milwaukee restaurant, one in a Madison bathroom, and another handcuffed and beaten for showing solidarity with gender-and-species-identity-fluid humans. Simply stated, Milwaukee is ground zero for Islamophobia in the United States.' "

"Thank you."

"Brilliant. Just brilliant!"

Roland Cheek had returned to the *Milwaukee Journal Sentinel* building a few blocks from the Police Administration Building. The lobby was empty. He took the elevator up to the newsroom. As he stepped into the cavernous room, three people sat typing on their keyboards next to fifty-five other reporter desks, which were now empty. It was as chilling as the sight of an abandoned cathedral, deserted before an advancing Mongol army.

Cheek took his seat and opened his computer. His mandatory Home Page came on: 'Roland Cheek. Assignments: Crime, Football, Obituaries, Cooking, Court House, Opera, Women's Soccer, State Politics and Business.'

As he started to type, a bell sounded, followed by a recorded voice over a speaker in front of the room.

'This is your daily call from the principals at American Spring Hedge Fund, LLC, the owners of the *Milwaukee Journal Sentinel*.'

A few seconds later a person took over.

"Hi. This is Jonathan from American Spring? How are we today? Good I hope."

All four remaining reporters said, "Good."

"Excellent. Excellent. So, let's sound off. One at a time."

"Roland Cheek, *Milwaukee Journal Sentinel*. Present."

The other three did the same.

"Excellent. So, let's get to it. I have some good news and some not-so-good news. The good news is that four of our papers are doing worse than you are. In Pennsylvania, Texas, California, and Ohio. Unfortunately, we have to shut them down."

He paused. No one reacted.

"The not-so-good news is that Milwaukee is not profitable. Not profitable. So, we have to invoke the Jack Welch Rule. The bottom performer must be weeded out. We've made no decisions yet as to who that is. But three of you will have added responsibilities. Any questions?"

"That will be difficult," said a woman to Cheek's left. "We each have almost a dozen areas to cover."

"Let's think like a team," said Jonathan. "We send daily national feeds in all these areas. Your job is to throw in local color here and there. A guy who's been married seventy years visiting his wife in an old age home. A kid with a deformed foot becomes the kicker on the high school football team. That kind of thing. It just pulls on your heart."

"Okay."

Cheek resumed typing when Jonathan hung up. He put down the facts, but he needed an angle. Any angle. Any local angle.

I know! Asian resistance to jihad! China does the Uighurs. Myanmar does the Rohingya. And the local angle! The Milwaukee Hmongs! One of them hides in the bushes by a parking lot on a cloudy night.

He dialed Yang Vang, cultural leader of the Milwaukee Hmongs.

"Yang, Roland Cheek here. *Milwaukee Journal Sentinel.*"

"Yes! Roland. Good to hear from you."

"What have you got for me?"

"Hmong dance this winter. HmongFest next summer. You'll get publicity package. I'll personally deliver!"

"Thanks, Yang. But I have a sensitive matter. Two men were murdered in a parking lot of a coffee shop in Shorewood. People saw an Asian man nearby. Is there any talk in your community about who did it?"

"What? That's bullshit! We didn't do it!"

"I don't know, Yang. It had to be local. I mean, someone isn't coming to town just to knock off two guys. Right? And how many Asians do we have in this town?"

"Plenty of sushi restaurants. Did the guy use a knife?"

"No. A gun."

"Plenty of Chinese. In the college. In businesses. And plenty of Filipinos, too!"

"I don't know, Yang. You have the biggest community."

"It wasn't us."

"Well okay, Yang. But I have to keep looking."

"Leave us out of it. Don't print it! Don't want any shit."

"We'll talk again, Yang."

Cheek turned back to his computer. He started to type.

'Yang Vang, cultural leader of Milwaukee's Hmong community, pleaded with this reporter not to print the possibility that a person or persons in his community might be involved in the nighttime murders of two students behind the Colectivo coffee shop in Shorewood. It is important to note that this is only a theory at this point. The police did not directly state it, other than to say that an Asian man was seen in the vicinity of the parking lot at the time of the murders. They also said that the investigation continues.'

He sat back and read it again. Yang must be sacrificed. Once again, Cheek had saved his own sorry ass from another round of cuts.

Chapter Thirty-Eight

The door to the Nurse's office at Burden, Hefty was closed. The Nurse sat at his desk, staring out the window at Milwaukee's industrial valley, many floors below. He had no work. He barely heard a knock before Bigfoot lurched in and closed the door behind him.

"Foot!"

Bigfoot plopped down on a chair, his legs slightly spread, staring at the Nurse with small, porcine eyes,

"What's up, Foot?"

"Another complaint from a client. He fired us. You sent him a long memo about why there's no progress in his case."

"I have to keep him informed."

"You told him you were frustrated. You were nervous about the outcome."

"I am."

"Nurse, let me be blunt. We've carried you for a long time. Your work is shit. You should *never* tell the client bad news! You should *never* show weakness. If he gets fifty years, you boast that you saved him from getting life! You see?"

"Yes, but . . ."

"If he gets the electric chair, you boast that you saved him from hanging. It's less painful, etcetera. You see?"

"But I . . ."

"We've had enough of you. No more memos! No more bad news. If you lose a single client going forward, we're getting rid of you! Vote you out."

Bigfoot struggled to his feet.

"And stop sending associates to court! Go there yourself! *Do* something!"

The Nurse kept staring out the window long after Bigfoot lumbered out of the office. His eyes were moist.

My work is not shit! I'm a good lawyer! I need a win. I need anything. I need to impress a client.

He walked over to the bookshelves above his client chairs. They held a hodgepodge of statutes, administrative rules, and some of his books from law school. He took down his notebook from Trial Advocacy and opened it to Trial Prep. Halfway down the page, he read:

BRANDEIS BRIEF

"The Brandeis Brief was pioneered in 1908 by future Supreme Court Justice Louis Brandeis. It is a brief that relies principally on scientific, historical, or social science information. Brandeis once wrote a brief that was 100 pages long, and only two of them were legal argument. If objection is made that it includes material outside the record, ask the judge to take judicial notice. Even if he won't, he'll still be influenced by the information."

The Nurse flipped the page.

SUCKING OUT THE POISON

"Sometimes, your client will present an awkward fact that hurts your case. Always draw it out on direct examination. Do not let your adversary do it on cross examination. For instance, your client may have a felony conviction. On direct examination, right in the middle, say:

'Mr. Jones, you once had contact with the law when you were nineteen, correct? '

'Yes.'

'Tell the ladies and gentlemen of the jury what happened.'

'Well, a friend of mine lent me his car. I thought he owned it. Turns out, he didn't. So, I have a conviction.'

If you don't do it, your opponent will ambush you on cross examination, like this:

'Mr. Jones, you're a felon, aren't you?'

'Well, yes, but . . .' "

As a slow grin spread across his trembling lips, the Nurse sat back down behind his desk.

I will write a Brandeis Brief in the Saudi Arabian case!

And I will suck out the poison!

I will file it on my own, without telling Raptor, Hawk.

I will win the case.

He opened his laptop and went to work.

"Supplemental Brief in Support of Claims of Plaintiff Taqi Maghribi"

The claims of Taqi Maghribi have to meet and overcome the challenge of thirteen hundred years of history. This we acknowledge. The court will undoubtedly be thinking, *why should I give him relief when his culture has spent more than a thousand years invading and murdering people in Europe? Perhaps even the judge's ancestors?* Well, we welcome the challenge.

Let's start at the beginning. Islam was founded about fourteen hundred years ago. Almost from the beginning, jihadist forces overran Spain and Portugal. They attacked France, occupied Greece and the Balkans, and menaced Austria until three hundred fifty years ago. This we acknowledge. But . . ."

The Nurse's eyes gleamed as he typed. He was finally liberated. He would file something on his own. He would finally win!

Chapter Thirty-Nine

Bernie Weber and Maynard Gieck sat at a polished mahogany conference table in a small room near Wayne Hawkin's office.

"Bernie, Audrey told me about her conversations with you, how you're approaching the quantum cryptology problem. I have to say that I was astonished last time at the work you did for us on the Riemann hypothesis. With the Chinese. But if Audrey got it right, what you're doing now is jaw dropping."

"Okay. Thanks."

"But I need to hear more details. To see if there's some input we can give. Some computer resources that you won't find in Wisconsin."

"Sure. What do you want to know?"

"Well, as I understand what you're doing, you've somehow corrected or modified John Stewart Bell's equations? So, there's a vulnerability in the cryptography, based on his work?"

"Yeah. Let me start from the beginning. Everyone today believes that entangled particles affect each immediately over any distance. If one is measured, the other one produces the same measurement instantaneously. That theory is based on the math of Werner Heisenberg and Erwin Schroedinger."

"It's more than a theory, isn't it? Hasn't it been proven?"

"Einstein didn't think so. He argued that it had to mean that some communication went between them faster than the speed of light, which is impossible. So, he argued that whatever we learn about the first particle from the measurement of the second particle must have been a characteristic of the first particle, even if there had been no measurement of the other one."

"Wasn't that disproven by Bell?"

"Yes and no. Bell's math does seem to disprove it. The quantum cryptography that you need to break is based on Bell's work. But his math is incomplete. What I'm doing is to build on what he tried to do. And what I've done shows that Einstein was right."

"But weren't there physical experiments that showed instantaneous agreement between entangled particles?"

"Yes. But that isn't inconsistent with the one particle's possessing the characteristic all along, regardless of the measurement of the other one."

"So, where do you go from here, Bernie?"

"When the fundamental math supporting an encryption system is in error, the system can be penetrated based on that knowledge. I need to write an algorithm that exploits Bell's error and breaks the encryption."

"How far along are you?"

"Part way."

"Did Audrey tell you we have a hard deadline to get this done?"

"Yeah. My doctoral thesis is going to show how to break other encryption systems where other algorithms can't, so I've done some of the basic work. I'll get it done. No problem."

"Bernie, why do you think that so many top-flight mathematicians disagree with each other, and some get it so wrong?"

"You want to know what I really think?"

"Yes. I do."

"Guys get so swept up in their math that they try to project reality from it. Even when reality is different."

"Do you have an example?"

"Sure. You can't repeal the law of cause-and-effect. You can't repeal or increase the speed of light. If somebody's math requires that you do, they simply create a new reality. Some others try to unify the four forces and end up driving round pegs into square holes."

"What do you mean?"

"Think of the four forces that popped out of nowhere at the Big Bang: gravity, electromagnetism, the strong force, and the weak force. The deeper question is where they came from. The deepest question is why there is something rather than nothing."

"Bernie, you're amazing. Why don't we concentrate on quantum cryptography? Let's talk about what we're doing, and what computer assets we have that might help you."

Gieck's phone vibrated. He looked down.

"Audrey and Hawkin are going a little longer. We have plenty of time. So, let me describe where we're at on this in the NSA."

Wayne Hawkin turned off his phone. He sat with Audrey Knapp before a computer screen. A picture of Joanna Martinez in her office filled the screen.

"Joanna, tell Audrey what our surveillance found out about the people of interest in Milwaukee."

"Right. So. the people of interest are sending five more men to Milwaukee. They've talked about their casualties. They blame them on Audrey."

"How many people do they have in Milwaukee now, and what is their objective?"

"They have Taqi Maghribi and a man named Tamerlane. Soon, they'll have the five new men. All the others were casualties. As far as their objective, it's to neutralize the young man they're obsessing about, named Bernie Weber. They think that means neutralizing Audrey, too."

"You had information on where they're staying in Milwaukee."

"Yes. They've rented a house for them."

"How about the man named Tamerlane?"

"He stays with Maghribi. We have Maghribi's house well seeded. As long as he stays there, we hear everything."

"And the others? When do they arrive?'

"Tomorrow. They're coming in on different flights. They should all be there by evening."

"And where exactly are they staying?"

"They've rented a house on Keefe Street in the Riverwest neighborhood of Milwaukee."

"Describe the area."

"The Riverwest neighborhood starts at the Milwaukee River on the east and ends at Holton Street on the west. Its northern boundary is Capitol Drive, and its southern boundary is North Avenue. It's a racially diverse area, very bohemian, lots of artists, actors, singers, dancers, waiters, and bartenders. Politics is progressive left. Perfect place for them to hide. They won't stand out."

"Show us the house."

A picture of a two-story, wooden house appeared on the screen. It had been badly maintained. The weedy lawn hadn't been mowed in several weeks. Peeling paint and bare spots appeared all over the front of the house.

"One of Milwaukee's worst slumlords owns the house," Martinez said. "Or, I should say, that one of his LLCs owns it. He controls hundreds of units in the city. He's ignored repair orders, fines, and contempt citations. This is typical of one of his properties. The house on one side is boarded up. The house on the other side has a For Rent sign, but it's vacant right now."

"They obviously don't intend to stay there long," Audrey said.

"Right. One of the most crime-plagued areas of Milwaukee is on Keefe Street a few blocks west of this area. Nobody looks out-of-place here. Nobody will care about who their new neighbors are. And if they leave suddenly, nobody will notice or care."

"Got it. Thanks, Joanna. Keep us informed."

"Will do."

"So, let's talk about our objectives, and where we are."

Hawkin turned off the screen.

"If we could convince Bernie to stay out here in protection, he could do his work with no risk. The question would be, should you even go back to Milwaukee?"

Audrey nodded.

"Right. Except for two things. First, Bernie isn't willing to stay here. He let us fly him out to meet with Maynard Gieck, but he wants to go back to Wisconsin. His Mom's there and his studies, too."

"Can you protect him out there? And yourself?"

"I have so far. And Wayne, there's another consideration. These men are part of the February 1st threat. The more of them we neutralize, the more their plan is compromised."

"Right. All right, go back there with Bernie. Make sure he's secured. That he doesn't go places without you knowing."

"Agreed."

"And not an Asian man this time."

"Right."

"You have all the equipment you need?"

"All set."

"Good luck."

Chapter Forty

Three men sat widely separated in a row of seats just inside the main terminal of Mitchell Field in Milwaukee. The display of incoming and outgoing flights was right over them. They didn't acknowledge each other. Two were reading newspapers. The other typed into his phone.

A fourth man came walking out from a concourse with a group of arriving passengers, pulling a small suitcase behind him. He sat in the row with the others and pulled out a magazine without paying them the slightest bit of attention.

A half an hour later, a fifth man walked up to the row, also pulling a small suitcase. He sat down. One of the men got up.

"I'm getting the van now. I will be out front in fifteen minutes."

The others didn't even look at him as he spoke. One of them finally stood up and walked to the outer door. Each rose separately to follow him.

They all got into the van. It drove to the airport exit and headed north. At Layton Avenue, it headed east to Highway 794 north into downtown Milwaukee.

"Our equipment will be in the house?"

"Taqi has placed it there."

"Will he join us tonight?"

"No. He is busy. He will meet us at 10 a.m. tomorrow to give us orders."

"Does he know where the boy and the woman are?"

"He knows their residence and the boy's office. We will put them under surveillance."

"I understand that Taqi said we have wider latitude than he gave the others to take necessary action?"

"Yes. He will explain tomorrow. Taqi does not want to wait for the perfect time to take them out. Delay was fatal before. Even if there is risk, we must terminate the boy and the woman the moment we see them alone."

"Very good."

The van sped across the Hoan Bridge into Milwaukee's east side. GPS guided them to Prospect Avenue, to North Avenue, over the Milwaukee River to Humboldt Avenue, and up to Keefe Street.

There was no traffic on Keefe Street. They pulled into the driveway of a shabby house with a front lawn full of tall weeds. They got out with their luggage in the backyard.

"We need to get some supper."

"We'll get it delivered. I want to go over our plans. To prepare for the meeting with Taqi."

"Good."

The five men carried their bags into the house.

A handsome young African American man of medium height, dressed in blue jeans and a sweatshirt, carried a musical instrument in a long case down Keefe Street. There were no other pedestrians. His hair was covered by a large red, black, green, and yellow wool cap. He saw the van pull into the driveway as he walked past on the other side of the street.

The five men walked into the living room. Badly stained, sheer curtains hung on the front window. One of the men stood, speaking, while the rest sat on the sofa and in two chairs.

The musician walked into the alleyway between two houses across the street. One of the houses was completely dark. The other showed a single light on the second floor.

The musician opened his case and removed a fat tube about four feet long. He held it on his shoulder and knelt down. The tube had a firing site. He closed one eye and zeroed in on the man standing in the living room across the street.

He fired. The missile blew apart the center area of the downstairs and destroyed the living room. He fired again. Flames roared out onto the lawn.

The musician turned back and trotted away from Keefe Street with his instrument and case to a car parked at the other end of the alley.

Chapter Forty-One

The Milwaukee Police Department spokeswoman looked out at the wolfpack of journalists with their notepads and cameras and microphones.

"I will make a statement. Last night, at about 10 p.m., five men were murdered in a rented home on Keefe Street. They were all Saudi Arabian nationals, in the country on student visas. Homicides are still beneath last year's level at this time. Some sort of missile was used in the attack. The house is almost completely destroyed. There were no other casualties beyond the men inside. We are working with the FBI to solve this. We do not have a motive or a suspect at this point. I will take questions."

Roland Cheek jumped up.

"Cheek. *Journal Sentinel*. Have you interviewed the landlord?"

"Not yet."

"Does he have insurance, and, if so, when did he buy it?"

"Don't know and don't know."

"And a follow-up question. I talked unofficially with an officer who was at the crime scene. He said it reminded him of his father's story about Viet Nam. When the Viet Cong pinned them down, they called in a C-47 gunship they called 'Puff the Magic Dragon.' It mowed down everything in its path. Was that the kind of weapon used here?"

"I don't know anything about weapons back then. Or if they even had missiles. The FBI is investigating."

She looked around the room with unfriendly eyes.

"Yes?"

"Woke Fetish, *ProgCheck*. It has been reported that the Milwaukee Police Department has received surplus military equipment. Did this equipment include missiles, and has the Department ever used any military equipment?"

"The answer is no and no."

"And second question; there was a report from a neighbor that a musician was seen on the street just before the attack. Have you investigated whether there are any musicians on the police force?"

"Not really. Most of them can't sing Happy Birthday. Yes?"

"Cenk Rut, *New York Times*. This is the tenth Saudi scholar who has been murdered in the state in the last month. Nine in Milwaukee and one in Madison. I have two questions. First, has the Police Department investigated the presence of far right Islamophobic hate groups in Milwaukee, and second, is there a far-right presence in the Milwaukee Police Department, as there is in certain areas of Germany?"

More crazy shit from these assholes.

"I don't know that they were scholars. We have plenty to do. Don't know about hate groups in Milwaukee. None of that in the Police Department."

"One follow-up question. In Germany, they have a unit in the military, the KSK, that has been infiltrated by far-right extremists. They give themselves code names, such as Little Sheep. Do you hear nicknames in the Milwaukee Police Department? Such as Little Sheep?"

"No. Never heard of Little Sheep or any other kind of sheep. Thank you. That concludes our press conference."

The reporters scattered to their workstations. Roland Cheek began to type.

You want local? I give good local.

"There were five more horrific murders Tuesday evening; five more lives snuffed out at the dawn of their careers. Five men were murdered by a missile fired into a house on Keefe Street, while children slept nearby, and their parents watched TV. A police spokeswoman denied knowing whether the landlord had insurance, and, if so, when he bought it. The landlord has a lengthy citation record with the city for failing to even respond to orders to repair his many unsafe properties. We are not naming him because no charges have yet been issued. A musician was also seen near the targeted house just before the inferno. The police spokeswoman admitted that the department hadn't investigated whether there were any musicians on the police force, and she joked about it."

Woke Fetish worked at a station further down.

"Five students were murdered in their apartment in Milwaukee Tuesday night. This time, it was a missile into the living room while the roommates sat around, catching up on the day. A spokeswoman for the Milwaukee Police Department denied that the MPD had received any missiles in the shipments of military equipment that the federal government had given them. She denied that the Department had ever used any military equipment. This has been contradicted by several protesters who said they witnessed Milwaukee Police riding in vehicles that appeared to be of a military nature."

Cenk Rut worked nearby.

"In another shocking Islamophobic attack in Milwaukee, five scholars visiting from Saudi Arabia were blown up by a missile Tuesday evening as they sat relaxing in their home in a diverse part of town. A police department spokeswoman admitted in response to a question that the Milwaukee Police have not even investigated hate groups in Milwaukee. She denied any presence of far-right hate groups in the Milwaukee Police Department itself. She specifically denied any similarity to the KSK in Germany that has been linked to far-right hate groups. When asked whether nicknames are used in the Milwaukee Police Department, such as Little Sheep, used by the KSK, she denied any knowledge of such names. Yet Milwaukee is the most segregated city in the country, and the least susceptible to the influence of modern culture. A Black man, named Cecil Brown, recently decided to dress in a cowboy outfit and ride around Milwaukee on a horse to show that Black people do activities that are not frequently associated with them. He was immediately arrested for stealing a police horse. It took two days while he stayed in jail to prove that he had bought the horse, and that no horses were missing from the police stables. This reporter has also visited various high school soccer games to immerse myself in the local culture. I did not see a single player kneel during the national anthem, unlike almost everywhere else in the country. When I asked a player what would happen if someone did, he responded, 'I'd kick them in the ass.'"

He got a text.

'Ed meeting will start shortly. Can you join in ten minutes?'

Zoom information followed. Ten minutes later, the editorial board of *The New York Times* appeared around a conference table.

"Welcome, Cenk," Fatima said. "We have some preliminary issues to discuss. You're welcome to stay. You're second on our agenda."

"Great. Fine with me."

"So, first we will discuss our editorial for this Sunday, 'Can Trans Label Apply to Race; Is Transracial Identity Legitimate?' Bruce, you wrote the draft. Your comments, please."

"I'm wrestling with some depression issues. I wrote that transracial identity should be defended like transgender identity. But the reaction in the newsroom when I floated it to some of them crushed me."

"Do you have examples?"

"One of them accused me of transmisogynistic violence! Another accused me of epistemological insiderism."

Bruce wiped his eyes.

"And another one said it's okay to write that something exists, like a lake, but on racial oppression or trans oppression, different analytics are mandatory."

"That's sobering."

"Right. But the worst came from an intern."

"Yes?"

"He's only been here a week. He's twenty-one years old. And he said, 'You speaking to you ancestors. We here before you. We built these cities. We had civilization way before you out you caves. You have the F-in nerve to F-in dehumanize my ass?"

The board members exchanged grave looks. Bruce lowered his head.

"It's a demographic we need," Fatima said. "But Bruce, he wasn't saying that your guilt is your identity as a cis white het male. It's the structure of your thinking. In his mind, you're guilty of illogical incivility."

Several board members nodded.

"Rework it, Bruce. Take it back to him and some of the others. Get buy-in. If it isn't there by tomorrow, we'll go with the draft on parochial schools. And now, Cenk Rut! Welcome, Cenk!"

"Good to be with you."

"Cenk, I looked at your piece on the murders of the five men just before the meeting. It's terrific. Just a few comments."

"Okay."

"Do you have any personal info on the murdered scholars to humanize them further, to put them in context? For instance, did any of them write on racial oppression or the rights of indigenous people?"

"It's very likely, Fatima, but the short answer is, I don't know. I'll write an update when we learn more."

"Right. Yes? Sir Basil?"

197

"Cenk, this is Basil. It blew me away that the Milwaukee Police Department hasn't even investigated hate groups in Milwaukee. Is it because the ideology is so pervasive that no one notices?"

"Good point. I'll dig further."

"Good work, Cenk," said Fatima. "Let's put a piece together ASAP with the pictures of the ten murdered scholars in Madison and Milwaukee, their names, and whatever we know about them. The theme is the attack on the First Amendment and intellectual independence itself when scholars are murdered out of hate."

"Great idea. I'm on it."

In an apartment nearby, another text came in to Taqi Maghribi.

'Can you talk?'

'Yes.'

'Are you secure?'

'Yes.'

'Is anybody with you?'

'No.'

'What are you doing out there? I send five men and you lose them on arrival?'

'It was a tragedy. Unthinkable. The woman got them.'

'How did she know they were coming? Our communications are encoded beyond their ability to penetrate.'

'I don't know. Someone has been indiscreet perhaps.'

'Not here. And you haven't been able to get the woman?'

'Now I have only Tamerlane. He's only one man. He can't have her building under observation constantly.'

'And the boy? He got away last time.'

'My men were not aggressive enough. And they paid for it with their lives.'

'Maghribi, my superiors are dissatisfied with you. It's time we pulled you from Milwaukee before we lose you too. You can redeem yourself when Cordoba succeeds.'

'But what about the boy?'

'Leave Tamerlane in Milwaukee. Tell him to concentrate on the boy. You know his building?'

'Yes.'

'Tamerlane must break in and end this. Even if it's risky.'

'I will give him the order. When do you want me to leave Milwaukee?'

'Tomorrow. You will tell the college that your father has died in Riyadh, and you must return immediately. Rent a different car. Drive to Washington. Stay in motels. You have different identifications?'

'Yes.'

'Eat at diners. Pay in cash as we have discussed.'

'I will obey. But I have one suggestion. The court hearing on our lawsuit against the police and others has a hearing tomorrow. The city is moving to dismiss our claims. We oppose it. Raptor, Hawk says we are certain to win. It would look strange if I didn't attend.'

'Agreed. A good article about you would help our cause. Permission granted. Stay another day and attend the hearing tomorrow.'

'Thank you.'

'And Tamerlane must not fail.'

'He will not fail. Just as he did not fail in Istanbul.'

'Goodbye.'

Chapter Forty-Two

The Nurse answered his phone.

"Yes?"

"Sir, a Mr. Weaver Dane from Raptor, Hawk is at reception to see you."

"Tell him I'll be right out."

The Nurse stood up and massaged his chest until the pain subsided. He opened his briefcase to check its contents: copies of the motion papers, sunglasses, collapsible white cane with the red tip.

Weaver Dane stood up in the reception area when the Nurse arrived.

"Are we all set, Champ?"

His tone was derisive. The local cretin could not have fucked it up. He had not had the chance. The Nurse would introduce him, sit down, and shut up. The motion was trivial for Raptor, Hawk. He was Babe Ruth lining up for batting practice.

"All set."

As they waited for an elevator, a small man, a dead ringer for Herve Villechaize on *Fantasy Island*, stood near them. He appeared to have worked a small jar of Vaseline into his jet-black hair, which he parted directly down the middle.

"This is Tattoo," the Nurse said. "He inherited the Serpent's clients. Tattoo, this is Weaver Dane from Raptor, Hawk. We're in trial."

"Ze plane, ze plane," said Dane.

He chuckled as they shook hands. Tattoo scowled but said nothing. When they reached the first floor, a tall thin man with an absurdly narrow face and nose stood waiting to get on. He could have popped out of a Rembrandt painting of a Dutch burgher from the seventeenth century.

"And this is our Hollander, Calvin. Calvin, Mr. Weaver Dane from Raptor, Hawk. We're in trial."

They shook hands.

"Pleased to meet you."

"Same."

Calvin's tone was as expressionless as his demeanor.

"You have an interesting assortment of nicknames," Dane said, as they walked to the parking garage.

"It's good corporate bonding."

"Do you have a nickname?"

"Yes. They call me 'The Litigator.' "

"Aha."

The Nurse drove them to the County Courthouse. When they got out of the car, the Nurse opened his briefcase, put on the sunglasses, and took out the cane.

"My eyes have really been bothering me. My ophthalmologist advises complete shielding from light. Of course, that is not always possible. I have an appointment next week. We want to avoid surgery."

"Of course."

Dane held his elbow as they navigated their way out to the courthouse lobby and through the metal detector. They arrived fifteen minutes early at the courtroom on the fourth floor. The benches for the public were already crowded with spectators. The lawyers for the city and the Police Department were already seated at the rear counsel table reserved for the defendants.

The Nurse and Dane set up at the forward table. They motioned to Taqi Maghribi in the front spectator row to join them. No pleasantries were exchanged with opposing counsel. They put their notes and motion papers on the table.

The courtroom was silent. Everyone waited for the presiding judge, the Honorable Frawley Watkins, to come through the door behind the bench.

The door burst open suddenly. The judge's court reporter, bailiff, and clerk walked out, with the judge in his black robe right behind them. The courtroom rose to its feet. The bailiff called for attention.

"Hear ye, hear ye, hear ye. All persons having business before this honorable court are admonished to draw near and give their attention for this honorable court is now in session. God save the United States and this honorable court. Please be seated and come to order."

The spectators sat and the lawyers sat down.

"Appearance of counsel, please," said the clerk.

Weaver Dane stood up.

"If it please the court, Weaver Dane of Raptor, Hawk on behalf of the plaintiff Taqi Maghribi. We're here to oppose the motion to dismiss our claim."

The city attorney stood up behind him.

"And Adam Stephens on behalf . . ."

"Sit down," said the judge, waving at Stephens. "Mr. Dane, you're not from around here. Burden, Hefty is. I want them on the record. Let counsel from Burden, Hefty rise and put in his appearance."

The Nurse started to shake. He stood up to face the empty jury box, a ninety-degree angle away from the judge.

"If it please the court, Attorney Kevin Putz for the plaintiff, and . . ."

"Face the bench, Mr. Putz."

The Nurse turned to face his voice.

"I apologize, your honor. I have an eye injury. My ophthalmologist advises caution. It is my honor and pleasure to introduce Mr. Weaver Dane of Raptor, Hawk, who will argue against the motion to dismiss on behalf of the plaintiff."

The City Attorney Adam Stephens stood up, but the judge waved him back into his seat.

"This will be a short proceeding. I do not need argument. The briefs are sufficient. Mr. Putz, stand up."

The Nurse stood back up. Weaver Dane's sphincter tightened.

Danger! Something is fucked up!

"Mr. Putz, I want to congratulate you. When you filed an eighty-page untimely brief that also exceeded the page limits prescribed by circuit court rules, I was about to reject it and fine you. But when I read it, it completely changed my mind. Congratulations!"

"What brief?"

Weaver Dane was on his feet. *The cretin had managed to find a way to fuck it up!*

"What brief? I didn't authorize a brief beyond what we had filed!"

"Mr. Dane. Burden, Hefty signs all pleadings. They do not need your permission to file anything. You need their permission to file anything."

He turned back to the Nurse.

"Mr. Putz, I want to thank you for your candor. I was all set to deny the motion of the city attorney to dismiss Mr. Maghribi's claims. But your candor in your brief completely changed my mind. As you acknowledge in your supplemental brief, under the Supreme Court Rules, you have a duty of candor to the court and opposing counsel."

"Moron!"

Dane hissed toward the Nurse sotto voce.

"You managed to find a way, didn't you? You unspeakable piece of shit! I'll wear your balls for a bowtie!"

Maghribi tried to shrink under the table.

"Counsel, could you speak louder please," said the court reporter. "I only heard the word 'bowtie.' "

"Don't speak when the court is speaking," said Frawley Watkins. "Mr. Putz, I had no idea of the history of jihad over thirteen hundred years! I'd heard stories. My grandmother was half Serbian. And you know what hit me the hardest?"

"What?" said the Nurse.

"When you included that devastating Bulgarian poem!"

The judge looked out over the silent courtroom.

"I did not know until I read Mr. Putz's brief that the Ottoman Empire used to kidnap ten-year-old boys in the Balkans, take them to Turkey, and force them to convert. They called them Janissaries. Then they'd send them back as young men to Serbia and Bulgaria to kill their relatives."

Emotion crept into the judge's voice.

"The Bulgarian poem that Mr. Putz presented to the court was about a Janissary who was about to kill a kneeling Bulgarian woman: It had these lines from the woman:

'Spare me, my son. Do not kill your mother.' "

Frawley Watkins' eyes were wet. His voice trembled.

"I grant the motion of the city to dismiss all claims against it and against the police department. I award costs and actual attorney fees to the city for having to defend the frivolous claims of Taqi Maghribi!"

The judge glared at Maghribi, who tried to lean behind the Nurse.

"And I want it known that I was tempted to refer this matter to the district attorney! We do not need this in America!"

The judge stood up. He snatched up his papers and stalked back into his chambers.

Bitter tears ran down Weaver Dane's cheeks.

"You lantern-jawed imbecile! My partnership! You hornet eyed homunculus! We had it won! We had it won! And you managed to find a way to fuck it up, didn't you!"

"I wrote a Brandeis brief. I sucked out the poison. The judge praised me."

"You grotesque unspeakable piece of shit. I should kill you!"

Maghribi hurried out, not daring to look at the spectators. As Roland Cheek approached him with a notepad, he waived him away and kept walking.

Chapter Forty-Three

Taqi Maghribi stared at the message appearing on his PC.

'Are you secure?'

'Yes.'

'Are you alone?'

'Yes.'

'How did it happen?'

'I didn't hire the lawyers. They were incompetent.'

'Was the judge bribed?'

'Very likely.'

'I've fired Raptor, Hawk. There will be no more lawsuits.'

'Good.'

'Leave Milwaukee immediately. Travel as we discussed. Rent a different car. We've lost ten good men in Milwaukee already. We can't risk another.'

'What about Tamerlane? And the boy and the woman?'

'Tamerlane will stay. He will be joined by Sadaf. She should be there soon.'

'I don't know her.'

'She is one of the skutnicks embedded in Minneapolis. She has expertise in explosives. She will stop in Milwaukee on her way to Washington. She will assist Tamerlane in surveillance and elimination of the boy and the woman.'

'Excellent.'

'Notify the college and leave immediately. I will contact you each evening.'

'I understand. I will do so.'

'Goodbye.'

Maghribi heard the door open. He held a gun at his side as he went down the stairs.

"Who is it?"

"Tamerlane."

"We have news. Slightly changed orders. I am leaving for Washington this afternoon. A woman named Sadaf is driving from Minneapolis. She will join you when I'm gone. She will help you in disposing of the boy and the woman."

"Good."

"When you are done, you and she will drive to Washington to join me. Further orders will be issued then."

"I understand."

"I will contact you as necessary. I'm leaving now. I wish you success."

"And I to you."

Maghribi packed his belongings into a duffel bag and a box and loaded them into his car. He took out his phone and dialed as he drove to the car rental.

"Gravegoods?"

"Yes."

"Maghribi. How are you?"

"Blessed and increasing."

"Happy to hear it. Gravegoods, I have some bad news you should know."

"How bad?"

"My father died. I must return to Saudi Arabia."

"Condolences, my brother. Sorry for your loss."

"Could you cancel my classes?"

"Of course. You coming back?"

"That depends on circumstances."

Maghribi's phone rang.

"Yes?"

"Tamerlane. Sadaf is here. She arrived just after you left."

"Put her on."

"Here she is. Just a minute."

He heard the voice of a very young woman.

"Hello?"

"Sadaf?"

"Yes?"

"Maghribi. You understand your orders?"

"Yes, but I have a question. How much collateral damage . . ."

"Stop. We will communicate by messages only. No details on the phone."

"I understand."

"Discuss with Tamerlane. Message me tonight with your plan."

"I will do so."

"Until this evening then."

Chapter Forty-Four

A plump woman in her sixties sat working at a laptop in the Colectivo coffee shop. She had placed her oversized handbag on the seat next to her. She occasionally sipped her coffee as she slowly nibbled a piece of toast.

Colectivo was crowded. Students from Community College chattered away or worked on their laptops. Older Riverwest lifers with grey beards and man buns sat staring at nothing in particular. Some older women wore long grey hair to their shoulders, looking more country than ingenue. Others had surrendered to very short hair, lumberjack shirts, and corduroy pants.

Tamerlane and Sadaf sat at a table by the window, sipping expresso.

"So, you understand the plan?" said Tamerlane.

He spoke barely above a whisper in the Badawi Najdi dialect of the nomadic community in Saudi Arabia.

"Yes. I am ready."

"How long will it take you to plant your packages in the building?"

"It depends. Perhaps ninety minutes. Will I have access to the parking garage?"

"Yes. You will walk in when a car exits. You will be in a housekeeper's uniform. There will be no issue."

"Will I have access to the lobby?"

"Yes. There is a restaurant on the ground floor. People walk around the lobby at will."

"I'd like to get to the middle and upper floors."

"You will be able to. You are housekeeping. I am delivering packages."

"What is security like?"

"Nonexistent. In New York, it would be more difficult. Here, not so much."

"Cameras?"

"In the garage, yes. But I observed the guard who sits at a desk outside the restaurant. He talks to people. He doesn't look at the screen very often."

"If we park a car outside, how long can it stay before they remove it?"

"How long do you need?"

"Perhaps fifteen minutes."

"That will not be a problem."

Tamerlane got up to get more coffee.

The plump woman paid no attention to anyone beyond her screen. A message came through.

'Are you alone?'

'Yes.'

'There is urgency. They have targeted your apartment building. Perhaps as early as tonight.'

'I understand.'

'The woman I told you about is the expert. Pay attention to her first.'

'I will.'

'Act quickly.'

'Understood. Out.'

She stood up. No one paid attention as she closed her laptop and walked out the door.

Tamerlane returned to the table with two more cups.

"When the building comes down, we will be nearby. Watch closely for anyone who gets out. If we see the woman or the boy, we have to fire immediately."

"That will be dangerous. The police and firemen will come quickly."

"On the contrary. There will be utter confusion. More sounds in the night will go unnoticed."

"You're probably right. It's unlikely that anyone will be coming out."

"Right. And then we leave for Washington immediately."

"Our schedule is arranged there?"

"Yes. We meet with Maghribi and Malouf and the operation team. All of them. The ones that will penetrate the Capitol. The support staff. The pilots. This is the dawn of a new Caliphate! Noble lions are remembered! History will reward us!"

Tamerlane's eyes were especially intense.

Sadaf trembled slightly from excitement, from the romance of the moment.

"History will remember us! We will do our duty!"

When they finally finished their coffee, they walked out onto the sidewalk and turned the corner onto Chambers Street. They walked toward their car on the next corner, past a shuttered industrial building and an empty lot. There were no pedestrians and no traffic.

"I must have left my sunglasses," Sadaf said. "I'll be right back."

She hurried back toward the coffee shop. Tamerlane walked to the car and opened it. He sat waiting for her as he looked at his phone.

Sadaf walked back to the table where they had been sitting. Two stoners were sitting there as they read the menu on the wall. One wore long hair under a fedora, a vest over a T shirt, and jeans. The other had multicolored hair and his head half shaved.

"I left my sunglasses. Did you see them?"

"No."

She knelt down to look under the table. The two men also peeked under it.

"Don't see them."

"You sure you didn't see them?"

"Way sure. Ask the cashier."

She walked over to the cashier, a girl with raspberry-colored hair and a nose ring.

"Did anybody turn in some sunglasses?"

"I'll check."

She turned to a server who carried a bin of cups.

"Could you check for sunglasses in the back?"

The server went into a back room and came out a few minutes later.

"No sunglasses. Sorry."

"Okay."

Sadaf walked out of the coffee shop, scanning the floor. She walked slowly back to the car, examining the sidewalk. She looked up as she approached the car. A blanket of shattered glass lay on the street. There was something in the front seat, peeking just above the dashboard.

Sadaf felt vomit rising in her throat. She ran around to the driver's side. Tamerlane was covered with blood, lying on his side, his head partially blown off. Sadaf screamed and clutched her chest. She saw a few people two blocks away, walking in her direction. She turned to run the other way.

Chapter Forty-Five

Sadaf sat at her computer. A message appeared.

'Is this a good time?'

'Yes.'

'You are alone?'

'Yes.'

'Where are you?'

'In Maghribi's house.'

'What happened?'

'Tamerlane and I had a coffee.'

'And then?'

'We left to come here to prepare for the operation tonight.'

'How did it happen?'

'I went back to find my sunglasses. Tamerlane stayed in the car. When I got back, he had been shot.'

'You left him there? And the car?'

'Yes. There were people approaching. His body was sprawled across the front seat. I couldn't move him.'

'You acted correctly. There is nothing in the car or his wallet that could lead to us.'

'What do you want me to do now?'

'Our plan is too much for one woman to execute on her own. You've only seen pictures of the boy and the woman. You don't know the city. You're too valuable to Cordoba to risk losing you. Come to Washington now.'

'But the threat to the encryption?'

'It's not certain that the boy can ever pierce it, much less by February 1. It's a greater risk to Cordoba to lose you now.'

'Give me my orders.'

'Rent a car tomorrow.'

'Yes.'

'Do not go out tonight. Drive to Washington tomorrow. Meet us in the place we designated.'

'I will not go out tonight. I will leave for Washington tomorrow.'

'Good.'

It started to rain, first softly, then very hard. Sadaf got up to go to the kitchen. She had a sandwich and a glass of juice. She walked up the stairs to the bedroom, locked the door and lay down on the bed. She held a gun in her lap. The rain pounded fiercely on the roof.

Suddenly she heard a noise. A thud. Probably a branch breaking off and hitting the house. Almost certainly a branch. Definitely a branch. She heard another noise. A faint noise. She looked at the doorknob. It wasn't turning. She held her gun pointed at the door.

Sadaf finally turned on the television.

'WISN TV EVENING NEWS WITH KATHY MYKLEBY.'

A woman's face appeared on the screen.

'Good evening. I'm Kathy Mykleby and this is your news for today. A gruesome murder near a well-known Riverwest coffee shop this afternoon. We go right to the crime scene and our reporter, Colleen Henry. Colleen?'

'That's right, Kathy. I'm reporting once again from a Colectivo coffee shop, this one on the corner of Humboldt Avenue and Chambers Street. A man was gunned down in a parked car on Chambers Street just down the block. I'm standing here with Stacy Gums, a server who saw the victim leave. Stacy, tell us what you saw."

Gums was nervous, darting glances back and forth between Henry and the camera.

"Like, I saw two people? A man and a woman? Like, they both left? She came back and said she was looking for her sunglasses? And somebody must have did him in."

"What did they look like, Stacy?"

"They were foreign? I don't know what language they were talking. They both had dark hair."

"Were they arguing?"

"I couldn't tell, the way they were talking."

"Kathy, the police officers I spoke to here on the scene wouldn't comment or answer questions. The manager of the coffee shop declined to go on camera. Back to you."

"Thanks, Colleen. We now go live to a briefing by the Milwaukee Police Department."

The screen turned to the spokeswoman for the department, standing at a lectern. A small group of reporters sat facing her.

"A man was shot and killed in his car that was parked on Chambers Street this afternoon. He was a Saudi Arabian national, here on a student visa. Two pedestrians came on the scene and discovered the body. They are not suspects. Detectives are searching the scene for evidence. We have no leads at this time. The investigation continues. I will answer questions. Yes?"

"Roland Cheek, *Milwaukee Journal Sentinel*. The two pedestrians who claim to have just come on the scene. Who were they?"

"A man and his wife out for a walk. They were questioned, but they are not suspects."

"Did they see anyone else?"

"An older woman taking a walk. No one else."

"The staff here said the victim had coffee with a woman. Who is she?"

"We don't know. We want to speak with her."

"Is she a suspect?"

"Too early to tell. Yes?"

"Cenk Rut, *New York Times*. Eleven Saudi Arabian scholars have been murdered very recently, one in Madison and now ten here. Isn't it obvious that the MPD should be investigating white supremacist groups as possible suspects?"

"The detectives follow all leads. We don't comment on what they're investigating."

"Do you know if any Proud Boys or Boogaloo members were in the coffee shop at the time?"

"Don't know at this time. Yes?"

"Woke Fetish, *ProgCheck*. What kind of weapon was used?"

"We don't know yet. We're working with the FBI on that. It must have had a silencer. Nobody heard anything. MPD's ShotSpotter didn't register anything."

"Are any silencers missing from the MPD's arsenal?"

"We don't have any silencers. Thank you. That concludes our briefing for today."

Sadaf turned off the television. The rain had let up to a drizzle. She turned off the light to try to go to sleep. She heard a noise downstairs. Sadaf sat up against the headboard with her gun pointing at the door. When no further sound came, she leaned back into her pillow and started to doze off. She woke immediately at a sound at the door. She held her gun with two hands as she looked around the room.

She stared at the knob. Had it turned slightly? Definitely not. Probably not. Possibly not.

Sadaf dozed off again. She woke suddenly many times throughout the night, gun pointed at the door, sweating. At last, the faint light of early dawn came through the window.

The bathroom was at the end of the hall. Sadaf undressed. She opened the bedroom door slowly, gun pointed straight ahead. The hallway was empty. Sadaf walked down the hall slowly, gun in hand. There were two bedrooms off the hallway on the way to the bathroom. She kicked open the door of the first bedroom. It was empty. She walked slowly toward the second bedroom. It was empty, too.

Sadaf walked into the bathroom and closed the door. After she used the toilet, she ran the shower. When it was hot enough, she stepped in with her gun and propped it up on a ledge away from the stream of water. She relaxed for the first time under the rush of hot water. She washed herself and her hair, and finally turned off the shower.

As Sadaf opened the shower curtain to reach for her towel, she stared into a woman's face, just a foot away. Before she could scream, she collapsed to the shower floor under a barrage of bullets.

Chapter Forty-Six

Gravegoods Beaker rapped his knuckles against the table. Two men in ties and sport coats sat on either side of him. Members of the Victim Studies Department sat around the table.

"I want to introduce these two gentlemen," Beaker said. "They are detectives from the Milwaukee Police Department, here to question us about Taqi Maghribi. On my left is Detective Vince Bobot, and to my right is Detective Frank Cortez. I'll let them take it from here."

"Thank you Professor Beaker. Folks, I'm Vince Bobot, and this is my partner, Frank Cortez. We're detectives with MPD. We're investigating leads in the recent murders of Saudi students in Milwaukee. It's important to know that just because we ask questions doesn't mean someone is a suspect or has done anything wrong. We just want to get as many facts as possible. In particular, we want to know more about Professor Taqi Maghribi, who taught here until he recently left. What can you tell us about him?"

The table was silent. Bobot pointed at Bronwyn Ferkwell.

"Ma'am?"

"I'm Professor Bronwyn Ferkwell. My question is, have you read Taqi his rights?"

"He doesn't have any rights."

"What?"

"I mean he doesn't have any rights when we interview other people. We don't have to give him notice."

"What do you want to know?"

"What was he like? Did you trust him?"

"He was very progressive," said Digby Brayboy. "Kind of intense. Didn't get to know him well."

"Two people were murdered recently who were staying in a house he rented. One was a man named Tamerlane. The other was a woman named Sadaf. Did anybody here ever meet either of them?"

They all shook their heads.

"You sir," said Cortez.

He pointed at Pronoun Jackson.

"Did you know either of those two people?"

Back in Detroit, it was not a prudent thing to know people. Pronoun Jackson had once denied even knowing himself.

"Didn't know them. Don't know anybody."

"Taqi Maghribi left the college suddenly, just as these murders were occurring. He said his father died and he had to go back to Saudi Arabia. But there's no record of his ever leaving the United States. And we aren't even certain that he ever left Milwaukee. Other than to Professor Beaker as he was leaving town, did Mr. Maghribi ever mention to any of you that his father died?"

No one had heard a thing.

"How about a woman? The victims were staying at his house. Did he ever mention a girlfriend?"

" 'Girlfriend' is a complex term," Uri Diggleboots said. "I was helping Taqi explore a more fluid universe."

"Let's cut to it," said Cortez. "A woman was staying in his house. She was murdered while Maghribi was supposedly out of the country, which he never was. Did he ever mention a woman, any woman, for any reason?"

"No."

"We interviewed some of his students," Bobot said. "He taught some violent ideas. To your knowledge, did he ever advocate violence?"

Brayboy frowned.

"Now when you say 'violent,' what do you mean? We promote the free exchange of ideas."

"Well, one of his students said he discussed the answers to twenty-seven frequently asked questions."

Bobot looked down at his notes.

"For instance, Maghribi stated in class that the answer to one of the questions was 'It is permissible to buy, sell, or give as a gift female captives and slaves, for they are merely property which can be disposed of.' Did you ever hear him say that?"

"Not really."

"How about this answer to another question? 'It is permissible to have intercourse with the female captive.' Did you ever hear him say that?"

No one had.

"Basically, he kept to himself," Beaker said. "He came in, dropped some knowledge on the Crusades, and took off. He didn't go out at night."

Bobot stood up.

"He's been criminally charged by the D.A. for murder of the woman and the man who lived with him. Very likely a love triangle that went tragically wrong. We have a warrant out for his arrest."

"Are you done with us?" said Beaker.

"For now. If Maghribi contacts any of you, call us immediately."

He gave Beaker his card.

"We'll call you if we need to talk with you again."

Gravegoods Beaker gestured to the table as the detectives left.

"Hold on. A reporter for *The New York Times* wants to interview us."

Beaker stepped out of the room and returned with Cenk Rut. He motioned to a chair. Rut sat down.

"Go ahead."

"I'm Cenk Rut, reporter for *The New York Times*. I'm here to do a feature story on Milwaukee. One thing that interests me is the treatment of one of your visiting professors, the Islamic scholar Taqi Maghribi. Professor Maghribi was attacked by police while he was checking into his motel. He was attacked at a festival. He was handcuffed and thrown on the grass in front of a theater. Now, he's disappeared. Do you attribute this to Milwaukee's culture? Is it too insular?"

"Not insular," said Digby Brayboy. "Taqi was always in the wrong place at the wrong time."

"But are you worried for his safety? Eleven Saudi scholars have been murdered in Wisconsin in the last few months. Ten of them in Milwaukee. Two were murdered while they were staying as guests in his house. Now, as I said, he's disappeared. Isn't it a reasonable inference that he was also murdered, and his body hasn't been found yet?"

"Have to ask the police. I don't know."

"Let me ask a different question. Are any members of the Proud Boys here as students?"

"No clue," Ferkwell said.

"How about the Boogaloo?"

"Don't know," said Brayboy. "Never heard that."

"Let me switch topics. I also interviewed several of his students. He exposed them to recent scholarship on the pernicious effects of the Crusades on non-Western civilizations. Do you think he was murdered by the alt-right in retaliation?"

Gravegoods Beaker shrugged.

"Where's the body? Won't know until we find it. Show me the body."

"Well, I want to thank you for speaking with me. I'm on deadline. Is there an office or classroom where I can work?"

"Yes. Ask my secretary. She'll set you up in my office."

"Thanks very much."

Uri Diggleboots waited until Rut left.

"I will say this. Taqi was a peculiar sumbitch. That's all I'll say."

"He spun some crazy shit," Beaker said. "But then, who hasn't? Meeting's over. Thanks for coming."

They could see Rut typing in Beaker's office as they filed out.

DATELINE MILWAUKEE.

'A beacon of reason in a fog of hate may have been snuffed out in Milwaukee. The distinguished Islamic scholar, Taqi Maghribi, visiting professor of public policy and culture at Milwaukee Community College, is missing, following the murders of his two colleagues and nine other Islamic scholars, here and in Madison.

'Maghribi was last heard from in a call to the chairman of the Department of Victim Studies at the College. He was leaving to attend the funeral of his beloved father in Saudi Arabia, but he never made it. Instead, two of his colleagues who were staying with him were shot, and Maghribi has not been heard from since. One of his colleagues was shot while sitting in his car near a coffee shop. The other, a woman, was shot while naked in a shower. No witnesses came forward, and no one in the vicinity admitted to hearing anything. There have been no arrests.

'Milwaukee has a large population of people of German, Austrian, Croatian, Serbian, Polish, Italian, and Irish descent. It is not easy being a minority here. Milwaukee has the reputation of being the most segregated city in the country, clinging to its ethnicities and religion. It was hoped that the introduction of visiting scholars, such as Professor Taqi Maghribi, would have exposed Milwaukee to new ideas of diversity and inclusion. But that was not to be. Taqi Maghribi, a symbol of the modern, has disappeared.'

Cenk Rut proofed it and hit 'SEND.' The distant scent of the bitch goddess Pulitzer wafted into his nostrils.

Chapter Forty-Seven

Bernie and Audrey sat with Maynard Gieck in his office at the NSA. Bernie had a notebook spread open in front of him.

"Bernie, Audrey told me you made a breakthrough? How close are you?"

"Close. Want me to explain where I'm at?"

"Absolutely. February 1st is six weeks away. You think you can do it before that?"

"Yes."

"Convince me."

"Okay."

"Start from the beginning, Bernie," Audrey said. "Even though we've gone through pieces of this before."

Bernie looked down at his spiral-bound notebook, which said 'Milwaukee Community College' on the front.

"There are three problems we have to overcome to break this quantum encryption. First, prove that John Stewart Bell's theorem is incomplete. He was a smart guy, but his theorem only involves a few pages of high school algebra."

"Where does that get you?" said Maynard Gieck.

"If the basis of the cryptography is incomplete or has faulty math, it opens up lines of attack on the cryptography itself."

"So, what did you do?"

"To prove that Bell's theorem was incomplete, I had to prove that the math it was based on was faulty or incomplete. That meant proving that Werner Heisenberg's math that is the foundation of quantum mechanics is at least incomplete."

"Slow down. What do you mean it's incomplete?"

"Heisenberg said a lot of things, but the two most important for cryptography are uncertainty and entanglement. He tried to prove that a particle, say an electron, doesn't have a specific location until you observe it. It's just a wave function that is potentially in different places. It's only when you observe it that it pops into a specific location."

"And you don't agree with that?"

"I think it's ridiculous. The fact that something is in a specific location when you observe it is obvious. That doesn't mean it wasn't there when you didn't observe it."

"I thought the box experiment backed him up?"

"Not really."

"Are you familiar with the box experiment?"

"Yeah. Here it is. Let's say you take a box and put an electron in it. According to Heisenberg, it doesn't have a specific location in the box. It exists in a potential state until it's observed. That's when it pops into some location or other. Then, let's say you put a partition in the box to divide it in half. According to Heisenberg, the electron doesn't exist at any specific location in either half. It's only a wave function. Then, let's say you cut the box in half and send me one half to Milwaukee. You keep the other half here in Washington. If I open my half, I have a 50-50 chance of having the electron pop into a definite location in Milwaukee. It's random. If it pops into a location in Milwaukee, when you open your half, there is no electron in Washington. And vice versa."

"Hasn't that been proven many times?"

"Sure. But what does it prove? That result is consistent with the electron being in one half of the box or the other all along. So what? It's random. 50-50."

"What's the second Heisenberg conclusion you're disputing?"

"The effects of entanglement. He said that if two particles are entangled, they somehow communicate instantaneously, even if they fly off billions of light years apart. If you observe and measure one, it snaps out of its possibility haze into a definite state. Its correlated particle, billions of light years away, instantaneously pops out of its haze into an exactly correlated state. If you measure one, the other provides the same instantaneous measurement. If you do an experiment on one, the other gives the same result."

"What was your conclusion?"

"Quantum mechanics is more philosophy than reality. We deal in reality. Two particles can't communicate with each other faster than the speed of light. That means that the correlation was preprogrammed. It's a hidden variable that quantum mechanics hasn't accounted for. What I did was complete their equations. And that showed me a weakness in the encryption, which we can exploit."

"You completed your work on that problem?"

"Yes."

"You said there were three problems you had to overcome. What are the others?"

"The second one is this. They've achieved certifiable quantum randomness. There are different algorithms for prime factorization and computing discrete logarithms on a quantum computer to break an encryption. But they don't work against this encryption. I'm writing an algorithm that will work."

"How close are you?"

"Very close."

"Less than six weeks?"

"Yes."

"What's the third problem?"

"In quantum computing, the adversary is instantaneously notified when someone touches his encryption."

"What do you mean by 'touches?' "

"Looks at it. Tries to open it. Tries to get into it in any way."

"But wouldn't you still be able to read their messages?"

"Maybe. But they may have it programmed to instantaneously destroy everything if that happens. Or instantaneously change everything, so we'd have to start over."

"What's your solution?"

"I'm writing an algorithm to trick them. Their program will think that I'm not external. That I'm them."

"How close are you on that one?"

"Really, really close."

"Less than six weeks?"

"A lot less."

"Bernie, we haven't had any success with this. What you're doing is astonishing. I hope you can bring it home really soon. "

Audrey's phone showed a message.

'Call me. Wayne.'

She stood up.

"Have to call Wayne. Bernie, we'll leave for the airport when I'm done. Maynard, could you brief Bernie on the approach you've taken?"

"Sure."

Audrey walked down the hall into an empty office. She closed the door and dialed.

"Wayne, it's Audrey."

"We caught a break. Maghribi's been arrested in Virginia. The Milwaukee police had a warrant out for him."

"What was the warrant for?"

Hawkin chuckled.

"You won't believe it! The killing of Tamerlane and Sadaf!"

"You're kidding!"

"No, I'm not. He was arrested in Falls Church. They're holding him in a local jail. He has a hearing tomorrow in Arlington County Court to extradite him to Wisconsin."

"Why was he arrested?"

"He was weaving in and out of traffic. An officer pulled him over to give him a ticket. He was argumentative. The officer ran his name and saw the warrant."

"You think a judge would hold him with no real evidence?"

"Don't know. But we have a window here. Let's not waste it."

"I'll go down there tomorrow. Bernie and I will stay here another day. He can talk some more with Maynard."

"Good. Call me when you're done."

"Will do."

Chapter Forty-Eight

Taqi Maghribi was led into court, handcuffed, dressed in a loose-fitting orange shirt and trousers. The sheriff's deputy directed him to a seat at the defense table, next to a middle-aged lawyer, wearing an Armani suit, white shirt, and silver tie. He leaned in toward Maghribi and whispered to him.

Sitting on the spectator benches were lawyers waiting for their cases to be called, retired courthouse regulars, greedy for the spectacle at the ultimate reality show, two men with dark hair and moustaches, their faces rigid and staring straight ahead, and a stout, elderly woman holding a notepad. A sticker, reading, 'FALLS CHURCH NEWS-PRESS.' was displayed on the side of her briefcase. She sat by herself to the side of a rear bench.

Maghribi glanced at the two dark-haired men and nodded as he spoke with his lawyer.

"All rise."

A door opened behind the judge's bench. A court reporter and bailiff came out first, followed by the judge. The bailiff stepped out in front.

"Hear ye, hear ye, hear ye, the Circuit Court for Arlington County is now in session. All persons having business before this honorable court are admonished to draw near and give their attention. Please be seated and come to order."

Everyone sat down. The judge looked through some papers while the courtroom remained silent.

"Call the first case."

"In re extradition request by the State of Wisconsin for Taqi Maghribi. Appearances please."

A young and nervous new Assistant D.A. stood up.

"The Arlington County District Attorney by Alan Weisenborn for the State of Virginia, your honor."

Maghribi's lawyer stood up.

"Williams and Porter, your honor, by Peter Harris, on behalf of Taqi Maghribi."

"Thank you, gentlemen. Mr. Weisenborn, you may proceed."

"Your honor, the state of Wisconsin issued an arrest warrant for Mr. Maghribi in connection with certain murders in that state for which he's been charged. Mr. Maghribi was pulled over and cited for inattentive driving in Falls Church. When the officer ran his license, he noticed the outstanding arrest warrant and took Mr. Maghribi into custody. We notified the district attorney in Milwaukee. They then issued a governor's warrant, requesting the extradition of Mr. Maghribi to the custody of the Wisconsin Department of Corrections. The Milwaukee D.A. said they will come here to pick up Mr. Maghribi. We filed the arrest warrant and the governor's warrant with the court. We ask that the court sign the extradition order so we can turn custody of Mr. Maghribi over to the individuals sent by Wisconsin."

"Very well. Mr. Harris? Objections are normally waived at this stage. Do you object to extradition?"

"Yes, we do, your honor. The underlying arrest warrant was issued without probable cause. In fact, without a shred of good faith. Twelve people from Saudi Arabia were murdered in Wisconsin. Mr. Maghribi knew some of them. He has a valid visa to be in the United States as a visiting professor. He left Milwaukee a few days ago. So, on those facts a court commissioner in Wisconsin orders him arrested for murder? For leaving town? No physical evidence, no witnesses, no motive? It's absurd. We ask that the court release Mr. Maghribi and declare that the underlying warrant for his arrest lacked probable cause to issue."

"Do you contest the authenticity of the governor's warrant to return Mr. Maghribi to Wisconsin? Do you think it was forged?"

"I take no position on that."

"You've seen it? You've been given a copy?"

"Yes."

"Mr. Harris, the court where you can raise objections to the arrest warrant is the Wisconsin Court. Mr. Maghribi will be accorded full due process there to argue about probable cause. I'm not ordering him extradited to Russia or Turkey. Wisconsin's one of ours, you know. We all follow the same constitution."

"We note our objection."

"So noted. The court orders that Mr. Maghribi be turned over to the custody of the agents sent by Wisconsin to bring him to Milwaukee. He will be held in custody here, pending their arrival."

The judge put the file off to the left.

"The court is adjourned for a ten-minute recess before we call the next case."

"All rise," said the Bailiff.

Two deputies walked over to Maghribi to take him back to jail.

"I'll visit you this afternoon," Peter Harris said. "We'll discuss next steps."

The two dark-haired men walked up to Harris as Maghribi was led out.

"We are friends of Taqi. What happens now?"

"We should probably step outside."

The reporter and several other spectators were leaving. The two men and the lawyer followed after them. The reporter sat on a bench at one end of the hallway, her open briefcase next to her. She spoke on her phone, looking down at the floor.

Harris walked with the men to the other end of the hallway.

"This was fully expected," he said. "The judge just complies with the governor's warrant. We'll have no trouble getting this dismissed in Wisconsin. The police can be very aggressive. But when a judge looks at it harder, I guarantee that the charges against Mr. Maghribi will be dropped."

"How long will this take?" said one of the men. "We have work to do with Taqi."

"Well, let's see. Milwaukee will send people, probably a commercial van transport service, to pick him up. Their only deadline is that the court can't hold him here for more than thirty days. They'll probably come a lot sooner than that. They'll drive him back to Milwaukee."

"Why not fly?"

"I checked. The state budget is underwater. It's cheaper to drive than fly. Milwaukee is about eight hundred miles from here, and it takes about twelve hours to drive in light traffic, if they drive straight through, but they may not."

"Why not?"

"The prisoner transportation services that the states use drive large vans. They may stop several times to pick up other prisoners who are going to the Midwest. Could take a few days."

"Is Taqi in handcuffs the whole time?"

"Basically. They'll get him food at a McDonald's, let him use the bathroom. But they'll handcuff him in the van."

"That is inhuman!"

"It's all relative. Anyway, we'll file a motion to release him before he even gets there. We'll ask for an emergency hearing. I would say we should have him out in a week to ten days after he arrives in Milwaukee."

"Can we see him before he leaves here?"

"You can try. The jail has visiting hours. Call them and check hours and who can visit. I don't know whether extradition holds can even get visitors."

"Okay."

"And one more thing. Everything you say or do with him will be on video and audio. Everything."

"Okay."

Harris walked away. The men stayed talking.

"What should we do now?"

"We have to inform Malouf. Will he hold our meeting without Taqi?"

"I don't know. Shall we visit Taqi?"

"Why not? But be careful what you say. They'll be listening."

"There's no hurry now. Let's have a coffee."

The men walked out to their car. They drove a few blocks to a restaurant. The parking lot was full. They finally got a space on a residential street a block away. They spoke in subdued tones as they stood in line for a table.

"What if they don't get Taqi out in time?" one said in the Badawi Najdi dialect.

"Malouf will decide. We may have to execute Cordoba without him."

The receptionist came up to them, holding menus.

"Gentlemen. Two?"

"Two."

A server came to their table and poured two glasses of water.

"Do you need time with the menu?"

"No."

They both ordered.

"When Cordoba succeeds, there will be widespread violence."

"It is necessary. The Crusaders will destroy themselves from within."

They ate quickly, paid in cash and headed out the door. No one else was near where they parked as they got in the car. When the driver tried to start it, there was no sound. He tried again. Still no sound.

"What is the matter? Is the battery dead?"

"I don't know. There is no sound. Perhaps someone stole the battery."

"What?"

"The kaffirs steal everything. Batteries, hubcaps, the car itself."

"I'll call Malouf. Tell him to send a car to get us. You call the rental company. They'll have to have this one towed."

"All right."

The driver dialed.

"Hello," said a woman.

"Yes. I rented a car from you. It's defective. Won't start. Come and get it towed."

"Okay. First, I'll need your name and the rental contract number."

"Yes, my name is . . ."

There was a loud sound of breaking glass.

"Hello? Hello? What is your name and contract number?"

Total silence.

"Hello? Hello? What is your name? Where is the car located?"

More silence. The woman hung up.

Chapter Forty-Nine

Late in the evening, as Audrey was reading on the bed in her hotel room, her phone rang.

"Wayne?"

"Good work. A little aggressive on location. Have you watched the news?"

"No."

"A neighbor remembered part of a license plate number on the street after hearing breaking glass, with an old woman driving the car."

"And?"

"It was part of a diplomatic plate. The network reported that sources said it was Russian. Moscow denied it, of course. Said it was stolen."

"Good. You got my message? With the audio of the hearing and their conversation in the hallway?"

"Yes."

"Can you ID the van service and get their route? How many other prisoners are they picking up, and where? Do they have scheduled food stops?"

"Already on it. Back to you soon."

Chapter Fifty

A few dozen Congressmen filed into a large conference room in the Capitol. A whiteboard in the front said "Democratic Skutnick Selection Committee."

A man sat in a leather armchair at the head of the table. The sign in front of him said "Chairman Langdon Tusch (D Maryland)," He had a righteous mane of thick, white hair that he combed in a wave back over his head with no part. He looked like the antebellum Mississippi Senator, Beauregard Plushbottom.

Tusch had an overall righteous look to him, having practiced feigned candor over a forty-year career in the House. He was perfectly groomed in tan makeup, a light grey suit, blue shirt with white collar, silk mauve tie, and a matching pocket handkerchief. He occasionally yawned like the lion he was, looking out over potential meals.

He frowned slightly at some of his colleagues walking in. The Krew entered as a posse: a short, dark woman in a head scarf with laser sharp eyes that seemed to convey centuries of pent-up, anticolonial anger; a short, doe-eyed spitfire who regularly busted Tusch's balls; a foul-mouthed, gnarly looking individual who was widely avoided; and several other of the Krew's running dogs, who he knew were plotting to primary him.

Sitting down on the other side were the guys representing blue collar districts in the Midwest and the West, who got blowback for suggesting that statues of George Washington, Abraham Lincoln, and Ulysses Grant should not be torn down by a mob because, well, George had created the country and Abe and Ulysses had preserved the very place that gave their attackers the freedom to tear their statues down.

More Congressmen walked in and filled in the seats, most of them rookies, and most elected by primarying Tusch's friends.

Tusch finally banged the gavel.

"Welcome, colleagues. We're here today to vote on our skutnicks for the State of the Union, coming up in four weeks. We have to get the names in to the Secret Service for security checks by tomorrow, or they'll be barred. We are allotted ten skutnicks. Twenty-two names made the final cut. We have to winnow them down today."

Tusch saw a hand raised.

"Yes?"

"How many of our skutnicks will be publicly recognized?"

"We're negotiating still. Probably not many. President Trump controls that. But the commentators are starved for content. Our skuts will get plenty of exposure."

No more hands went up.

"All right, let's look at our first candidate."

Tusch clicked the PowerPoint to a picture of a woman with a mournful, defeated look.

"Here . . ."

A hand shot up from the coven who was out to get him.

"Yes?"

"I have a motion?"

"Well, technically we're not running this by Robert's Rules, but . . ."

"I move to pick our skutnicks in the same way the Democratic Party picks its convention delegates."

"Second! Second! Second!"

Damn! I don't know what those rules are. I'm a Superdelegate. Automatic. How bad can they be, though? Might get these people off my butt.

"Is there unanimous consent?"

A few "yesses" were shouted out. Many heads nodded.

"All right, we'll pick our skutnicks by the DNC delegate selection rules."

One of the Krew's running dogs hurried over to Tusch with a piece of paper. Some of the others passed them out to the rest of the Congressmen.

"Thank you."

Tusch looked down at the sheet. He'd been had.

"Read the percentages," said several members of the Krew.

"Delegate Selection Rules," he said. "50 percent women, 13 percent African American, seven percent Hispanic, three percent Native American, five percent Asian/Pacific Islanders, 10 percent LGBTQ+, 15 percent people with disabilities, 35 percent Youth (Under 30), and three percent Muslim Americans."

"Keep reading!"

"Threefers are forbidden. Twofers are discouraged but permitted."

Several of his colleagues clapped.

"As I was saying," Tusch said, "this woman has a compelling story. She was evicted . . ."

"Point of order!"

"Well, technically this is collegial. We're not constrained by parliamentary practice, but what is it?"

"She looks like she's cis white het. That's a tiny percent of the total. She doesn't look like she's under thirty. Looks healthy. I move we table her and take a second look if we need her at the end."

"Second! Second! Second!"

"Don't you want to hear her back story?"

"No! No! Call the question!"

"All in favor of tabling her, even though I haven't even gotten to her name yet, say aye."

A chorus of ayes filled the room.

"Okay. Let's move on."

Tusch clicked again. A picture of a young man wearing a durag popped up on the screen. There were scars on his cheeks, but his smile was broad and genuine.

"This gentleman is a long shot. He killed a man in Louisiana when he was nineteen years old and served time. The governor pardoned him for self-defense. While he was in prison, he took some courses. On the other hand . . ."

"We want him!"

"Pick him!"

"We need him!"

"Remember, we only get ten. Don't we want to see the whole field before we start picking?"

"No!

"Pick him!"

"Call the question!"

"All right. All in favor say 'aye.' "

"Aye! Aye! Aye!"

"All right, hearing no 'nays', Mr. Jamal Daniels is selected. But I just want to tell you that a source let us know that the Republicans have selected almost half their skutnicks from the Middle East. Heavy foreign policy play. We need some skutnicks with the chops to match them."

Tusch clicked again. A picture appeared of a man in a suit and tie, glasses, with a friendly smile, holding a book.

"Now this is Professor Geoffrey Greene of NYU. He serves on the Council of Foreign Relations, has authored twelve books on American foreign policy, and will likely be short listed for Secretary of State in any future Democratic Administration."

One of the Krew raised her hand.

"Looks like a corporate democrat. We don't want folks who feed into the post-colonial narrative of condescending to indigenous people in other countries."

"I agree," said another. "Doesn't fit into the selection criteria. He's part of the small percent. Move to defer until we see what we have left."

"Just so you know," said Tusch. "His work is in arms control with the Russians and the Chinese. His latest book lays the groundwork for a comprehensive treaty that . . ."

"Don't care about corporate treaties!"

"Move to table!"

"Second! Second! Second!"

"All right. All in favor?"

Another storm of "ayes" rang out.

"Okay. Okay. We'll move on."

Tusch clicked again. A picture appeared of a woman staring into the camera with her lips parted to show her teeth.

"Some of you suggested this person. I disagree, for reasons I'll mention. She is an activist who organizes boycotts to make grocers stop branding ethnic foods with their names. For instance, Trader Ming for Trader Joe's brand of Chinese food, Arabian Metro for Metro Mart's brand of Middle Eastern foods, and so forth. She said, 'branding is racist because it exoticizes other cultures and makes us the default normal.' Now, my objection is that we want the media focus to be on the Democratic message. Jobs and healthcare . . ."

"Pick her."

"We want her!"

"But let's discuss . . ."

"Call the question."

"There is no question . . . all right; all in favor, say 'aye.' "

Once again, the ayes had it.

"Just remember," Tusch said, "our intelligence is that the Repubs are going full frontal foreign policy on their skutnicks. At least four of them are scholars with expertise in Middle East policy. We have to match them somehow."

He sighed and clicked on the next picture.

Chapter Fifty-One

Malouf looked out at an audience of nearly sixty people, mostly men, seated inside an amphitheater in the Saudi Arabian embassy in Washington. As they began to quiet down, he knocked his water glass on the table a few times to signal for complete silence.

"We will begin. In three weeks, Operation Cordoba will be launched. The heroism of the lions of the Ummah will determine if it succeeds. The restoration of the thousand-year Caliphate begins now."

He took a sip of water as he inspected his audience. Their faces glowed with excitement. They were ready. A hand went up in the first row.

"Yes?"

"Taqi Maghribi. He is our field commander for the night of Cordoba. What is his status?"

"Here is the status of Maghribi. The Crusaders assassinated Tamerlane and some of our soldiers. The Crusaders framed Maghribi for the murders they committed. Maghribi drove to join us but was arrested in Virginia on a false traffic charge. They are driving him back to Milwaukee in a police van."

"Will he be available for Cordoba? That is the question."

"I hope so, but we must plan as if he won't. We have hired a lawyer to represent him. The lawyer says that Maghribi is certain to be released. The charges are false."

"But when will he be released?"

"That is unclear. The van taking him to Milwaukee will make stops to pick up other prisoners. We do not know when he will get to Milwaukee to appear before a judge."

"How do we know the Crusaders won't kill him on the way?"

Malouf chuckled.

"The Crusaders are stupid. They pride themselves on what they call 'due process.' We have used it to free many of our soldiers. For stupid reasons, Maghribi is safer in their custody than he would be elsewhere. But if he is not returned by the night of Cordoba, I will assume field command of the operation."

There were no more questions.

"All right. I will show you an historic video before we begin."

Malouf clicked on a remote. A video started on a screen against the wall. It was titled, KAMIKAZE: THE DIVINE WIND. A Japanese narrator started to speak:

"It was 1944. Hsiao Horiyama volunteered for the kamikaze mission of the Japanese Air Force. Kamikaze, "the divine wind," was named after a sacred typhoon that destroyed an enemy fleet in the thirteenth century."

The picture of a Japanese man in his nineties came on the screen. He sat in an armchair, wearing a sweater, and began to speak:

"I was twenty years old. I had been drafted into the Japanese Army. One day, they started recruiting volunteers from our unit to train and become kamikaze pilots. The Showa Emperor Hirohito visited our unit, riding a white horse. I took it as his personal request. I had no choice but to die for our country."

A video of young Japanese pilots wearing headbands with the rising sun picture on them stood in a group, drinking from small cups.

"This is the kamikaze ceremony," Horiyama said. "This was the fulfillment of our destiny. We were ordered not to return. Each plane had a crew of three men. Each plane had an eight-hundred-kilogram bomb strapped to its undercarriage, and only enough fuel for a one-way flight. We were instructed to disengage and drop our landing gear when we took off so it could be used by other pilots."

His voice broke slightly.

"Our flight two days later was to be out of Kushira Airfield in Kagoshima Prefecture, to attack the Americans who were bombing Okinawa. That particular operation was called Kikusui, which means Floating Chrysanthemum. The next day, all of us flew around the Holy Mountain and dropped flowers. I was sure that night would be my last on Earth."

He paused.

"But the next day, the Emperor announced that Japan had surrendered. I remember I was sad and angry when I heard the news. I wanted to do my duty."

Malouf stopped the video.

"The Samurai are also infidels. But they showed a path to fighting the Crusaders. Unfortunately, they were unsuccessful. I will start by asking questions. Who of you are flying out of airfields in Maryland?"

Eight men stood up.

"Who of you are flying out of airfields in Virginia?"

Ten men stood up.

"Out of Delaware?"

Seven stood up.

"Out of West Virginia?"

Six men.

"Out of Pennsylvania?"

Fourteen men.

"And you have under your command more pilots at more airfields."

Heads nodded.

"Is anyone in doubt about your airplane? When you will get it, and when you will land it at your airfield?"

No one responded.

"Is anyone in doubt about the synchronized time you will all take off?"

No one.

"Is anyone in doubt about what to say when air traffic control contacts you?"

No one.

"And is anyone in doubt what to do when military jets approach you?"

No one.

"We need as many of you as possible to get through to crash into the Capitol. Is that understood?"

Heads nodded.

"All right. I am satisfied. Now, who among you are crew on the tanker ship that will land the shoulder-held launchers earlier that day?"

Ten men stood up.

"Is anyone in doubt about where to go with them and where to hide until the synchronized time?"

No one responded.

"Very well. And now, the skutnicks. Stand up."

Three very young women stood up.

"You are the lionesses who fight to restore the Caliphate. And we lost one of you, Safan, who died bravely fighting the Crusaders."

They nodded.

"Skutnicks, are you in doubt about what to say when you are asked to be searched when entering the Capitol?"

They all shook their heads.

"Are you in doubt as to where and when you will get the chemicals and materials that you will wear under your clothing, and where to place it on your bodies?"

They shook their heads again.

"You will defer to your male escorts. You will cite the correct objections that have been upheld by the courts, if asked. And you will state the permission to be free from any search that you received from President Trump as Saudi Arabian guests and friends of his administration."

They nodded.

"And who are the escorts who will accompany the skutnicks?"

Three men stood up.

"Are you in doubt as to the procedures to employ, and where to deliver the skutnicks?"

Heads moved left and right.

"And are you in doubt as to how to leave the Capitol before the President's speech begins without arousing suspicion?"

They shook their heads again.

"And now, I invite you to stand and describe why you volunteered for Operation Cordoba. If you choose to do so."

There was silence until one man stood up.

"The Crusaders bombed Syria!"

He sat down. Another man stood up.

"I speak for many of us. I saw a broadcast of the celebration in Malazgirt of the anniversary of the battle in 1071 when an army of Seljuk Turks defeated the army of the Byzantine Empire. We are proud of our ancestors who walked with glory, honor, and victory into the center of Europe after entering Anatolia from Malazgirt. They held the red flag of Turkey in one hand and the green Sanjak in the other. Like them, we, too, summon the spirit of the Sultan Alpaslan. Operation Cordova is the new Malazgirt!"

Another man rose.

"I have lived in America for two years. As I walk past their bars and night clubs, I become ill at the sinister places where the Crusaders gather to drink alcohol and commit vices throughout the night, feeling secure from the wrath of Allah that awaits them."

One of the women stood.

"I am willing to live in a tent under an Islamic State instead of all the luxuries under an infidel state. When my family learns the news of Cordoba, they will know that I have been killed in battle and am now with our Lord Allah."

Another man rose.

"The Zionist state has hypnotized the world. May Allah waken the people and help them see the evil doings of the Zionist state and of the Crusaders."

Malouf nodded.

"I am well satisfied. I will now review the battle plan for the three prongs of the attack. Pilots, skutnicks, and launchers. On to Cordoba!"

Chapter Fifty-Two

Audrey and Hawkin studied a map in his office.

"The van is going to pick up three more prisoners on the way to Milwaukee," he said. "One in Indiana and two in Ohio."

Hawkin clicked on a remote. An enlarged map of Ohio appeared.

"Their first stop is Cleveland. They pick up a prisoner at the jail at this address. I sent you a copy of this. Cleveland is 374 miles from Washington. In light traffic, the drive is six hours."

He clicked again.

"Their next stop is Toledo to pick up another prisoner at this jail."

He clicked again.

"Their final stop is Fort Wayne, Indiana. They pick up their final prisoner at this jail. Then, they drive to Milwaukee."

"That's how far?"

"About 250 miles from Fort Wayne. You can drive it in a little over four hours."

"All right."

"Let's talk about opportunities to access Maghribi."

Hawkin clicked again.

A large van the size of a small truck appeared.

"Here's the van they use. Milwaukee uses the cheapest vendor with the most spartan accommodations for the prisoners."

He clicked again to show the interior.

"There are no windows. There are twelve metal seats. The prisoners are handcuffed to the seats for the entire trip."

"Do they stay overnight anywhere?"

"Not this company. They have a bunk behind the driver's seat. One guard sleeps while the other one drives. A tail car with two drivers follows the van the whole way."

"What about the prisoners? Where do they sleep?"

"Sitting up."

"So, they never go into a motel along the way?"

"No."

"Okay. What about meals?"

"They stop for McDonald's. One of the drivers goes into the restaurant and brings the food out. The prisoners have the cuffs taken off them one at a time to eat."

"What about bathroom stops?"

"They stop every three hours. They'll bring the prisoners in one at a time to use the facilities."

"Do they remove the cuffs in the bathroom?"

"Yes. One at a time. If it's a larger bathroom, like at a McDonalds, one driver goes in with him and stands guard inside. The drivers are mostly retired police officers, and they're armed. If it's a single-occupant restroom, the driver keeps his foot in the doorway."

"Do they ever stop for any other reason?"

"No."

"What do they have planned when he gets to Milwaukee?"

"They'll bring him to the Milwaukee County Jail. We've monitored the filings in their Circuit Court. His lawyers have already filed motions to release him. The argument date is not set. We have to assume that they'll press it the minute he gets there."

"Pretty limited points to access him before Milwaukee."

"That's true. We had Agency legal counsel look at the warrant and the motions. They say that the court is liable to dismiss any charges against him and grant the release. The evidence against him is obviously thin, to put it charitably. That will give him time to get to Washington well before February 1st."

"Got it. Will you authorize support personnel to assist me?"

"Yes. Call Joanna and tell her what you need."

"Good. Maghribi won't be coming to Washington."

Chapter Fifty-Three

An unmarked van rolled to a stop on Ontario Street in front of the Cleveland County Jail. The car trailing them pulled in behind. The driver of the van turned back to the seating area.

"Maghribi!"

Taqi Maghribi opened his eyes and sat up. He started to move until the handcuffs stopped him.

"What?"

"Wake up. You're getting company."

The guard in the passenger seat got out and headed into the jail. He was gone for twenty minutes.

"Pull in the back," the guard said. The guy's ready. Paperwork's done."

The driver drove around to the back. Three guards stood with a handcuffed man in a loading bay. The driver backed in, got out and opened the rear door. The guards walked the man out to the van and up into the seating area. The driver handcuffed him into a seat a few rows away from Maghribi.

"Next stop, Toledo," the driver said.

"When do we stop for the bathroom?" Maghribi said. "When do we eat?"

"We did a bathroom stop an hour ago. We'll be in Toledo in under two. We'll stop for food and the john after that, between Toledo and Fort Wayne."

The new passenger didn't say anything. Maghribi closed his eyes again.

The van finally pulled up in front of the Lucas County Correctional Center in Toledo, with the trailing car behind them. Once again, the guard in the passenger seat hopped out and went into the building.

"All right, wake up!"

Maghribi and the other passenger sat up.

"You're getting more company."

A half an hour went by before the guard came out and walked back toward the rear of the van. He opened the door.

"All set," he said.

Three guards walked a handcuffed prisoner out to the van and hand-cuffed him into a seat apart from the other two men. When they were done, the driver drove slowly out onto the street.

"We'll stop for food and bathroom soon," he said.

They drove toward Fort Wayne for forty-five minutes, passing a food sign with the logos of a few restaurants and signs with logos for gas and lodging. They finally pulled into a McDonald's and parked along the perimeter, away from other cars. The trail car pulled up next to them. A handful of other cars, two motorcycles, and another van were parked around the lot.

"All right. Here's the drill. I'm Lou. Marty, here, is going in to get the chow after you're done using the can. You'll eat in the van. This is your chance to use the can, one at a time."

He pointed to Maghribi.

"You're first."

Lou walked around the back and opened the door. He helped Ma-ghribi down the step.

"Can you take off the handcuffs?"

"In the bathroom. And remember something. I'm armed. I'll be in the bathroom with you. If you pull any bullshit, I'll use it. Understand?"

"Yes. My arrest is unjust anyway. The judge will free me."

"Good luck with that."

As they walked into McDonald's, a Toledo police officer was behind them, leading an old man in handcuffs. The officer and the old man followed them into the bathroom. The officer carried a "CLOSED" cone and put it just outside the door.

"Prisoner?" said Lou.

"Yeah. Hard to believe. The asshole's eighty years old, and he's still passing bad checks."

Lou chuckled.

"It's always something."

"I got to go in here," said Maghribi.

He nodded toward the toilet. Lou unlocked his cuffs. Maghribi went into the stall and closed the door. The old man held out his hands to the officer. He unlocked his cuffs. The old man walked around a partition to the urinal.

"You look familiar," said Lou to the officer. "I swear to God! You look exactly like Brett Favre! You related?"

The officer smiled and looked down, embarrassed.

"I'm his brother, Scott. His older brother."

"That's amazing. You're on the Toledo force?"

"Yeah."

"I'm a huge fan of Favre. In my opinion, he's the best the Packers ever had. Better than Starr. Rodgers isn't close."

He looked closer at the officer.

"I don't mean to pry, but didn't you get in some trouble once? You okay? They still let you on the police force?"

The officer looked embarrassed.

"Yeah. Drunk driving in Pass Christian. My best buddy died in the crash."

The officer bumped into the hand drier, and it blasted out.

"Sorry. Bumped it. Anyway, I got house arrest, but the governor pardoned me. Haley Barbour. Can't say enough good things about that gentleman. So, I got the charge expunged."

"Wow."

"Say, could you help me on this map?"

He spread a map out over the sinks, behind the partition with the urinal. He bumped the hand dryer again.

"Sorry. Damn. We're going to Minneapolis. Now, when I get to Chicago, should I go to Milwaukee and over to Madison, or is it quicker to head west and up through Janesville?"

Lou bent down over the map. The eighty-year-old man walked out, zipping his fly.

"Could I go out to the van, officer?"

"Yeah. Go ahead. Report to the guard there. I'll be right there."

The officer looked down at the map with Lou.

"So, I think it's faster to go west and then up to Janesville," said Lou.

"Last time I went through Janesville, there was bad road construction. Single lane."

"I remember. But that's done now."

"Now, when I get to Madison, I head to La Crosse and then on to Rochester. Do you know if there's any construction there?"

"Don't know. But even if there is, there isn't as much traffic compared to Madison.'

"Got it. Thanks, brother."

The officer folded the map and opened the door.

"Tell Brett he's the best," said Lou.

"Will do."

Lou washed and dried his hands. When he stepped around the partition to look at the stall, he saw something on the floor under the door.

"Maghribi?"

There was no answer.

"What are you doing in there?"

Lou got down on his knees and looked under the door.

Maghribi had fallen off of the toilet, his trousers still down around his ankles. His head and upper body were wedged in between the wall and the toilet. Blood was spattered on the wall.

"Jesus Christ!"

Lou ran out into the restaurant.

"Where's the manager? Where's the manager?"

"In the back."

"Get him! Emergency in the bathroom!"

The kid behind the counter went in the back. A young man in his early twenties came out.

"What's the matter, sir?"

"There's a man on the floor in the toilet stall. He must have fallen and hit his head. Call 911. Get in there and open it up. Now!"

The manager pulled out his phone. He called 911 as he ran into the bathroom. He crawled under the partition and opened the door.

Lou stared down at Maghribi's body. His head and chest were covered in blood.

"What happened?" said the manager. "What the fuck happened?"

"I don't know. Suicide? But how did he get a gun? Call the police!"

The manager dialed again. Lou ran out to the van and yelled at Marty.

"Call management! Maghribi's dead!"

"What happened?"

"Don't know. Call them!"

Lou ran back into the restaurant as Marty dialed. Two squad cars finally pulled into the parking lot. Lou stopped them at the door and showed them his badge.

"Retired Milwaukee Police. Prisoner Transport."

"Okay."

The officers hurried back to the bathroom. One of them knelt down to examine Maghribi's body.

"Shot. Multiple."

He looked up at Lou.

"Did you hear anything?"

"Nothing. I was standing here talking with one of your officers. Scott Favre, Brett's brother."

The officers looked at each other.

"You sure it wasn't Eli Manning? Peyton's brother? Now, him we have on the force."

"Are you pulling my bobber?"

"Me? How about you? Mister, we're going down to the station to talk about this some more."

They escorted Lou out of the restaurant while the EMTs hurried past them.

Chapter Fifty-Four

Wayne Hawkin sat reading a headline on the front page *of The New York Times*.

"Another Islamic Scholar with Ties to Milwaukee Murdered."

The byline was Cenk Rut.

'The most dangerous place for an Islamic Scholar to teach or take courses is not China. It is not North Korea. It is not the Middle East. It is Milwaukee. The noted scholar Professor Taqi Maghribi, an expert on the Crusades and the glory years of Spain under the Ottoman Empire, is dead. Murdered sitting on a toilet in a McDonald's bathroom.

The story of his murder starts with his arrival in Milwaukee less than a year ago as a visiting professor at Milwaukee Community College. The day he arrived, he was tased and beaten by Milwaukee police while trying to check into a motel. Weeks later, he was arrested and beaten again by police at a diverse festival of people exploring intersectional identities. Not long after that, he was kidnapped, stripped, handcuffed, and dumped in front of a Milwaukee Theater. Twelve other Saudi Arabian scholars were murdered in the few months that Professor Maghribi was in Milwaukee. He knew he would be next. He fled Milwaukee to return to Saudi Arabia for the funeral of his beloved father, to no avail. His pursuers caught up to him in Virginia, arrested him, and, in a cruel irony, charged him with murdering his own countrymen. They started to drive him back to Milwaukee on the pretext of a court order. And so it was, in a lonely McDonald's between Fort Wayne and Toledo, that they finally succeeded in getting their man. The scholar Taqi Maghribi is dead."

Hawkin's phone vibrated.

"Audrey?"

"Yep!"

Her voice was almost giddy.

"I'm sitting here with Bernie. He solved it!"

"What?"

"Get Maynard on the line!"

"Right! Hold on."

They heard a phone ring. Maynard Gieck answered.

"Maynard? Hawkin! Audrey and Bernie also on the line. Audrey?"

"Maynard! Bernie solved it! I'll put him on now, but we've only got a week to go. What's the fastest way to get Bernie's material to you?"

"What? Bernie, what did you do?"

"It's a long story. I can send it to you."

Hawkin jumped in.

"Audrey, here's what I want you to do. Show Bernie how to send his info immediately to Maynard on your secure access. Bernie, stand by for a call from Maynard if he has any questions. Maynard, when you get it, we need to apply it and get that traffic read in a nanosecond. Can you do it?"

"If it's what Bernie describes, yes, of course. Bernie, send it to me through Audrey immediately. My team's standing by. Hold on."

Gieck stepped off the line for a moment.

"Back. They're covering my screen. Can you send it now? Audrey?"

"Right. Hold on. Bernie, forward it to this address."

"Okay."

There was a pause.

"Okay," Audrey said. "Maynard should have it now. Maynard?"

"Okay. Right. The team's on it. Bernie, give me an overview of what you did."

"Yeah. Like we talked about before, there were three problems to solve . . ."

"I get that. No need to go over that again. But how did you attack the underlying math? Heisenberg and Bell? I can't figure out why that occurred to you."

"So, their math proved that two entangled particles would react to the measurement of one of them, identically and simultaneously, even if they were separated by billions of light years. There were only a few theories about how that could happen. I had to eliminate each of them as being impossible."

"Go on."

"The first possibility is the magic dice theory. Two magic dice always agree when they're tossed simultaneously. But we rule out magic. That theory is impossible."

"Agreed. What's next?"

"The second possibility is that at the quantum level the speed of light is not a barrier to communication. But that's impossible because of Einstein's work. I ruled that out as impossible."

"I agree totally. What's the next one?"

"The third possibility is an analogy to genes. If the particles were preprogrammed with something like genes, they would act similarly. For instance, two brothers might have the same color hair or eyes."

"What about that?"

"Genes don't act simultaneously. Just because something is done to one brother carrying the gene doesn't mean that an identical reaction will instantly occur in another brother with that gene. It's impossible for preprogramming to produce instant effects without communication, and communication is bounded by the speed of light."

"Where did you go from there?"

"There's a fourth possibility. That there's a field at the quantum level that we haven't discovered but is showing up in our math. For instance, Newton really didn't understand gravity as a field, even though his equations were terrific. No one understood electromagnetism as a field until Faraday and Maxwell came along. But there are a couple of reasons why an unexplained field at the quantum level can't possibly be the answer."

"What are they?"

"Well, electromagnetism and gravity are still subject to the limitations of the speed of light. So would any other mystery field."

"What else?"

"Electromagnetism and gravity are two of the original four forces that came into existence at the Big Bang. But there are two others, the strong force and the weak force. They're also subject to the limitations of the speed of light. The strong force binds together what makes up subatomic particles, like protons and neutrons. The weak force governs the interaction between subatomic particles that's responsible for radioactive decay of atoms. That's it. There is no other mystery force or mystery field. And the four that do exist are subject to cause and effect and the limit of the speed of light."

"Maynard," Hawkin said, "I don't understand much of this, and I want the damned messages read! Now or sooner! We've got a week to the State of the Union!"

"Right, Wayne. We're on it. My guys are working it. I'll head back there now. But Bernie, one last question. You've eliminated all the possibilities. Then what?"

"That's simple. Say you're given the only five possible answers to a problem. Four of them are impossible, and one is so improbable that everyone laughs at it. In that case, the improbable one that everyone laughs at has to be the answer."

"And what was the improbable one?"

"That Heisenberg's and Bell's math was wrong or incomplete. When you supposedly prove in your math that something impossible is true, there's an error in your math. And that's what I found. Because their math is the basis of quantum encryption, I found a way to penetrate it."

"Bernie," Hawkin said, "thank you more than I can ever say. Audrey, all hands-on-deck for our meeting tomorrow at the Farm. Two p.m. I need you there in person. Maynard, I need a transcript of the messages as soon as possible. No later than six a.m. tomorrow. If you can't do it, notify me immediately. That's it for now. Thanks all."

Chapter Fifty-Five

A large brick building of Eschweiler Jacobethan architecture with a cedar shingle roof stands not far from the airstrip on the Farm in Williamsburg, Virginia. From a distance, it looks like a stately private home.

Audrey Knapp pulled open the front door and walked up to a man in a suit, sitting behind a desk.

"Which room is the meeting with Director Hawkin?"

"Conference room down the hall to the left. Agent Knapp?"

"Right. Thanks."

Audrey walked down the hallway. Several dozen people were already seated when she arrived. The chairs were arranged in rows, facing a table in the front. Audrey sat in the back on the end. Wayne Hawkin finally arrived. The room quieted as he arranged some papers.

"Welcome back to the Farm. I've already spoken personally to most of you about this meeting. The rest of you got word from your mission chiefs."

Hawkin looked down at his notes.

"We have intelligence that there will be a jihadist attack on the Capitol during the State of the Union speech by the President five days from now. They call it Operation Cordoba. It will come by air and by ground attack on the building. I've already set the battle order in response. I'm going to go through it now. First, Cordoba intends to fly small suicide planes packed with explosives from many of the airports in the states around Washington. Their theory of attack is that if even a small number get through, they will destroy the Capitol."

Hawkin paused.

"Who of you is in command of the land response at all the airports in Virginia?"

A man in the front row stood up.

"I want a team at every airport in Virginia. No matter how small. And I mean every single one. Is that understood?"

"Yes, sir."

"Keep it under surveillance all day. If anyone even approaches a plane, arrest them. Use whatever force is necessary. If they manage to get on the plane, destroy it on the ground. Do you have the weapons to do that?"

"Yes, sir."

"Good. Thank you. Who here is in command of the Navy air response over Virginia?"

A man stood up.

"You and your pilots have your orders from COMNAVAIRLANT?"

"Yes, sir."

"There is a no-fly order over Virginia that day. If you see a small plane in the air over Virginia that evening, shoot it down. If you see a commercial jet, intercept it, and guide it away. It may be mistaken. You'll have to judge. But if it continues, shoot it down."

"Yes, sir. Question, sir. This is in addition to normal air cover over the Capitol and metro area during the speech?"

"Right. Good question. For all of you, your mission supplements standard ops that day. You will coordinate flight patterns with the usual air surveillance assigned to the Capitol that evening."

"Yes, sir."

"Let me ask the same questions of the rest of you. Who here is in command of the land response to all the airports in Maryland? In West Virginia? In Delaware? In Pennsylvania?"

For each state, different men and women stood up.

"There will be a no-fly order for each of those states on February 1st, just like Virginia. You will secure every airport in your state. Every single one. Arrest everyone even approaching a plane. And destroy the plane ASAP if they manage to get on. Understood?'

Everyone nodded and responded with "Yes, sirs." One woman raised her hand.

"Yes?"

"Sir, when we arrest them, where shall we transport them?"

"Right. Good. Everyone you arrest will be transported to Guantanamo for interrogation. They'll be flown right out of here. So, when you take somebody, restrain them in your van. When the day is over, drive them here to The Farm for further processing."

"Thank you."

"Okay. Now, who here is from the Navy with orders to cover Maryland? Delaware? West Virginia? And Pennsylvania?"

At the mention of each state, different people stood.

"Okay. Any questions? Do you understand your instructions?"

One man raised his hand.

"I have a question. Say a small plane flies into one of the five states from out of state and may not know of the no-fly. How much latitude do we have?"

"Good question. First of all, they should know of the no-fly. It'll go out nationally. You're playing safety. Every airport in the five states should already have been secured. We will not permit any plane to even take off from the states surrounding the District. So, of course you will use discretion and judgment. I'm not looking for cowboys. Escort them away if your judgment is that they strayed into the airspace. If they continue on to the District of Columbia, shoot them down."

"Yes, sir."

"Good. Who here is from Seal Team Six with orders from the commanding officer of the Naval Special Warfare Command?"

Two men stood up.

"A Bulgarian tanker named the Grozdana is en route to the Port of Norfolk. It has a small crew. About half of them are Kosovars, who are smuggling in missile launchers along with the regular cargo."

Hawkin looked back at his notes.

"Screening at American port entries for commercial ships is lax on all our coasts. We don't know how these crew members plan to do it. At night in a small boat? Mixed in with cargo that rarely gets fully searched? In the personal effects of crew members on liberty?"

He paused.

"I want the Seals to board the ship as it enters the harbor. Secure the bridge and the ship's communications. Secure the crew. Handcuff them in their quarters. Use whatever force is required. Then search the ship. Confiscate the launchers and any weapons."

One of the men standing raised his hand.

"Yes?"

"Sir, after we're done, will we require their captain to bring the ship alongside the pier, or shall we do it?"

"Don't let them do anything. Handcuff the captain in his quarters under guard. Bring in a Navy quartermaster to navigate it in."

"Yes, sir."

"The Grozdana is scheduled to put into port on January 31st. They obviously want to limit the time in which they could be discovered. I want to keep the commanders of Cordoba in the dark as long as possible about what happened to their men on the ship. One of our agents will accompany you. He will take over their communications."

"Yes, sir."

"Thank you all. That concludes this briefing. Go home and brief your teams. Five days from now, we have to smother Cordoba. Not a single plane or a single missile can hit the Capitol. You are dismissed."

Audrey walked up to Hawkin as the rest filed out.

"I got your message. Where do you want to meet?"

"I'm using Joanna's office. I'll be there in five."

"See you there."

Joanna Martinez's office was dark when Audrey entered. She flipped on the lights and looked over the pictures of the various disguises. A plaque with a quotation caught her attention.

"March 28, 1786, letter by John Adams and Thomas Jefferson, Diplomats, to Sec. of Foreign Affairs John Jay, re discussion with Ambassador from Tripoli in London, regarding Piracy by Barbary States."

The full quotation was underneath.

"We took the liberty to make some enquiries concerning the ground of their pretensions to make war upon nations who had done them no injury. The Ambassador answered that it was founded in the laws of their Prophet; written in their Koran; that all nations who should not have acknowledged their authority were sinners; that it was their right and duty to make war upon them wherever they could be found; and to make slaves of all they could take as prisoners; and that every Mussulman who was slain in battle was sure to go to Paradise."

Hawkin walked in minutes later and closed the door.

"We have a problem."

"What is it?"

He sat down.

"Cordoba has a third line of attack at the speech. Jihadist agents will be placed in the gallery at the Capitol."

"Well, that's easy. Arrest them at the door."

"Right. But it's not as simple as that. Each political party gets ten guests. They call them skutnicks. The origin of the name is irrelevant. But four of the Republican guests are from Saudi, and we don't have full information on how they will be armed. Or, I should say there were four. There are three now."

"What happened?"

"You. The woman you terminated in Milwaukee was one of them. Well done."

"Thanks. So let's arrest the other three and interrogate them."

"Here's the problem. They're sponsored by officials in the Saudi government. Those officials are very close to the Trump people."

"Why?"

"The Trump administration says it's because Saudi Arabia is the most effective counterforce to Iran and Iranian Shiite terrorism. But the Saudis continually export Sunni Wahabi terrorism into Europe and the United States. We trained their pilots in Florida, and they murdered our sailors in the classroom. The President didn't even criticize them."

"It's got to be more than geopolitical alliances in the Middle East."

"You're right. The President has a personal financial motive. Why do you think he fought like a starving wolf to keep his tax returns private? I've seen those returns. He wants to hide his foreign money."

"Well, at least you'll search these women before they go into the Capitol."

"Not exactly. Of course, they'll go through metal detectors like everyone else. But they're not stupid enough to bring in weapons. I'm afraid they'll bring in explosives that won't register on a metal detector."

"Trained dogs can smell it. And matrons can search them."

"The Saudi government opposes any search other than a metal detector. Donald Trump supports them. He overruled our objections. The Saudis cite religious reasons and claim it would defile their women. Remember, we ran into that when the police in New York arrested a woman from India who had beaten her maid. Lower caste maid. An untouchable. They did a matron search on intake into the jail, and it caused a riot in India."

"Are you telling me that our government is going to let three jihadists into the audience for the State of the Union speech just because they passed a metal detector? Did you tell the White House what we suspect and what we know?"

"Of course, I did. Staff is on our side, but Trump overruled them. Said the metal detector was enough. The procedure for all the other guests is to go through the metal detector at the entrance of the Capitol. They're escorted to the office of the member of Congress who invited them. The member then escorts them to the gallery if they are invited to watch in person. Otherwise, they're escorted by security out to the exit of the building."

"But here we have advance info that they're a threat!"

"Right. And President Trump simply said that we're wrong about the women. He pointed out that they were vetted by the Secret Service in advance, like all other guests. He doesn't acknowledge that he instructed the Secret Service to approve them on the request of the Crown Prince."

"But Wayne! The threat!"

"I've argued with the White House. They say that the President's orders are that the women have to be treated like all other guests. He overruled the staff. Just like he overruled Defense and State and abandoned our Kurdish allies to be slaughtered by the Turks. All because Erdogan of Turkey called him in his golf cart to ask him to withdraw from Syria, and Trump wanted to get back to his game. Just like he met with the Russkies alone in his office with no Americans present. He's impulsive, lazy, crooked and unprepared. A lot of people have died as a result."

Audrey was silent for a moment.

"So, what do we do?"

"You mean, what do *you* do? You're going into the Capitol as a skutnick. Here's a diagram of the Capitol where the speech is given. Look, here are the bathrooms. Here are the corridors they'll walk in."

"Where are the women now? And where will they be during that day?"

"They're on their way to Washington. On the day of the speech, they'll be staying at the Mayflower Hotel. When they go to the Capitol, the Speaker of the House will be holding a reception in her office for distinguished guests. Sort of a receiving line. The chairs of some of the House committees will be there. So will some of the skutnicks, along with some Senators who are friends of the Speaker and major donors to her party. The Saudi skutnicks are on the list to greet her."

"Then what?"

"Then, they head to the gallery. Escorted by a Congressman. They'll be seated in the front row of the gallery, looking out over the floor."

"Got it."

"We'll have our personnel in the Capitol during the speech. They may appear to be security, or aides. They're there to support you. Here's a briefing book with locations where they'll be."

"Who am I the guest of?"

"That's in the briefing book. And who you'll be. What you'll look like."

"One question. How am I going to get a weapon into the Capitol?"

"You're not. Our people inside the Capitol will have everything you need. It's also in the book. Keep in mind you may have to use methods you learned in training."

"What weapons will the women have? Specifically."

"What we expect is in the book."

Audrey didn't respond.

"Audrey, I want those women terminated. No matter how it's done. I don't care if you throw them off the balcony onto the Wyoming delegation. I'm just kidding."

"Actually, you're not."

"Actually, you're right."

Audrey stood up, holding the briefing book and the Capitol diagram.

"I want to digest this. I'll call you with any questions."

"Good. And a couple more things. Try not to do it on national television. And leave yourself a route to get out of the Capitol before they find out what happened."

"I understand. I'll get it done."

Chapter Fifty-Six

Milwaukee Television Anchor Kathy Mykleby looked into the camera as it went live.

"Good afternoon. President Trump is set to give his State of the Union address in a little over two hours inside the Capitol. We have team coverage, and live video from the pool camera. We go to the Capitol now."

The Congressional chamber in the Capitol came on the screen. A few members were already taking their seats. An occasional aide walked in the background.

"This room will be packed very soon. Congressmen, Senators, cabinet members, Supreme Court justices, ambassadors, and guests will squeeze in to witness the President's speech. We go to my colleague, Colleen Henry. Colleen, what do you think the President will emphasize?"

Zulkifar Malouf, joined by three women in traditional dress and three men, sat in his room at the Mayflower Hotel in Washington, watching the same pool camera pan the Chamber. When it went to a commercial, he opened his laptop. The others stayed silent.

To: Grozdana

Re: Docking

'I have not heard from you since this morning. Is there something wrong?'

An answer came back quickly.

'Nothing wrong. Docking delays unrelated to us. We docked this morning. Cargo off loaded and is in place at final destination.'

'Good.'

The words BREAKING NEWS suddenly spread across a diagonal banner on the screen. An anchor for the Washington, D.C., ABC affiliate came on.

"We interrupt this broadcast for breaking news. A small plane accident in Charlottesville claims the life of the pilot within the last hour. His plane burst into flames as he tried to take off. No cause of the accident has been determined so far. The pilot's name is being withheld, pending notification of next of kin. We go back to the pool video of the Capitol."

Malouf typed quickly on his laptop.

To: Virginia Commander

Re: Charlottesville

'Was it one of ours? If so, why was he engaging so early? What happened?'

'Yes it was ours. Zoran. He wanted to go up early and practice his movements. He said he had plenty of fuel. I do not know what happened. But we still have many planes in Virginia. I have instructed them to take off at last minute to reach coordinated 9:30 p.m. EST arrival at destination."

'Need more discipline. Keep me informed.'

Malouf looked back at the TV. The anchor was still talking.

"At precisely 8:30 p.m. EST, the President and First Lady will get into this limousine at the White House and proceed to the Capitol."

The pool camera showed a limousine sitting in front of the White House, surrounded by Secret Service agents.

"When they get to the Capitol, the First Lady will be escorted to the Gallery, overlooking the floor. She is expected to sit with guests, including some of our allies in the Middle East. The President will make his way to the podium through the center aisle, shaking hands with members of Congress along the way."

Wayne Hawkin watched the broadcast from his office in Langley, nine miles away. He opened his laptop.

To: TANKER FROGS

'Request status.'

'All secured. Cargo located and secured. Crew secured. Ship is docked.'

Hawkin sent another message.

To: NAVAIR COMMANDERS

'Need status.'

Several replies came back immediately.

'Pennsylvania secure.'

'Delaware secure.'

'Maryland secure.'

'West Virginia secure.'

A few minutes later:

'Virginia secure. Difficulty in Charlottesville. Resolved.'

A middle-aged woman sat watching the broadcast in her room at the Mayflower Hotel, two floors below Malouf. There was no luggage in the room. She looked at the clock and left.

Zulkifar Malouf turned off the volume of the broadcast and started to quiz his guests.

"You are sure of your orders? What you will say at the entrance to the Capitol if you are questioned?"

"Yes," said one of the men.

The women nodded.

"When you enter, you will be met by security. He will lead you to the office of the Congressman in your briefing book. The Congressman will take you to the offices of the Speaker, who will greet guests. From there, you will be escorted by the Congressman to the gallery, where you will sit in the seats you are shown."

The men and the women all nodded.

"When you are seated, you will ask to use the bathroom. You will go together. Your three escorts will accompany you and stand outside in case others try to enter."

He looked at the men.

"Do you know what you will say if someone else tries to enter?"

"Yes. The women using the lavatory have the highest security. They will be out shortly. In the meantime, there is another Ladies' rest room down the hall. And we point."

"Good. They will need fifteen minutes."

He turned back to the women.

"You know every detail of how you prepare the explosives on your body?"

The three nodded.

"And you know exactly how to detonate it?"

They nodded again.

"And you know the precise time to detonate?"

"9:30 p.m. EST," said one.

"Correct. You must be precise. Other lions will attack the building at the same time. You must not be late by a single minute."

"We understand," said another.

The rest nodded. Malouf smiled broadly at them.

"You are defenders of the Ummah. Your obedience will bring you great rewards! Now, let us go!"

The women's eyes shone with almost romantic intensity as they left the room. When they got to the elevator lobby on their floor, a workman was kneeling in front of one of the doors, looking at a diagram he'd laid out on the carpet.

"This one's out of order. So are these other two," he said. "There's only one working."

The workman took out his phone and texted.

"I'll be right back."

He walked toward the stairwell.

"Shall we use the stairs?" asked one of the women.

"No."

Malouf pointed to the overhead light.

"The good one's almost here."

The six of them stood close to the elevator door. As it opened, they saw a woman alone inside, facing them with a weapon. Malouf hit the floor. The woman blasted silent rounds into the group. She hit a woman and two of the men. The door closed. Malouf jumped up. The women and the remaining man trembled on the carpet.

"Get up! Get up! Before someone comes. Drag them back to the room."

Malouf and the man each took one of their dead companions by the feet and dragged them back to the room. The women dragged the remaining body. They started to cry when the door closed.

"What do we do?"

"Steady. We have to leave here quickly. Can't wait for our car. We only need a few hours. There is blood on the carpet. We can't be trapped here."

"We're leaving them?" said the man.

He pointed to the bodies.

"We have no choice. They have died in combat in defense of the Ummah. They have their reward. But we are the living. We have work to do."

He pointed at the dead woman.

"Undress her. Take what she was carrying. Conceal it. Quickly! Quickly!"

Malouf and the other man turned their backs to avoid seeing her undressed.

"We are ready," said the women.

"Good. Go! Use the stairwell and hurry!"

They trotted down the stairs. When they walked out into the lobby, a crowd had congregated at the elevators. All of the doors were open. The cars were dark. A few maintenance men in forest green shirts spoke into walkie talkies.

"They're all out? What was it?"

"Checking. Don't know yet."

Malouf hurried them out to the street to the front of the cab line.

"There's a line, Mister," said a doorman.

"Diplomatic corps. This is the ambassador's family and ministers."

He handed the doorman two one-hundred-dollar bills.

"Okay. Got it, pal."

He blew a whistle. A cab pulled up to the curb and the man opened the door.

"One of you can sit up front."

Malouf jumped into the front seat. The others squeezed into the back.

"The Capitol. Quickly," said Malouf.

The cab sped away.

Chapter Fifty-Seven

The cab stopped just before a police barricade, blocks from the Capitol. The driver turned to Malouf.

"This is it."

"What do you mean?"

"The police blocked off an area around the Capitol tonight. Vehicles can't just drive up to the building. Unless you're a limo. Dignitaries."

"We are dignitaries."

"Why are you taking a cab?"

"Never mind."

Malouf paid the fare. They stepped out of the cab onto wet pavement that shone under the streetlights. The light rain had stopped. They walked quickly through the street to the Capitol.

"Is this wise?" said the other man. "They killed Maghribi. They shot at us in the hotel. Won't they be waiting for us here?"

"I don't think so. They can't break our encrypted messages on Cordoba. Maghribi was lazy and careless. They must know about his involvement with Khashoggi. He messaged me too often with light security about other matters. I chastised him."

"Why did they shoot us at the hotel?"

"They were trying to get me at the hotel. They have no idea about the women and where we're going. Besides, we have to try. A joint air and land action will occur at the same time. We can't walk away."

Dozens of uniformed security guards were fanned out around the entrance to the Capitol. Malouf led them to the front of the line.

"Excuse me. These women are guests of the Congress to view the President's State of the Union address from the gallery."

He gave the women's names.

"And who are you?"

"I am Mr. Zulkifar Malouf. We are escorting them."

"Are you also invited?"

"As escorts only. We will leave once the ladies have been delivered."

The man looked at a list.

"Do you have credentials for the women?"

"Yes."

Malouf handed him two envelopes.

"Stand here."

The man pointed to a spot. He left to talk to a man in a suit near the entrance. He turned and waved them over.

"Mr. Malouf?"

"Yes."

"The two ladies and the gentleman escorting them may proceed to the security checkpoint. They will wait there for you. You will come with me to clear up the access points on their credentials. You said you believe they will sit in the Gallery?"

"Yes! Absolutely. We have clearance from Congressman . . ."

"No problem. We need confirmation. Come with me to our command post."

Malouf followed the man in the suit. The two women and their escort followed the security guard into the Capitol entrance. The man and Malouf walked up to a large guard shack. It had no windows. The door was closed. The man opened the door. A middle-aged woman in a uniform was sitting behind a desk. Several large canvas bags lay along one wall, next to what looked like a long, oversized golf bag on wheels.

"Yes?"

"This is Mr. Zulkifar Malouf. We need to confirm the Gallery credentials of two women he is escorting."

He handed the envelopes to the woman.

"Yes. Sit down."

She pointed to the chair in front of her desk. The man in the suit closed the door and left. The woman opened the envelopes. She scanned them and sat back, her hands on her lap.

"You are not requesting to join them inside? Just the two women will go to the Gallery?"

"Right. Of course. I will not . . .

She stood up. He started to jump at the sight of the gun, but multiple silent rounds blew him back onto the floor. The woman concealed her weapon. She walked out and closed the door. The man in the suit stood nearby.

"He can be removed," she said.

"Very good."

The woman walked toward the Capitol entrance. The man in the suit signaled to a workman, standing near a large dolly. The workman went inside the guard shack. He came out a few minutes later, locked the door behind him, and loaded the golf bag on the dolly. He pushed the dolly slowly away from the Capitol into the darkness. The man in the suit walked alongside him without speaking.

The woman from the guard shack walked into the Capitol. Malouf's two women and their escort had passed through security and were standing off to one side. The guards manning the metal detector were processing a growing line of Congressmen and spectators. Two men in suits sat on stools, supervising the area. The woman from the guard shack beckoned to them, and after a brief discussion, one of them walked with her into the Capitol. The other one approached Malouf's companions.

"You two ladies are cleared for entrance. Mr. Malouf has left. He said to tell you that he will join you at some point in the future. And you, sir, you may escort the ladies to the check point for Gallery access. They will be escorted to their seats, and we ask that you exit the building at that time."

"We were told that the Congressman who invited us will escort us. And the ladies were invited to a reception in the Speaker's office."

"The Congressman is out on the Chamber floor now. There has been a schedule change. The Speaker's reception has been canceled. The Congressman will meet the ladies after the President's address. The ladies should remain in their seats in the Gallery. He will come to escort them out."

"All right."

The man in the suit led the three of them down a corridor to the entrance of the Chamber. Several Congressmen walked by them onto the floor. Their guide directed them toward two men and a woman in uniform, who were standing on the side.

"These women are guests in the Gallery. The gentleman will leave with me."

"Very well."

The woman in uniform stepped forward. She wore plastic gloves.

"I will pat you down. It is required for guests in the Gallery."

"You may not touch them!" said their escort. "It is not permitted. This was specifically arranged with the Congressman!"

"Why not?"

"It is not permitted to touch a woman! To defile her."

The three guards conferred briefly.

"Okay," said one. "The women may enter. I'll show them to their seats."

Their escort watched them be seated.

"All right. I'm ready to leave."

"There is a holding room near the entrance where you can watch the address on television," said another guard. "Would you be more comfortable there?"

"No! No. I have an urgent matter to attend to. Thank you for the invitation, but I must leave immediately."

"Very well. This way."

"I thought the entrance was back down that corridor."

"It is. But the exit we use for all guests is separate. This way."

The man followed the guard down a different corridor. The guard stopped in front of an unmarked door.

"I have to collect another guest in here who is also leaving. Step inside with me."

"I can wait in the hall."

"It's not permitted for a guest to be alone in the building without an escort. Step inside."

He gestured for the man to go first. The man stepped inside. The guard pulled the door shut behind him. There was a muffled sound, a thud, and then silence. The door opened. A young woman in a Navy captain's uniform came out and closed the door behind her.

"The janitor should tidy the room."

"Yes.

The Navy captain walked to the entrance to the Chamber. In the background, a workman was pulling an oversized golf bag toward the room. The Navy captain approached the Chamber entrance and handed an envelope to one of the guards, who studied it and waved her through.

"You know your assigned seat?"

"Yes. Thanks."

"Wait a minute," said the female guard. "Shouldn't I pat her down?"

"Not necessary," the other guard said. "She went through all of that when she met with the Speaker."

"Oh. Okay."

The captain walked up into the Gallery and sat next to one of the two women. They looked at each other.

"This is exciting, isn't it?" said the captain.

One of the women mumbled something. The other stared straight ahead.

"Are you skutnicks too? Crazy name. What was your angle to get here?"

They didn't answer.

"My deal was I'm the CO of our medical support unit in Afghanistan. One day, I get a call. They want me as a guest at the President's address. Can you believe it? Me! I'm still pinching myself."

"Interesting," said one.

The other stayed silent. The Navy captain looked around and down on the Chamber floor. The two women started to whisper in the Badawi Najdi dialect.

"I'm uneasy."

"Why?"

"Something strange is going on. Malouf should not have just left without speaking to us. To say goodbye."

"There's a lot going on. It was not necessary. We have our orders."

"I think we should go to the restroom now to prepare ourselves and be ready."

"Our orders are to activate at 9:30 p.m. We have a little time."

"If everything is normal, we have time. But it can't hurt to be prepared."

"I agree. Let's go."

The two women stood up.

"Bathroom," one said to the guards. "Which way?"

"Down the corridor on the left."

"We will be right back."

The women walked down the corridor and pushed open the bathroom door. It was a small room with two stalls and two sinks.

"Go into that stall. I'll go into the other. We'll pass each other the chemicals under the partition."

The door opened as she spoke. The Navy captain walked in and stood in front of the mirror, fixing her hair.

"There's something wrong," said one woman in Badawi Najdi. "This bitch is after us. They know."

"What should we do?"

"Kill her. Then we must work fast. We will have to detonate early."

"As you say. One, two, three!"

They rushed Audrey, knocking her to the ground. One kicked her in the side. Audrey got up and kicked the woman between the legs.

The other woman delivered a savate kick to the head. Audrey moved in time to miss most of the impact. The two women started to circle her. They rushed. Audrey went down. Their fingers gouged her face, grabbing for her eyes, while they kneed her in the stomach. The larger of the two grinned down at her as she kneed Audrey again.

Suddenly, blood started to trickle from the woman's mouth. She tried to lift herself up. Audrey drove the knife deeper, up into her belly as she shoved her into the other woman. Audrey got up first. She kicked the other woman in the head. Then the stomach. Then the head again. She dragged her by the hair into a stall and forced the woman's face into the toilet. She slammed the lid down on her neck and sat on it. The bubbles and sputtering finally stopped.

Audrey left the stall. She stepped over the body by the sink. When she left the bathroom, a sign that said "Out of Order" had been placed in front of the door. A guard was sitting in a chair nearby. He walked over to her.

"All set?"

"All set. The Ladies' room has to be cleaned. Careful with the chemicals."

"Roger."

A woman walked up to them.

"Powder room?" she said.

"Sorry," said the guard. "Out of order. Plumbing problem."

"What's the closest powder room?"

"Try that other corridor. About halfway down."

"Why, thank you."

The woman walked away. Audrey hurried back toward the entrance. A TV monitor on the wall showed the President and the First Lady walking toward a limousine.

"The President and the First Lady are about to get into their limousine," the anchor said. "They will drive from the White House to the Capitol. The First Lady will take a seat in the Gallery. The President will be announced at the door of the Capitol Chamber. He will walk down the aisle, shaking hands with members on each side who have positioned themselves there. He will then . . ."

As a light rain started up again, Audrey walked slowly out into the darkness.

Chapter Fifty-Eight

Inside a Stone Creek coffee shop on Milwaukee's East Side, Audrey sipped her coffee as she read the editorial page of *The New York Times*.

'ISLAMOPHOBIA IS A THREAT TO OUR STRATEGIC ALLIANCES'

By Assistant Editor Cenk Rut

'It has come to this. Fear of violence has caused guests invited to the President's State of the Union Address to abruptly leave the Capitol. Saad Khan, a spokesman for Saudi Arabia's Crown Prince, confirmed today that it was the threat of violence that caused two representatives of the Kingdom to leave the spectator Gallery before the State of the Union address and return to their country. 'They became frightened and left the Capitol,' Mr. Khan said. 'We have full confidence that what occurred earlier will be investigated, and the perpetrators will be brought to justice.' Mr. Khan was referring to an incident earlier that evening in Washington, at the storied Mayflower Hotel, where a third Saudi woman and her two bodyguards were shot to death in an elevator lobby. That woman had also been scheduled to attend the President's address in the Capitol. A source in the FBI said that the matter was being investigated. At long last, when will this country come to terms with the corrosive phobia that is undermining our national interest? When will we learn to embrace multicultural customs that will enrich our own culture and from which we have much to learn?"

Audrey looked up as Bernie sat down next to her. She leaned in and hugged him.

"Bernie, I love you! You saved us! Again!"

"I'm glad I could help. Did you stop them?"

"Totally. You saved us from a lot of trouble."

Audrey opened her laptop.

"Wayne wants to thank you, too."

Wayne Hawkin appeared on the screen.

"Wayne, Bernie's here. We're not secure. Coffee shop. No one immediately around us."

"Right. Bernie, I really can't thank you enough. Your country can't thank you enough. You did it!"

"Thanks."

"How are your studies going?"

"Good. I'm almost done."

"Bernie, I want to tell you two things. First, at some point you'll want to publish your work. What you've done for us in every matter you've handled will seal your reputation forever. Have you thought about that?"

"Kind of. But yeah, I think I will."

"I have two requests of you. Before you publish anything, give me a heads up."

"Definitely. I'll let you know."

"Call Audrey. She's your contact."

"Okay."

"And second, we'd like to hire you as a consultant. You'd be paid. You wouldn't have to be in an office out here. We'd just like to call on you from time to time with problems."

Bernie hesitated.

"Well, you know, I want to teach and do my work here. The spy stuff gives me the shivers. But you can always call me with a real problem. I don't need to be paid."

"Understood. You're a good man, Bernie. A very good man."

"Thanks."

"Audrey, I need you out here tomorrow morning. In my office."

"Sure. Everything okay?"

"For now. I want to talk with you about the future. The committee we've discussed is extremely pleased with your work. They've authorized your similar involvement in some pending matters."

"Got it. See you tomorrow morning."

"See you tomorrow."

Hawkin's picture disappeared. Audrey put her hand on Bernie's arm.

"Bernie, let's have lunch."

"Sure! Where do you want to go?"

"You pick it. I have a feeling we'll be seeing each other again."

Bernie smiled.

"Let's go!"

They walked together out onto the street.

Coming Soon!

CHINA CODE
BERNIE WEBER: MATH GENIUS SERIES
BOOK 2
BY

MATTHEW J. FLYNN

Milwaukeeans are inherently tactless and naturally suspicious. They don't believe in nuance or "going easy" on someone. So when foreign spies invade their city, they sure as hell aren't going to take it lying down and they may not even behave like typically polite Midwesterners.

In this darkly comic thriller, the CIA and the Chinese Ministry of Intelligence go head-to-head in a battle to reap the rewards of Bernie Weber's mathematical genius. The secret to cracking China's encryptions lies in this unassuming college student's proof of the Riemann Hypothesis, and the Chinese fear that his findings could take down all of their operations…

For more information
visit: www.SpeakingVolumes.us

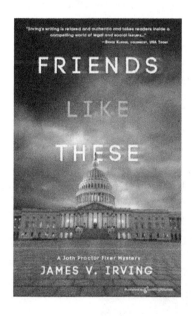 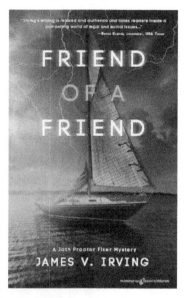

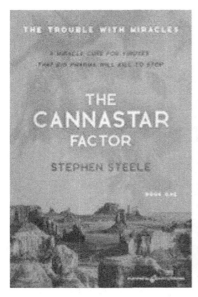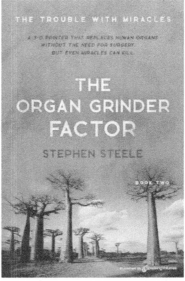

Made in the USA
Las Vegas, NV
16 March 2022

45749832R00173